This book is dedicated to
Gary & Geraldine Hughes

Thank you for your help and support

OUROBOROS

Danny Hughes

Ouroboros: Copyright © 2017—2019 by Danny Hughes
All rights reserved. No part of this publication may be reproduced, distributed, or transmitted without the express consent of the author.

"The Earth is the cradle of humanity, but mankind cannot stay in the cradle forever"

- Konstantin Tsiolkovsky

3ʳᵈ Cycle – ETA: 70.2 Yrs

Part One: The World You Left Behind

His vital signs began to resume their normal rhythm.
"Good morning, Maintenance Engineer: Gilbey" ADAM; the ships A.I. computer's voice was clear and not too inhuman.
He felt hazed as he wiped his face and tried to pull himself out of his stasis pod. His legs began to buckle beneath him, causing him to grab hold of the oxygen pipe leading out. "Please try and refrain from breaking the equipment Sir, you do not want to have to spend the next seventy point two years of our journey awake with no one but myself as company".
Gilbey would have laughed, were it not for the currently overwhelming task of staying on his feet.

Every time he woke up and waited for his limbs to feel like his own again, he would experience the same pang of nostalgia; he couldn't help but think of that little deer that ran out onto the ice in that ancient film. He'd never seen a real deer before or a block of ice bigger than a cube floating in a drink for that matter. It was all just memories built from the huge archive of films and pictures stored on his community's bunker computer, back on earth.

ADAM began to speak "Maintenance Engineer..." before Gilbey cut him off.

"I told you in the last cycle to stop calling me that" he managed to state despite his mouth feeling as dry as a sand dune. He coughed but it was coarse and painful.

"My apologies Sir. What do you mean?" ADAM questioned.

His eyes felt almost as dry as his mouth and feeling began to painfully return to his legs, in a cold rush of pins and needles. "Stop using the whole damn title" he grunted.

"Playback" ADAM stated and the recording from the previous maintenance cycle began to play. "Just call me Gilbey" His own voice echoing back to him after two decades, the playback finished and he was left with the electronic hiss of his small stasis pod.

He remained silent and he motionless for a while. For the first time in twenty years, his mind was able to be truly empty.

Unfortunately, before long he couldn't help but notice that only the emergency lights were on.

"ADAM" Gilbey called out in no direction in particular. "Lights" and with that the stasis bay lit up. It was so bright that it felt like they were flying past the sun; something he had done a few times back in his days of deep-space salvaging missions, back when it was still safe to get ships to break atmosphere and still have to worry about getting them back.

The stasis bay was white and lifeless; a common feature on the Eden. The various computers around could be heard humming softly as they recorded and monitored his time held in suspended animation. Various displays could be seen on the walls showing innumerable pieces of information running endlessly like the Solar systems themselves. Flickering lights and buttons littered one side of the wall in amongst more displays showing his own heart rate, blood pressure, and brain activity. A macabre art project that would make sure that he completed the trip to Delta Tauri.

The lights felt for a moment as if they were growing stronger. They began to burn right into Gilbey's retinas. His dry eyes felt as if they were going to catch alight. He screwed his eyes up and flapped his half recovered arms over his face groaning at the annoyance of the pain.

"Goddammit... ADAM dim lights forty percent" and as he said it the room grew slightly darker once more, but even that felt like his eyes were on fire.

"Be careful Mainten..." the computer seemed to think for a moment and remember the man's request. "Gilbey... your eyes will take some adjusting to this. You haven't used them in over two decades".

Gilbey scoffed at the remark. "This isn't my first dance kiddo" he replied as he grabbed the sachet of coolant ADAM had deposited beside the stasis tank kindly before he had woken. Even the sachet felt refreshing in his hand.

"Yes, but not for this long. No human has ever been in stasis for longer than fifteen years, and even then it was under the watchful eye of an advanced medical team who were standing by... and it was safely back on Earth" ADAM informed him.

Gilbey paid the machine no mind, instead he ripped the seal of the sachet and poured the contents into his mouth. Instantly his mouth became a whirlpool. In a euphoric moment, he breathed deep through his nose before spitting it into the drainage port beside him. A small jet of ice cold recycled water rinsed the port clean once more. Gilbey was pleased to see that the water systems did not need repairing, at least in this section of the ship. It was a surprisingly disgusting job and, quite possibly, one of the most convoluted tasks he could get stuck with. Something like that would have taken nearly the entire cycle to complete.

"Work". Gilbey didn't want to even think about half the tedious little repairs he knew he would have to make, but the reality he had to face was: that is the reason he and the other members of the maintenance crew were even here.

"Where are the others?" Gilbey asked the AI, as he felt his legs begin to return to normal. ADAM took a few moments to answer, almost as if he was gathering precise coordinates on the ship to give him the exact locations at that moment in time. Gilbey decided to just go ahead and change the question to avoid the inevitable complex answer that was inbound. He was still tired despite sleeping just over twenty two years, and was not in the mood for dealing with an over thinking computer.

"Belay that." Gilbey dragged one of his hands down his face and scratched at his facial hair. "Is everyone awake?" he asked. He did not want to ask the machine if anyone had died as a result of being stasis for too long. The few deaths so far in the last few cycles had made the entire team concerned about returning to stasis.

The monitor closest to him blinked as the window for his medical charts was closed remotely and another opened. The faces of the ship's maintenance crew began to appear, displaying their vital signs and key information on them. The names Dietrich, Reids, Carter, Gilbey, Eckhart, Lane, and Graves were all displayed. All appeared alive and well.

"All members of the Eden Maintenance Unit are healthy and out of their stasis pods with the exception of Dr. Reids, who appears to be suffering from Awakening Sickness and is currently still residing inside his personal stasis bay".

Gilbey smiled to himself. He had suffered a mild case of A.S. on his first cycle, but thankfully it had only lasted for a few hours. It is a horrific ordeal where your body fails to adjust to the length of time you have been in stasis for. It feels as if your stomach is desperately trying to claw its way out of your body. Long distance space travel had been done many times before, but nothing quite like this. Gilbey had no idea how the colonists on board were going to feel once they reached their destination. Being asleep for nearly a century and a half is going to do tremendously awful things to your body. He imagined that most of them would suffer with some form of Awakening Sickness, if not all. He did not envy them. All he knew, was that they were going to need to dig a lot of sick buckets out of storage at some point in the next century.

As for Dr. Reids, Gilbey could not think of a nicer person it was happening to. The good Doctor was the unit's chief medical officer and thought himself higher than the rest of the crew. Even though Officer Dietrich was the highest ranking member awake during the cycles, Reids acted as if he was in charge.

During the first and second cycles the Doctor's attitude had rubbed Gilbey the wrong way and he was now, in his own words "Tired of his crap". His main role in this mission is to check the conditions of the Eden's flight crew and the colonists still held in stasis; ensuring that everyone is still alive.

Being a crew of only seven on an interstellar star ship that was over fifty miles long and weighed in at over a thousand tons dry, the maintenance team do find themselves short-handed and too often struggle to complete the necessary tasks during a single cycle, even with ADAM's help. Dr. Reids often believes that anything other than his own primary task is beneath him. Gilbey saw it in the way he flared his nostrils slightly when you asked him. The Doctor usually makes up research jobs to preoccupy himself during the weeks that the rest of the crew work on the ship, claiming it to be for "the good of the new world".

Thinking of him retching into the drainage port of his bay brought a well needed smile to Gilbey's face, but at least now he had a good enough excuse not to get into the thick of it.

Gilbey walked over to the sink and held his hands below the sensor. He pulled away suddenly, jerking his already sore muscles.

"Ugh! Fuck off." He groaned.

The water was ice cold. It was clear that the ship's functions were still taking some time to warm up at the start of this cycle, and so the water had not reached the right temperature yet. It was still refreshing none the less.

"ADAM, can you give me a very brief sit rep, please?" Gilbey asked splashing the water onto his face. His dry skin absorbing it instantly and he began to feel human again. He saw his reflection staring back at him in the mirror and thought to himself how strange that his beard and haircut had not changed in over twenty years. He tried to think about how many years it had been since he was born, he had lost track a very long time ago. As far as he was concerned, he was 34 years old, give or take a few months. Though even that could be wrong by a year or so. He appeared older. His eyes looked deep and dark, like he hadn't properly slept for the last few decades, which was kind of how it was when you went into Stasis, although you do find yourself dreaming. It is almost like one of those restless night's sleep where you wake up feeling even more tired than when you originally went to bed.

"The Eden is operating at ninety-eight point seven four percent with no change to our current flight time" replied ADAM.

"That's a shame." Mused the engineer. "I could have done with being there now". Gilbey smirked at his own reflection as if to congratulate himself on his terrible joke.

"There does appear to be a minor hull breach in section C on the western Sigma wing" ADAM informed him.

The moment the words touched Gilbey's ear his gradually improving mood took a nose dive and his stomach sank and for a brief second, he felt as if he was going to suffer the same fate as Dr. Reids and begin throwing up. "Oh for fuck sake!" he croaked, as loud as his vocal cords would allow, before kicking the panel below the basin, for he knew that this would mean a ridiculous amount of repair work that would be involved in such a job on top of his scheduled maintenance tasks. "This cycle is going to suck" he said to himself as he wiped his dripping face with his vest before putting it on. Leaving the garment even more stretched and shapeless than it already had been.

"What was that Sir?" ADAM asked inquisitively.

"Nothing" Gilbey said and waved his hand as though brushing away a bothersome insect. He was already deep in thought about the work he had already had to do since they first left Earth over sixty years ago and what a 'small hull breach' would mean if they didn't get to work on it right away would do to their flight time, not to mention their lives and the lives of the thousands of colonists currently held in stasis on board.

"Thank you, ADAM. That will be all for now."

"Of course, sir." With that, Gilbey heard the faint white electrical hiss of ADAM's intercom system fall silent.

During the first cycle, they only had a few engine issues that were expected from the fallout of leaving Earth's atmosphere and turning the primary thrusters on. There is the make or break moment in leaving the poison filled atmosphere of earth, the main thrusters fire and the ship is carried by the blast for the next twenty years before they need to fire again and the maintenance crew is awoken to make the always needed repairs. Unfortunately on occasion the thrusters don't fire; the ship is left to orbit the planet with both a flight and maintenance crew awake, while they wait for the optimal time to try and plot a course once more. This can take any time from a year. With the longest recorded time of a craft being held in Earth's orbit being six years.

The problem is that cutting through the smog caused a fair bit of damage to idling thrusters while they waited to be fired, especially once the jet stream caused the methane clouds to combust. This means that although the explosions actually helped the craft to be propelled out of the cloud and leave the atmosphere, once the rockets are turned off, the tail back will always over heat the stern and aft of the ship. It was a common issue and of course countermeasures have been developed and are taken to reinforce the exhaust ports, but there are weight limits. So strategically placing the main engine in the amidships is necessary and even a ship like Eden, fitted with huge launch rockets and a powerful engine to match her size couldn't carry enough plating to keep the flames from reaching the engine; twenty miles and countless decks deep.

These were the things you needed with off-world trips, more so since the Gloom had worsened over the year. Thankfully they didn't need to worry about re-entry or they would have been in serious trouble.

After their first awakening ADAM had informed Gilbey and the rest of the maintenance crew that the heat had caused one of the cooling ducts in the Lambda deck to warp to the point where it had stopped working completely. Meaning the ships engine could not begin to power up for the next thruster blast until repairs were complete. It took them the better part of a week just to stabilise the pressure in the maintenance tunnel before they could get in there to actually do the repairs.

ADAM had sealed the area after the initial thruster blast, to keep the gasses from affecting the sensitive network of cabling that ran through the entirety of the ship and not only powered ADAM but all other systems, resulting in catastrophic damage. This had kept the workload to a gratefully received minimum, but they had nearly reached their maximum maintenance cycle time before by the time the duct was repaired and some of the routine system checks had to be put off till next cycle so that the next thruster blast wasn't delayed. Thank fully nothing was missed and ADAM did not have to wake them up prematurely for emergency repairs, as this would have meant that they would spend over four months awake and working before their bodies were allowed back into stasis so as to avoid heart failure, which was the most common cause of death whilst in stasis, unless of course the ship suddenly exploded; which was second. ADAM would have woken them up before that ever happened, Gilbey hoped.

It took them nearly the whole cycle to get everything up to scratch. ADAM assured them that he had run various calculations and said that the cooling duct had a good percentage chance with the repairs they had made of keeping the ship from tearing apart in space, which had almost put Gilbey's mind at ease.

As for the second cycle, the repairs the crew had previously made to the primary thrusters meant that they were still on time for reaching Hyades star cluster. If they hadn't managed to repair them, then it could have added nearly a decade to the flight time. Gilbey was pretty sure that no one wanted to spend any more time inside this tin can than they needed to. Unfortunately the thruster damage had caused multiple issues in the engine deck which took the entire cycle time to complete. They had to replace ignition coils and a starter solenoid, on an engine the size of a house.

The team watched as the ship drifted passed the star cluster from a completely new perspective. No other humans would ever get to see this. Unfortunately upon making the belated system checks Graves came to realise that the ships magnetic deflector shields had begun to flicker and lose power for a few seconds at a time once every two or three years. The magnetic field, which covered the entire ship, had flickered and lost power for a few seconds at a time. Without it, any piece of debris could easily crash through the hull of the ship and bring the whole thing down from the inside. They were lucky that it was only a small hull breach this time around, but it was most likely the long lasting effects from the damage to the shield generator previously. Gilbey was sure they had fixed it perfectly, but these things were still a little temperamental. They had spent all of the second cycle working on the interplanetary magnetic shield Generator, so surely they had done the job, but regardless of that, something had managed to break through in-between the second and third cycle.

Fortunately the person in charge; Senior Maintenance Office Dietrich, wasn't as big a slave driver as Gilbey had endured on previous journeys over the Sol, so the crew did get some downtime during the cycles. Being the only people awake on an interstellar transport for a couple of weeks every twenty two years was something to behold, especially for a trip like the one that the Eden was taking. It was a journey that no human had ever done before, but also most likely one that no one will ever do again, so they may as well enjoy it.

The thought brought Gilbey back to the moment. He had tried to block out what this journey really meant for the human race. All the people that were left behind, and all the people on board who would never see most of their friends or family again, leaving them to their fate in the overpopulated underground metropolises buried deep in the ground.
He could feel the sensations of dread growing inside of him and beginning to clog his throat, as if someone had their cold fingers wrapped around it. He breathed deep and pushed his way through his feelings, sending them back into the dark recesses of his mind. He finished getting dressed thinking all the while that these thoughts were trying to remind him of the truth; there was nothing there for him any more. Not that there ever had been.

It was the furthest anyone had ever ventured outside of the Sol. He had been on deep-space salvages before. Maintaining the engine and making repairs as he had done here, but those ships always returned back to Earth, which you'd think would have been the easy part, but cutting through the smog safely was always tricky. Gilbey could remember all of the times he had thought that he was going to die as whatever ship he was on attempted to break through.

The Eden was not coming back. It had left Earth and they had not heard a single word from it since the maintenance and flight crews first went into stasis shortly after leaving registered space over sixty six years ago. The world they had left behind would not be the same one they remembered. The pollution had brought civilisation to the brink of destruction. They had become the engineers of their own downfall. The cyanogenic smog that covered the face of the planet and the trauma they had caused to the atmosphere were mankind's punishment for trying to create a way to reverse the incurable effects that humanity had caused the planet over the last few thousand years.

"Senior Officer Dietrich and the rest of the unit are in the Operations Room and are awaiting your arrival. Dr. Reids has been medicated and will be joining them soon".

"Thank you ADAM" Gilbey replied as he zipped up his jacket and went to the door, glancing over to the locker where he kept his own Industrial Rivet Gun, wondering what tiresome task would it be needed for this cycle, but he dared not ask for any more information from the machine.

Talking to ADAM was like talking to your conscience. His voice was very human and only occasionally had a twang of computerisation to it. Sometimes Gilbey would forget that he was actually talking to a machine, as if he was simply having a conversation with a voice in his head. Instead it was in every gadget and computer that was on board the Eden.

"Open it up".

ADAM fired up the mechanism and the door slid open revealing the pre-lit passageway. Most of the team had already passed through here, which was why everything was now up and running. Gilbey had been the first awake during the second cycle and previously when he had opened the door of the stasis bay, had had been greeted with nothing but a cold and dark abyss before him, almost as if he was staring out into the dark emptiness of space itself. Now the corridor was a tunnel of always blinding white light. The great task of repairing the Eden's hull awaited him.

The passageway felt cooler than the stasis bay. It seemed that even though their awakening had been predetermined, ADAM had not thought to get the ship warmed up ahead of time. During the last cycle it had taken a few hours before the crew felt as if they could take off their jackets.

Gilbey remembered that he had meant to ask Carter about changing ADAM's functions to do so before they came out of stasis, but he had obviously been too busy with the shield generator repairs and it must have slipped his mind.

Carter was ADAM's Operator and if there was anyone to ask about getting ADAM reprogrammed, it was him.

Just then the door to another stasis bay opened across the way and Dr. Reids emerged from the entrance. He wiped his mouth in a rather improper way, which was uncommon for him. He was a very well-spoken man who rarely engaged with the rest of the grubby engine monkeys he had had the rotten luck of being stuck with. Gilbey imagined that back on Earth he was a respectable Doctor, which obviously landed him a spot on the Eden, but not respectable enough as he had been appointed to the maintenance crew.

As he brought his hand back down, Reids noticed the other man in the hallway. "Oh" he said, collecting himself and straightening his coat, clutching tightly his data tablet which he was never without. "I thought you would be in Operations with the others".

"I'm heading there now" Gilbey replied. "How are you feeling?" It was really a rhetorical question. He didn't really care how Reids felt or how bad the sickness had affected him, but if he was trapped inside an enormous interstellar spaceship with the man, he may as well try and keep it as civil as possible.

The Doctor tried his hardest to put on a brave show, but Gilbey could see the small muscle spasms he was suffering from whenever his stomach twitched as if the sickness was about to return at any moment. "I am fine" he told him in a tone that made Gilbey think that he was trying to regain some lost credibility due to the fact that, thanks to ADAM, everyone probably knew he had spent the last thirty minutes throwing up.

Gilbey did think of telling him that it happens to everyone in an attempt to reassure him, but he remembered Reids had basically trivialised his A.S. during the first cycle, making out as if the sickness was merely a mild headache that would pass momentarily, when in reality it was more like the hangover from hell, so he left the man to suffer in silence.

He decided to head to the Operations Room and not wait for the Doctor. The two of them had nothing to talk about anyway, and the very idea of a hull breach had Gilbey too concerned for the amount of work that was needing to be done this cycle for mindless chitchat with someone who looked down his nose at him anyway.

When he arrived he found the rest of the crew already reading through the diagnostics, checking on the status of the colonists, and reading through various other data relating to the state of the ship and their current course settings.

Lane looked up from her computer terminal when the door had opened and smiled at Gilbey as he entered.

"Hey" she said. She too looked half asleep from her recent wakeup call. She yawned as she turned back to her work. Gilbey smiled and nodded. She was a nice girl, often keeping her own personal opinions on matters to herself to avoid any conflict, but it meant that she was always outspoken on everything. Gilbey had hung out with her quite a bit during the first cycle, but in the second, she had spent most of the time with Reids' understudy; Eckhart.

Carter was in the far corner of the room busy checking for network issues with ADAM. The two of them were deep in some conversation involving binary code that Gilbey could probably only understand a tenth of, but as far as he could tell, ADAM was operating at optimum efficiency, which was good as without ADAM, the entire ship would be like flying around with their eyes closed. Not to mention that all of the three thousand two hundred colonists would die in their stasis tanks almost instantly from heart failure. So it was good to know that they were being kept under the watchful eye of one of the most intelligent computer operating systems ever created.

"ADAM, troubleshoot the EVE" Senior Officer Dietrich called out as she stepped up to the middle control platform in the centre of the room. You'd have thought that this would have effectively ended Carter and ADAM's conversation, but a separate conversation from ADAM begun, allowing Carter and his beloved A.I. to continue their nonsensical computer talk.
"Checking the EVE Earth-Forming System..." ADAM replied as the rest of the crew stopped what they were doing and waited for the results. "Checking... the EVE System is functioning at maximum capacity, with a start time of thirteen point two minutes once we have reached our destination".

Gilbey noticed that everyone breathed a sigh of relief once they heard the words. It was the same repeated moment that had occurred in the previous two cycles that came before.
The EVE system was an enormous Earth-Forming molecular generator created by the best minds of the twenty forth century. Capable of manipulating an already established atmospheric planet to make it habitable for human life, the EVE System is able to recycle the regolith by adding organic material to the soil before redistributing it back onto the planet's surface allowing for vegetation to grow, whilst pumping oxygen and nitrogen into the air, making the atmosphere habitable over the course of twelve years.

Without the EVE, the thousands of colonists would be forced to survive inside the Eden, which will serve as a large habitation centre once the ship had landed, until they eventually died out, only venturing out as far as the Magnetic Field generator would offer a breathable atmosphere for.

The EVE itself is so large that the whole lower deck of Section A serves to house it and all the necessary sub-equipment needed to operate it. Enormous rib like appendages hold themselves in place during the flight, but upon touch down on the Delta, the ribs drive their way into the surface and the Earth-Forming can begin.

It was agony to think that the irreversible pollution damage caused to the Earth had begun to tear the planet's atmosphere so much that it did not have enough of an atmosphere left to get the EVE system working there. The smog, which the people on Earth called it; the Gloom, had completely dissolved it all. By the time the work had finished on the EVE system, it was already too late. The enormous gas giant that man had formed would be the harbinger of human races' termination.

This mission was mankind's final chance at redemption. To wipe the slate clean and start a-new. They needed to find a planet capable of utilising the EVE and creating a new home for mankind. Delta Tauri in the Hyades star cluster contained such a place, but one hundred and fifty three light years from Earth meant that it was going to take nearly a century and a half to get them there.

As soon as ADAM had finished stating the EVE systems' start time, everyone got back to their tasks. It was at this point that a cough behind Gilbey indicated that Dr. Reids had made it to the Operations Room.

"Dietr..." he managed to get out before coughing once more. In fear that the Doctor might start vomiting once again, Gilbey moved over to another section of the room near where he found Engineer Graves sitting looking at the data relating to the hull breach. It was the work that Gilbey knew he would be assigned for the majority of this cycle, so he thought he would get to it.

As soon as Reids composed himself, he continued with what he was originally going to say. "Dietrich, how are the colonists doing?" he asked.

The Senior Officer pressed a few buttons on the central control panel in the centre of the room and a holographic display brought up the ship complete with thousands of coloured lines beside it indicating every single person held in stasis on board the Eden. A small cluster of them were separated from the rest, these were flight crew. Looking over the entire ship nearly all of the coloured lines were blue, however a couple of yellow ones could be seen, which indicated that their vital signs were below normal, and, to the team's surprise, as soon as all of the lights showing the colonists and the flight crew appeared, a few of them flicked over to red.

"God damn it!" Eckhart called out as he got to his feet as if to get a better look at the holograph. Eckhart was the other Medical Officer awake during the cycles and the subordinate to Reids. His sudden outburst had caused the other people in the room to stop and look round to see what the matter was.

"Oh, are... are they dead?" a slightly shocked Lane asked as she turned towards Dr. Reids. The Doctor stepped onto the central platform. "ADAM, advise on stasis pods in critical condition".

"Michael James Burns, Olivia King, Faariq Bagheri; status... deceased. Cause of death: sudden change in cardiac arrhythmia resulting in myocardial infarction".

"Heart attack" Reids said aloud, almost as if he was informing the rest of the simple minded maintenance crew members what it meant in Layman's terms.

"Attempts were made at resuscitation" ADAM continued, "However all three cases were unsuccessful and resulted in loss of life".

"Did any of them have families?" Lane asked worrisomely. Gilbey knew that ADAM's answer would upset her. The thought that the families' of these people had left with their loved ones, expecting to start a new life together; a better one, only to come out of stasis a hundred and thirty seven years later to discover that their loved ones had died during the trip.

"Michael James Burns leaves a wife and three children" ADAM continued. "Olivia King leaves a husband and..."

"Okay, that's enough" Dietrich interrupted, most likely in an attempt to save Lane from wondering who was going to be responsible for informing the families of the departed once they reached Delta Tauri. "Reids, what do we do about the other critical ones?"

"I will monitor them from here for now" he replied. "But, if need be, a simple alteration in their stasis tanks should get their vitals back into sync".

"Well make sure that you are happy with their condition before the cycle ends". Dietrich went to move on, "When we get to..." but Lane interrupted her.

"ADAM how many is that now?... that we have lost on this trip?" she asked not really sure if she wanted to know the answer. The rest of the crew looked away awkwardly anticipating the difficult answer that was in bound.

"Calculating total number of colony or crew fatalities over the last 66.8 years of the Eden's travel time. One moment" ADAM informed the room. "Total number: Twelve. All casualties killed as a direct result of heart failure".

"This is bullshit!" Lane called out as she got up from her terminal and went to storm out of the room.

Eckhart caught her. "Its okay" he told her. "There isn't anything we can do about that. It is just the risk of being in stasis for so long".

"These people knew what might happen to them" Carter said. "They signed the consent forms before they ever got into the tanks".

"Shut up Carter!" Lane barked back at him, closely followed by the same uttered by Eckhart.

"I am just saying that these people knew the dangers" Carter replied trying to defend himself, before realising that the point was futile and turning back to his work with ADAM.

He was right. Out of everyone that the Eden was carrying, all of the three thousand and two hundred colonists, as well as the seven maintenance cycle crew and thirty eight members of the flight team needed for take-off and landing, each one of them had been carefully selected and evaluated before being asked if they wished to take part in this colonisation mission. Being in stasis for that long isn't good for anyone. It was the dangers of "prolonged suspended life", as the scientists called it. Every person on board this ship had to sign and agree to be in stasis for that long. It was a risk that every one of them took, including Gilbey when he was requested for this mission. None of them expected any casualties, but when they awoke during the first cycle and saw the red lights on the holograph, they all knew that there would be a lot more of them dead before they reached Delta Tauri, and they were right.

During the first cycle only two colonist died as a result of heart failure. On the second a further six died and one of the flight crew. Thankfully it was only one of the Landing Engine workers and someone who could easily be covered for, as horrible as it is to say, but it was still quite a shock to the system to see so many deaths.

"Isn't there anything we can do to prevent this?" Lane asked Eckhart. The young Doctor's face told her the answer, so Lane decided to ask something else. "Why doesn't ADAM wake us up so we can try to help?" This outburst was very unlike her.

"There's nothing we can do that ADAM wouldn't have already tried" Dr. Reids advised the sorrowful Engineer.

"Besides..." Carter added "ADAM's protocols on waking us are set to things might be a result of a catastrophic incident or malfunction, or something related either to the pods or the ship itself. Anything that might result in the deaths of multiple colonists or crew members would trigger him to wake us. A colonist suffering a simple heart attack isn't enough to create an additional cycle we really don't need and fuck up our lives by ageing us unnecessarily. We are already going to be older than any of the colonists we knew before".

The Operations Room fell silent. Once again Carter was correct but his cold hearted way of saying it made people feel irritated towards him.

"Look..." Dietrich decided to take control of the situation. "We are all saddened to hear of more people dying in-between cycles, but there is nothing we can do about this. Admiral Walker will be speaking to the families of those lost when we get to the Delta, so we don't have to worry about any of that. I am sure that one of the first things he does is bury the dead on the new world and create a sort of memorial to them... for their sacrifice. Let's just focus on what we have to do to get us there, okay?"

Gilbey decided that this was the perfect moment to change the subject to a more pressing issue. "How bad is the rupture of the hull in Section C?" he asked as he looked over Graves' shoulder at the monitor. He could see the four separate sections of the Eden split with one area displaying a flashing orb beside a large warning sign displaying the words 'Breach' and 'Oxygen failure' over and over. Graves selected this area on the touch screen and the picture zoomed in to the affected area.

"It looks like it happened quite recently" Graves told him.

"Approximately three months, seven days and six hours prior to your awakening" ADAM added.

"The damage relating to magnetic shield generator surrounding the ship during the previous maintenance cycle had clearly not been as fully repaired as we had thought" Graves told the crew, who were now hanging on his every word. It made him feel a little uncomfortable, causing him to slump back in his seat. "It appears that the, err... um... shield is... ADAM what's the shield's status?" he asked to help divert the awkward staring.

"The Interplanetary magnetic field is operating at ninety seven percent, which has resulted in a drop in power at irregular intervals".

"How long does the I.M.F go down for?" Dietrich asked.

"Just before the rift occurred, the shield generator failed for twelve point three seconds before a system reboot was automatically engaged and the interplanetary magnetic field continued to operate at...".

"ADAM, when did this first occur?" Gilbey requested interrupting ADAM from his full and unnecessarily long debrief. "And how often did we lose the Eden's shields for?"

ADAM took a short while to compile the data. After a few moments of awkward silence, ADAM spoke. "The magnetic shield generator failed a total of nineteen times over the course of the stasis sleep between maintenance cycles. Beginning four months and six days after you had re-entered stasis".

The room fell silent as they thought for a moment that for around once a year the shield generator had stopped working for, only at most, twelve seconds at a time, but within the last few months something had managed to use that small window of opportunity to cause a breach in the Eden's hull. It was a scary thought given that the shield was stopping all manner of space debris from completely tearing the ship apart and killing them all.

"So what the hell caused it? ADAM what is this I'm looking at?" Gilbey said, leaning over Graves and using his fingers to zoom in and rotate the strange image on the display which showed something in the Sigma wing of Section C. Graves leaned forward to get a better look.

"Upload to the central display" Dietrich commanded and suddenly the holograph in the centre changed from the image of the colonists coloured lines to a larger version of what Graves had displayed on his monitor. Here everyone could see the mysterious flickering orb.

"An object of unknown origin breached the Eden's hull at twenty one thirty three hours on April eleventh, twenty four ninety eight. It was stopped by the drop in velocity caused by breaking through the outer shell of the ship, before lodging itself into the wall of the Sigma passageway of Section C" ADAM informed the team. "There appears to be no hazardous gases or materials detected".

"Well that's a relief" Carter added.

"Has it managed to get into the Sigma stasis bay?" Reids asked. "There are eight hundred colonists next to that passageway".

"Although there is minor damage to the western wall, the stasis bay and all colonists residing there are secure. As protocol requires, I have sealed the Sigma passageway until the third cycle had commenced. There was no immediate threat detected, so I was not required to wake you from stasis".

"So what the fuck is it then?" Graves asked, appearing to get his courage back.
"I am afraid that without a sample uploaded and scanned, I simply do not have any relevant data at this time" ADAM admitted. This made Graves smile, hearing that the all-powerful machine that was in control of their lives did not have any clue as to what had managed to get on board the ship, but it made the rest of them feel concerned.
"Due to the size of the object; three point seven feet long, two point seven feet wide, and two point one feet high, I would presume that it was a meteorite of some kind. My preliminary scan reveals that the object is hollow and empty surrounded by a foot thick carapace, but I am afraid that I do not have any further information".

"Thank you ADAM" Dietrich said before closing down the holograph in the centre. "We need to get that shield generator working probably. Whatever we did to it during the second cycle was not good enough. We can't let this happen again as god only knows what else will crash into the ship. Any more of this and we will need to wake up the flight engineers, and those guys will be pissed if they have been woken up seventy years too early. We were lucky that this was just a small object, anything bigger could have ripped the ship in half, maybe even taken one of the middle sections of the ship out with it. One of those fall and we can kiss the tail end of the Eden goodbye".
"The Eden only needs Section A in order to fly" Carter added. "So long as the engine and the EVE systems are secure, then we would..." he stopped as he realised that it was not am appropriate thing to discuss.
"Thank you Carter" Dietrich stated as she walked over to Carter who was disconnecting his Programmer Interface from the ADAM port here in the Operations Room. "Carter, you and me will head down to the Gamma deck to try and sort the shield generator. We'll need ADAM to run diagnostics before we get there to try and pin point what exactly the problem might be". She turned her gaze over towards where Graves and Gilbey were located. "You two and Lane take a tram and head over to the hull breach. Take a look at the damage and, if possible, begin the repairs on it. We need to make sure no further damage will be caused to the outer wall of

the Sigma bay".

"What do you want us to do with this thing?" Graves asked pointing at the object that had broken through the hull on the monitor.

"So long as the ship is sealed and we ain't going to rip apart out here, I don't give a shit what you do with it". Graves face turned red following Dietrich's response. "If it's melting a hole in the floor, then use a Carrier to take it to one of the Storage holds and jettison the fucker". The Senior Officer turned to the Doctor. "Dr. Reids" she said in a calmer tone than the previous orders she had just given. "The people in the pods with the vital sign errors..."
The Doctor decided to continue her sentence for her. "Me and Eckhart will check their stasis tanks over. We need to check and see if any of them might be at risk of suffering heart failure after we finish this cycle".

"Can you do something about the deceased colonist?" The delivery of Dietrich's request felt almost as if she was asking him, rather than telling.
"Yes... yes" he struggled to say as Gilbey saw the Doctor's stomach twitch, causing him a brief moment of pain. Dr. Reids brought a hand up to his mouth before suddenly realising that everyone in the Operations Room had seen the spasm, so he proceeded to scratch his face, as if that was the reason he had brought his hand up in the first place. He cleared his throat and continued. "As with the others, ADAM has already cut off the oxygen to their pods and will continue to hold their bodies in stasis to avoid decomposition. This will allow their families to bury the bodies, or, alternatively, the ship's incinerator would be fine to cremate them, if they'd rather. So long as their deaths were not a result of any form of infectious virus, or the result of this meteorite, then it will be perfectly fine to preserve them here".
"Okay" Dietrich continued. "Look, we've got a lot to do and not a lot of time to get it done in. I know it is going to be tough, and after the amount of work we had on the last cycle, we were all looking forward to a nice easy one, but I think that..."

As Gilbey tried to listen to his commanding officer, a small flash caught his attention. Once he caught sight of it, Dietrich's voice became distant and almost muted, along with the constant humming of computers and machinery elsewhere on the Eden.
The small flashing light was coming from the Eden's communication uplink station. The uplink was designed to send and receive transmissions from over incredibly long distances. It is used

for ships venturing out to be able to communicate with Earth, or with one another, but the message could take days to travel from one location to another, depending on how far away the ships were. For something like the Eden, since the fact that they were travelling further and further away from the closest human-being with each passing moment, a transmission would have taken years to reach them.

The flight crew had used the communication uplink to speak to Earth as the Eden began their journey to Delta Tauri, but before they had gone into stasis, they had asked the maintenance crew to keep an eye on it for any future communications. The crew had checked it on the first cycle, but there was nothing. Lane took an interest in it over the first week of the second cycle, but other than that, they had not even bothered to pay it a second thought. They had not heard anything since a few days after leaving the Sol and now years had gone by. They figured that they had forgotten about them, but the small yellow light that was flashing on and off for a couple of seconds at a time made everything suddenly come rushing back to Gilbey. He felt his mouth almost drop open and his heart began to race.

"ADAM" Gilbey announced interrupting Dietrich who turned to him in vexation. "Have we... received any transmissions?" As soon as the words left Gilbey's mouth, he saw the crew's eyes grow wide and turn towards the direction of the communication uplink. A few mouths even began to drop in the same way as Gilbey's had done once they too noticed the small flashing yellow light, in the background, flickering like a lighthouse miles away, almost like a small beacon of hope.

"Oh... my god..." Eckhart muttered as Lane gripped his jacket tight, pulling him in closer to her embrace with a look of stunned shock on her face.

A few moments passed before ADAM spoke, passing seconds that felt almost like a life time. "Message received: August thirteenth, twenty four seventy six. Transmission destination coordinates; zero A.U. Sol System, Local Cluster".

"Earth" Lane said with a smile, a tear forming in the corner of her eye. Even Carter smiled as the word left her lips.

"It came only a few years after we finished the second cycle" Eckhart added as he too began to smile at the thought that they have had a message from home waiting for them all this time.

ADAM continued "Eighty two point three light years from our current location. Message Date:

December fifth, twenty three hours, forty nine minutes".

"Hey, thats like… fifty years old" Graves stated standing up from his station to get a better look at the communication uplink.

"Can you bring it up here ADAM" Dietrich asked pointing towards the central display once again.

Within seconds the holograph appeared in the middle of the Operations Room, only this time it was displaying data relating to the received transmission. "Sender: Daniel Hale. Clearance Level: C, one thirty seven. Dulce Bunker, New Mexico". An image displaying, what appeared to be, Daniel Hale's face, could be seen. The man's appearance was gaunt and balding, with deep sunken dark eyes. He appeared like someone whose face looked older than he actually was. The crew's faces began to change when they saw the image of Daniel's sickly appearance.

"Who the hell is that?" asked Gilbey as he tried to remember the faces of the people who had worked on the Eden but had not accompanied them on this mission, but nothing came to mind. His name rang a bell somewhere in the furthest corner of his mind, but he could not place it.

"Message playback…" ADAM proclaimed and the crew waited in nervous anticipation for the message to start. The sight of this unknown sender had made them feel a little on edge. Their hopeful message from back home had started to look like a foreboding transmission of despair.

The audio started and instantly filled the room with a bleak undertone. "Crew of the USC Eden" the hoarse voice called out as the holographic image of him remained motionless, hovering above the central display like a ghost. "This is Chief Daniel Hale of the United States Military… or what is left of it".

Gilbey could feel his stomach begin to clench and tighten the more he spoke. He felt as if he was starting to come down with a late case of Awakening Sickness once again.

"It has been a lifetime since you left Earth's atmosphere to travel to the Hyades start cluster in the great beyond. Your mission to colonise Delta Tauri brought hope to the people at the time. Carefully selecting and testing each colonist and their family members, picking only the elite who would be able to survive travelling that long in stasis to reach the new world… your new beginning… the last hope for the human race". His words brought uncertainty to the crew. Graves slumped back down in his seat. "I was not even born when you left this god forsaken place. I grew up in the world decimated by the Gloom; the pollution that poisoned the skies around the underground bunker which was my home with my father, David Hale, and son of; Commander Nathan Hale".

Now that was a name Gilbey did recognise. He was one of the high ranking generals in charge of the Eden mission. It was ultimately down to them to decide who would be able to come on board. He was an old man when Gilbey had met him before starting the trip. It was clear that he would not be going. Many of the "older" citizens were not allowed to accompany their families on the pretence that they would not survive the journey. Some proposed colonists even gave up their places to spend the last few years they had with their older relatives, rather than leave them alone in a dying world.

"My father would tell me stories his grandfather told him of the old world. The blue sky and white clouds that rained down water from above. Thick green grass that would grow from the soft soil beneath as animals, cattle and sheep grazed the fields as birds flew overhead".

It was not the life that they had remembered. Gilbey had grown up in one of the bunkered cities sitting just on the surface, with most of it buried underground. When he was a boy the animals had only nearly all but died out from the smog. He remembered seeing a lush grassy field once, but he couldn't recall if it was in real life or if he had seen it on a computer in some achieved footage. It was only when he was a teenager, when the air became so unbearable without the proper equipment that it became almost impossible for anyone to venture outside. That was when the government started to heavily invest their time and efforts into the various space programs, salvaging materials from old satellites, and mining minerals from floating asteroids in deep-space. This was the world that Gilbey had remembered leaving behind, one that was slowly being eradicate by the Gloom.

The transmission audio continued. "I grew up just as we lost communications from the last remaining bunker cities. The Gloom had changed since your time. The air was so acidic that it would burn right through your suit, and once it reached your skin, you were done for. Millions of bacteria and radiation forced its way into your bloodstream. A single infected could wipe out an entire bunker. We had heard it over the comms. Porton Down was lost within a month of bringing back someone who had been contaminated. We tried to build deeper underground, but we just didn't have the manpower. We had become weak by the lack of daylight, and with the contagion now becoming more of a frequent problem, we couldn't do anything but sit and wait to die". The crew could hear the sound of a cup of liquid being poured before the man on the message drank it. "Eugh... When the Gloom became more potent, we lost the chance to continue or research into the EVE system, in hopes that it could, somehow, reengineer what had been done to our planet. The technology was left stranded in the Utah complex when the smog managed to get in and kill everyone. We are all that is left... Right now, we haven't had a communication from anyone in over a year.

My father told me that you were the last hope for humanity. The Eden was the only shot Earth had of carrying on. He was a great man who took up the mantel after my grandfather passed. Thankfully he died before the Gloom could get to him. He left me in charge of the ruins. Half the facility was lost when the infection began to spread. We had to seal that entire eastern wing, just so we had a chance of living that little bit longer. There's not that many left now. It won't be long before we starve to death or become contaminated ourselves. The last of us who remain are sickened anyway. We were born that way; forced to live a life stuck down in this deep dark hole. How could they have children knowing that they were bringing them into this dying place? A lifetime of living beneath the ashes, just waiting around to die". His words were the stuff of nightmares to the maintenance crew. Their worst fears had come true and now the world they had left behind had fallen.

Gilbey looked over and saw that Lane was sobbing into Eckhart's jacket. He held her tight in an embrace, but his face appeared just as saddened as hers. Carter now had his hand over his mouth in disbelief at what he was hearing. Dr. Reids looked as if he was about to puke again.

"When we were children" the recording went on. "We were told not to send transmissions to you. You were a shining pillar of hope for the human race, and the last of the government wanted to keep it that way. They didn't want you to know how bad it truly was; the world you had left behind. I am sorry for telling you this. I know it must be difficult to hear. I don't know if you had expected this or if you thought that they would managed to get the project to save the planet up and running. I had heard stories of your mission and always believed that you would one day come back and save us, taking us to the new world where the grass was thick and green beneath a beautiful blue sky. I know now that you are probably not even at Delta Tauri yet. By my calculations, it will be years before you are even close. Most likely, by the time you receive this message, me and the last survivors of Dulce will be long dead. I only hope that this tells you not to come back. Don't send anything back to Earth. This world is dead and you will die if you come back here. Hear my warning Eden. Begin your new lives and remember the horrors that you have escaped from. The millions of people who have died because of what our ancestors had done to this planet. Don't make the same mistake at Delta Tauri. Live... please". The voice began to cough uncontrollably. A few gasps for air could be heard before Daniel managed to pull himself together again.

"End Transmission".

3ʳᴰ Cycle — ETA: 70.2 Yrs

Part Two: Lying in Wait

The morale of the group was low. It was the last thing they had been expecting, but in truth, they should have anticipated it. Earth was a dying world when they left. The people they had left behind were forced to live beneath the ground, breathing in recycled air and eating out of cans or harvesting from crops that grew in unnatural light. It was no way to live, not that they were doing much different presently, but once they reached their destination, everything would be different, at least they hoped. The world they had grown up in was gone. All that remained was Delta Tauri. If they could get the colony safely there, then maybe they had a chance of starting over, rebuilding humanity and truly learning the error of the human race's ways that had brought about their own destruction.

Gilbey had always felt like they were the only people in the universe at times, walking among hundreds of people suspended completely motionless as they stood inside their own individual stasis tank would have that effect on a person. At times he had disassociated himself from them, thinking of them as statues, if it was not for the computer monitors displaying heart rhythms and their vital signs nearby. It was easy to feel isolated on such a large ship, especially when there were only seven of them awake during the cycles, but now that they knew their home was gone and that everyone they had left behind were dead, it was much worse.

The message had come forty nine years after it had originally been written. If that was how the world was at the time, then by now it was nothing but a floating rock filled only with death, covered by a thick layer of man's own undoing.

The call had left the maintenance team feeling as if they too should give up the way that Daniel had, but they knew that they couldn't. They had to keep going. Like he had said, the Eden was the last chance humanity had of redemption.

Dietrich had noticed how down the group were feeling, as well as herself, and had decided to give them a few hours to go and get their thoughts together before they started work on the repairs. Lane had been devastated by the news and Eckhart, the handsome sympathetic Doctor with the excellent bedside manner, had decided to console her in the Recreational area.

Gilbey didn't want to think about it. Anyone he might have left behind was now surely gone. He had acknowledged that when he first accepted this job, and when he left Earth all those years ago. But now to know that they were all dead, all those left behind. It was not worth dwelling on. There was nothing he could do about it, and thinking too much into how they might have met their miserable demise would have been enough to drive him insane.

So with that in mind, he decided to get a look at this thing that had crashed through the ship and was now lodged in the Sigma wing of Section C. It was going to be a hell of a job to get it repaired, so he thought that he may as well go and have a look at what they were dealing with.

He had taken the Eden's tram system straight from Operations all the way to Section C of the ship. It was used to travel across the ship, as walking the distance would have taken well over two hours. Unfortunately the tram wouldn't take him straight to the Sigma wing. He would still have to walk the rest of the way. The trip from the Section C tram terminal would take him through the Sigma stasis bay. There he would find a quarter of the eight hundred colonists in this section of the ship that were being held in stasis there. Well give or take that many due to the fact that a couple of the deaths that occurred between cycles had been in this section.

"Arriving at Section C tram terminal" ADAM's voice announced as the tram slowly came to a stop. "The Sigma wing can be found on your right".

"Thanks ADAM" Gilbey replied reluctantly. He knew where the Sigma bay was from here. It had been part of the training that all of the Eden Maintenance Unit knew the layout of the ship from top to bottom. They did this so if there were any major issues on board, the crew would know the fastest route to get to where they were needed most. There was also only one tram terminal per each section of the ship, and one that leads directly to Operations, so in the event that the trams failed to work, the crew would know where to go.

Perhaps ADAM did not know what exactly the crew had been trained on, or maybe he was just practising for when the colonists wake and have to live in the Eden as the EVE Earth-Forming system gets to work. It was going to be a while before the planet was how they had envisioned it to be, and during that time everyone was going to have to get along inside the Eden itself and the surrounding protective field created by the Magnetic shield, if it managed to stay working that long.

"Why have you decided to work, may I ask?" ADAM questioned. ADAM was designed to adapt to his environments and the actions of the people on board, with the idea that he would be able to assist with any unexpected situation that might arise. With that in mind, he was known to ask questions about things that he might not have computed, something that he does not have yet on file, or something he could not solve mathematically. The idea that the others were grieving over the loss of their home world, yet Gilbey was still pressing on with his work, must have been quite peculiar to him.

"I…" Gilbey wasn't sure of how to answer in a way that ADAM would comprehend. He knew that if he told him the truth, the A.I. would not understand what he was saying or how he was feeling, which would have, no doubt, been followed up with more questions.

"I have a job to do ADAM. The breach endangers everyone". It wasn't exactly a lie, but telling him that he was doing it for any other reason than to just clear his mind of the terrible news they had just heard seemed like the easiest choice.

"Is that the truth Gilbey? I am detecting irregularities in your tone and voice octave, which often relate to a form of lying".

Gilbey couldn't help but crack a smile. After the news they had heard today, he had wondered if he would have ever smiled again. "Fuck off" he joked. "You really are too smart for your own good ADAM. Why don't you just leave it at that, okay?"

"But Dr. Reids..." ADAM went to say but Gilbey cut him off.

"Enough ADAM. That's enough". He was not in the right frame of mind to be arguing with a computer. "Stop talking to me".

When Gilbey reached the Sigma stasis bay of Section C, the door slid open to an already lit room. The bay was an enormous white hall with stasis tanks all around the edge, a few rows in the middle of the room, as well as a second tier of stasis tanks that lead onto a catwalk overlooking the entire room. It felt like a library of people or human sized dolls on a toy shelf just waiting to be opened and played with. Similar to the maintenance crew's own personal stasis bay, various terminals sat beside each one showing how they were doing, all in front of a green glow to indicate that all was well. The glow allowed the medical members of the maintenance crew to easily spot any who might be suffering from some kind of distress, which displayed the terminal as various shades of yellow, or who had sadly died whilst held in stasis, which showed a bright red light behind the text and monitoring windows displayed on the computers.

Each of the tanks had various tubes and cords feeding into them. It was through these that the person in stasis was able to be kept alive. One provided oxygen and cycled it back out to be used again after it had been treated, whilst others dealt with feeding and keeping the skin hydrated and healthy. It was strange as no matter what, you always felt as if you were shrivelling and drying up like a decaying piece of fruit whenever you came out of hibernation. It was why ADAM provided coolant sachets of specially designed liquid to help a recently awakened person. It was similar to going without food for a long time, which living in the bunkers and on long salvage missions, was something Gilbey knew all too well. If you started gorging yourself with food after not eating for days, then your body cannot take it and you will begin to feel worse, so, in a similar way, coolant was designed to rehydrate the colonists after exiting stasis, whilst providing them with enough liquid to not cause any damage. Drinking glass after glass of water, which is what you think you need, would actually be the worst thing you could do. The coolant is absorbed by your body and heads for the key places that it needs to go; the brain, the heart, and the kidneys, and then you simply spit out the left over liquid into a drainage port. Instant refresh and recharge, as the creators had sold it as.

With that in mind, it was horrible to think what the people in stasis would come out like if the tanks did not have a hydrating tube. Gilbey doubted that they would even survive.

Usually the lights being on meant that someone else was here. "Hello?" Gilbey called out. The word echoed across the cold floor, bouncing off each of the glass tank coverings. There was no response. The room was unnervingly quiet for a few moments before the sudden clang of something metal from somewhere in the distance shot all around. Because of the acoustics in the room, it really could have come from anywhere making it difficult to pinpoint.

"Hello?" Gilbey called out, louder, once more, but once again it was met with an ear piercing silence. "ADAM... who is down here?" he questioned, but that too came with no response. A moment passed. "ADAM!" Gilbey called out as the frustration began to build up inside of him. ADAM finally answered back. "You asked me to stop talking to you Sir".

"Oh for godsake" Gilbey blurted out almost automatically before laughing at the stupidity of the situation. "Maybe you ain't as smart as you thought you were".

"Who is..." Gilbey went to say, but a noise interrupted.

"Graves?" a familiar voice called out from behind one of the middle rows of stasis tanks. "I think this may take longer than I originally calculated. I will check out the object when I can".

"It is Doctor..." ADAM went to say.

"Never mind" Gilbey told the machine as he made his way to the source of the voice.

As he passed around the side of the last tank in the row, Gilbey could see Dr. Reids sealing a tear in one of the pipes with a small hand-held Weld-Pen. The intense heat was reattaching the tubing with precise perfection inside of the rich purple glow that stood out like a beacon in the white and blue all around as countless monitors beside their stasis pods shone out the colour status of the occupant inside.

The Doctor had not noticed Gilbey as he made his approach. He was too engrossed in his own little world. It was the first piece of work that required him to help with some repairs that he had seen the Doctor do since they left Earth.

A bucket lay beneath the terminal displaying yellow, indicating that this was one of the colonists in stasis who needed medical attention. At first Gilbey figured that the bucket must have been used to collect fluid discharged from the tubing, but as he got closer, he could smell the distinct foul stench of vomit. It was clear that the Doctor was not feeling one hundred percent just yet. It would have been another couple of hours before the A.S. began to wear off.

He was amazed that the Doctor had gotten down here so quickly. Gilbey felt as if he had left the moment the message from Earth had finished, but maybe, upon reflection, he had waited around for a while to see what Dietrich wanted them to do. Reids must have just decided to get to work, most likely before the messaged had even ended.

"But was Graves down here as well?" he wondered. Maybe he had been in the Operations for longer than he thought, stunned with emotion to learn the fate of the world back there.

"Hey doc" Gilbey said as he walked over, so as to avoid sneaking up on Reids whilst he worked. He wasn't sure if the man knew exactly how to use one of those weld-pens, as they had the power to burn through human flesh at a distance of about a metre.

The Doctor twisted his head around, took one look at the maintenance engineer, and turned back to his work, which instantly got Gilbey's back up, but in the interest of being civil, he decided to ignore it.

"How are you feeling?" Gilbey asked indicating towards the bucket. It was at that moment that he noticed Dr. Reids had a small stain on his jacket, possibly caused from when the sick had hit the bucket and splattered back onto him.

"I'm fine" Reids responded once again unbelievably. It was clear if he didn't want to talk about it in the passageway earlier, then he didn't want to talk about it now.

Gilbey was done trying to be the slightest bit sympathetic to what the Doctor was going through. He changed the subject. "What happened here? How did the tubing get a tear in it like this?"

At this point Dr. Reids had finished making the minor repair and flicked off the Weld-Pen, placing it back into the maintenance toolkit near his feet. A Beam-Saw casing was lying on the ground beside it. It was clearly the source of the noise Gilbey had heard earlier.

"Well it turns out that the stupid machine in charge of our fucking lives was wrong" Reids snapped.

"ADAM?" Gilbey asked.

"Do you know any other pin headed A.I. whose sole purpose is to ensure the lives of the colonists here are not lost before we reach the Delta?"

"What do you mean Doctor" ADAM's voice spoke out from all around.

"Oh, get lost!" Reids sharply told him staring up towards the catwalk, before turning his gaze back to Gilbey. "He is supposed to wake us if there are any issues with the stasis tanks beyond the ones who have died of heart failure" Reids went on. "This one had suffered severe damage from the piece of debris that crashed into us. A small fragment appears to have flown across the bay on impact" he said pointing off into the distance to where the piece of space debris was supposedly located. "... and torn through the tube here...." He pulled on the tube, holding it up so Gilbey could see the damage, which had now been welded back together, but the scar was still clearly visible. "It ripped right through and this poor girl would have died if we had left her any longer".

Gilbey looked over at the woman's face. She must have been around twenty five or so from the look of her, but it was difficult to tell given the completely motionless nature of her face as she stood, eyes open, coldly staring out beyond the glass of her stasis tank. He looked over towards the terminal display right beside the coolant distribution dock and the drainage port. "Jessica Kerrigan" the name read on the screen above flashing important medical words and number patterns, all in front of the glowing yellow light. Beneath her name was her colonist identification number; one-five-seven-three.

"Jessica's tubing had not been severely damage Dr. Reids" ADAM explained. "The tear had only caused a minor irregularity in her pulse, resulting in a slight decrease. I ran multiple diagnostic tests and calculated that she would have remained perfectly healthy until your next cycle". It was almost as if the computer was desperately trying to explain itself to the Doctor. "This woman would have died if she had not had this sealed soon!" Reids barked aimlessly towards the sound where he thought that ADAM's voice was coming from. "You should have woken me up to deal with this at once!"

"Given how you are currently handling your most recent awakening, I do not think that it would have been the best thing for your body Dr. Reids" ADAM responded amusingly, so much so that Gilbey couldn't help but chuckle, resulting in him receiving a look of disgust from the Doctor.

"Don't get cute with me you overpriced and overcomplicated calculator!" Reids fired back.
"It would have increased your cycle time by twelve percent resulting in..." ADAM told him before Reids cut him off.
"I am in my right mind to have you unplugged and fly the rest of the journey to Hyades myself".
Gilbey knew that it was a stupid thing to say to ADAM, as he was no doubt about to respond with a hundred reasons as to why that would not be a good idea and how much it would

endanger everyone on board. Not to mention that the Doctor would most likely die of old age before they even reached there.

It was then that he decided to sway the conversation elsewhere. He noticed something thick in the bottom part of the tubing stuff clutched in Reids' hand. "What is that?" Gilbey asked pointing towards it.

"The..." the Doctor tried to speak but the words caught in his throat. He looked as if he was going to be sick again. Gilbey contemplated stepping back. "The... the piece of shrapnel is still lodged in there?!" Reids proclaimed apprehensively.

"You sealed it without taking that out?" Gilbey asked in disbelief.

"I..." Reids looked embarrassed before his face turned to anger and he called out in an arbitrary direction. "ADAM!" His words echoed off into the distance. "You ensured me that there was no hazardous materials inside the tubing! I asked you before I began sealing it".

"That is correct" the machine answered.

There was a moment of confused silence that passed. "I..." Reids went to say but stopped. He thought for a moment before holding up the pipe with the large bulge inside of it. "Do you know what this could be doing to the colonist?!"

"I have checked and there appears to be no contamination caused by the piece of debris" ADAM responded. "Jessica is in perfect health now that the tube has been repaired".

"Perfect health...!" Dr. Reids repeated. He reached down and grabbed hold of the Beam-Saw, flicked the activation button on it and the blade casing lit up as a concentrated beam of high intensive lasers appeared. Gilbey could feel the heat coming off of it instantly. "I am not leaving that thing in there" Reids told them.

"Doctor Reids wait!" ADAM called out, flicking warning signs on Jessica's display terminal.

"Yeah hold up" Gilbey told him at the exact same time as he grabbed hold of the man's wrist, realising the danger that cutting the tube could have caused to the colonist in the stasis tank.

"If you make the slightest of errors, then you run the risk of damaging the tubing beyond repair, cutting the flow of oxygen into Jessica" ADAM advised. "Which can result in a permanent decrease of brain functions or even a loss of life".

"Yeah, cutting that pipe could do all kinds of shit doc" Gilbey added.

"Well what? What do you expect me to do? Just leave that foreign object in the fucking tube, lying in wait, ready to infect every single colonist on this section of the ship?"

He was right. Each one of the tanks' oxygen tubes fed back to a large air recycling processor that was connected to the cooling ducts that ran over the entire section of Eden. It was the same system they had used in the bunkers buried so far down into the earth that no new air from the surface could make it down, although they often had to change it as the Gloom had found a way.

With the small stone-like piece of debris caught inside this stasis tank's pipe, any contagions could affect every colonist in Section C.

"ADAM?" Gilbey asked looking up towards the ceiling as he let go of Reids' wrist. The Doctor let go of the activation button on the Beam-Saw and the laser dispersed, returning it to nothing but the cold metal casework.

ADAM took a few moments to answer, leaving Gilbey and Reids with the feeling that maybe the computer didn't have everything under control, before finally stating "As previously stated, I have scanned the debris and there appears to be no vapour or hazardous chemical discharge coming off of it. The drop in vital signs was due to a tear in the oxygen tube. The debris appears to be completely harmless and will be broken down over time, eventually being drawn into the recycle processor, whereby it will be separated from the clean oxygen and disposed of. I have calculated that the process will take a further twenty seven point three weeks now that the tear has been repaired".

This answer seemed to satisfy Dr. Reids. "Okay" he said reluctantly. "So we just leave it in there?" His words made Gilbey feel uncomfortable. He knew that if it was his stasis tank, he wouldn't want some piece of asteroid lodged in his breathing pipe. "But the next time something like this happens" Reids went on. "I want to know about it. I don't care if you have to wake me up separately for my own cycle and I'll age fifteen years! Do you understand me computer?"

"I understand you Dr. Reids. Please speak with the ADAM A.I. Operator and Computer Engineer; Carter, for a reprogram of my preliminary waking protocols, and he will be able to have these parameters redefined to suite your specific requirements" ADAM informed him.

"Oh, I will" Reids replied coldly turning to the computer terminal to check the condition of the colonist. "You can be sure of that!"

A sudden moment of realisation hit Gilbey. "And while you are at it" he added. "Can we set the heating to kick in a while before we wake up for the next cycle?" Reids turned around and gave him another disgruntled look, as if indicating that there were far more important matters at hand.

"It's fucking freezing in here when we wake up".

A while after Gilbey decided it was time to check out the cause of the breach in the ship. He left the infuriated Doctor and headed across the room to the far corner of the stasis bay, near to the Sigma wing of the ship. As soon as he turned out of the row of stasis tanks he could see the damage to the inner wall. A few shards could be seen lying scattered on the floor amongst pieces of the plastered wall in the middle of the walkway at various points between where Gilbey was standing and where the damage in the wall was. The wall had cracks running all the way from the bottom corner, almost as high as the catwalk overlooking the bay. Only a small piece of whatever had crashed into them was visible. Gilbey could see it poking through a tear in the wall. Graves was kneeling beside it, appearing to be giving it a preliminary examination.

It was hard to believe that a small piece of debris could have travelled such a distance on impact and landed so far away, embedding itself into the tube at the other side of the enormous room. He could see that the other pods looked unaffected, so it had only been the one tank affected by the meteorite, but they were going to need to scan the entire deck to be sure.

"Maybe it was just a piece of the wall" Gilbey wondered to himself, thinking about what exactly was the thing lodged in the colonist's oxygen pipe. He would rather it had been that, than a piece of meteorite in the tube that kept oxygen flowing to you over the years you are standing in stasis for. Although ADAM was known to have nearly every man made material on record, so he would have been able to analyse it already if it was.

Just then, in the distance, Gilbey saw Graves lean forward to touch the piece of rock sticking through the wall. Gilbey, realising how stupid it probably was for him to make contact with the unknown object with his bare hands, went to call out when something caught his attention beside him.

A terminal next to one of the stasis tanks he had passed was displaying a red glow, indicating that the colonist within the pod was dead. Gilbey stopped and turned to face it.

"Darren Wilson" he read off of the monitor screen before turning his gaze to the statue-like husk of the person behind the glass.

The man didn't look any different from any of the other colonists in the stasis tanks all around him. If it was not for the red display beside him, you'd have thought that he was still alive. Like all of the colonists in hibernation, his face looked in a permanent state of peace as his eyes stared out towards Gilbey. He didn't look dead. There was no obvious signs such as bleeding or contortion of the body, nor did he look like he had been in any pain, but there was something hollow about his eyes. The vacant stare did not have the same feeling of life behind them that the other colonists had. After a moment of staring into them, it was clear that he was now nothing more than an empty and lifeless shell.

According to the computer, Darren was one of the few colonists to have suffered a heart failure as a result of prolonged exposure to being suspended in stasis. This had happened nearly thirteen years ago, nine or so after the second cycle. All of the vital panels on screen showed nothing but flat horizontal lines moving from left to right. Apparently ADAM had made attempts to revive him, but each one had ended unsuccessfully.

Gilbey continued to stare into the corpse's eyes as his mind began to wander. If there was such a thing as a soul, then, like his body, Darren's would too be currently held in stasis until they reached Delta Tauri, at which time, when they finally found the planet to touch down upon, it would be released and free to soar high above the new world, along with all the others who had died to get them there.

"Another one gone" a voice said behind Gilbey. He had been so lost in thought that he had not heard anyone approaching him. He turned around and saw Eckhart standing there. His focus was on Darren's suspended body. "One of the first things we will do, when we get to where we are going, is probably build a grave for all of them. Not what I would have thought our first project would be". Gilbey stepped back as the young Doctor walked over to the computer and started to press a few buttons, bringing up various displays showing images of a woman and two young children. A few pods nearby lit up. From here Gilbey could see two smaller figures beside a tank with a woman in it. The woman was the same as the one on Darren's monitor. "His wife?" he asked.
Eckhart nodded. "It appears so". Gilbey couldn't bring himself to look at the faces of the two children who were now fatherless. Their suffering was all to come. "Admiral Walker will comfort them once they awaken when we get to the Delta" Eckhart told him.

Gilbey remembered Lane's sorrowful face when they mentioned Admiral Walker doing a ceremony the last time. She wanted nothing more than for everyone to make it and just to live happily at peace in their new world.

"Where's Lane?" Gilbey asked, changing the subject. In the background he could still see Graves as he was still unprofessionally examining the meteorite, so he knew he couldn't stand here chatting for very long, however, given how the shard in the oxygen tube across the bay had not caused any damage to the colonist the tube fed to, he was pretty sure that Graves was okay to touch it. All the same he had no idea what damage he might cause the wall further, as he did not have the steadiest of hands.

"I've given Lane a sedative to help calm her down" Eckhart told him. "The news of Earth had hit her a bit harder than expected. I figure she could take a day or two to..."

An abrupt voice boomed through the stasis bay causing both men to jolt suddenly. "On whose authority?!" Dietrich's shouted as she stormed across the hall towards them, her gaze fixated upon the young Doctor. Even from this distance they could see that a fire burned within her eyes. "Who said you could drug my crew?!" By the time she had reached them, Dietrich was breathing so heavily, unknown if it was caused by the journey here or the fact that she was fuming with rage, that she had to take a few deep breaths before she could speak again. At which point Eckhart went to answer, but she somehow managed to interrupt him. "We have just over three weeks to complete our job!" she went on breathing heavily in an attempt to catch her breath and continue her bombardment. "We have a major hull breach and an unknown object on board this ship. Our magnetic field could drop at any minute and leave us open for collision with any more of these fucking things floating around out there. We have limited numbers and limited time to get this done, and you are drugging my crew, leaving them out of action for god knows how long!"

"With all due respect..." Eckhart went to say, but Dietrich cut him off once more.

"No! I said you could have a few hours to get yourselves together. We were all shaken up by what we had just heard, but this mission is too important for us not to get done what we are supposed to do! If we don't get this ship repaired, then all this... all this is for nothing".

"My job is ensure the well-being of the colonists and Eden's crew, which includes all of us" he said gesturing over towards Gilbey. Dietrich gave him a cold glance before turning back to Eckhart. "Lane is suffering trauma from the news and she would be no good to anyone if she breaks down".

As the young Doctor and the Senior Maintenance Officer bickered at one another, Gilbey managed to slip out of the fold and head over towards Graves besides the small meteorite. He had known Dietrich to bust balls from time to time, but nothing like this. This was a side of her he had never seen and was glad not to be on the receiving end. Perhaps the message had gotten her more determined to reach the Delta and complete their mission to carry on the human race there. With Lane out of commission, it did mean that this might have taken longer than any of them would like.

He could still hear them going back and forth at each other as he made his way across the remainder of the stasis bay. After a few moments, Dr. Reids could be heard emerging from around the corner and managed to get himself involved in the debate. Soon all three of them were arguing with each other, however, it felt as if Dietrich was not disagreeing with the Doctor, only with whatever Eckhart was using to justify his actions.

"I should throw you out the god damn airlock for your insubordination..." was the last thing Gilbey managed to hear before he turned his focus elsewhere.

"What the fuck is going on over there?" Graves asked nodding his head behind Gilbey and towards the carnage. His face was filled with a profound curiosity as it always was, but really it was clear that he was making a mental note to not do anything that would piss their senior officer off the way that Eckhart had done.

"Just another squabble" Gilbey replied turning back to see that the situation back there looked as if it was starting to be resolved. The young Doctor was holding his hands up as if to say that what was done was done and they all needed to get on with it, which was really the truth of it all.

"What have we got here?"

Graves smiled a huge toothy grin at Gilbey. "Well..." he said as if to reveal some grand piece of information. "It's just an old piece of space rock". He laughed, seemingly amused with himself.

Graves was younger and less experienced than Gilbey, so naturally he did whatever he asked in terms of repairs, effectively making him his assistant. He was a good kid and helped out as much as he could, but he was prone to making a few mistakes here and there, as well as being slightly clumsy most of the time. He knew what was what when it came to engineering, especially in space. He apparently spent most of his time living on board some ship orbiting the Earth. There he worked making repairs to the hull on the outside of the stations in a full spacesuit, which was most likely why he had been selected for this job, so Gilbey was happy to have him under his wing for this particular type of task.

Gilbey took a knee beside it and looked at the damage to the stasis bay wall. A large fracture could be seen going halfway up the wall and the entire bottom corner was now lying in shards all over the floor nearby. The 'Space Rock' in question was bland and grey in colour. It looked no different from a boulder back on Earth, only this had more holes all across the surface that seemed to tunnel deep into its heart. There was no smell and no heat coming off of it, so it gave him the impression that it was harmless. Gilbey reached out a hand and placed it on it. Nothing happened. It felt just like a regular rock. It was not even cold. The Sigma wing, on the other side of the wall, was sealed, so it was not being heated. It was just an average room temperature.

Thankfully it looked as if no real damage had been done to the wall. All of the heating pipes seemed still intact. The closest one being visible thanks to the recently formed hole, and the steel floor looked relatively unscathed given the impact. It seems that the outside hull had taken most of the force when the small meteorite had hit the ship, which had probably caused the object to lose its velocity once it had broken through. It if hadn't, then this could have been catastrophic to the Eden and most likely taken her down.

Gilbey looked through the hole in the wall out into the Sigma wing. It was difficult for him to get his head around the meteorite and so he needed to almost lay on the floor to be able to see through a small opening. The hallway looked dark, most likely due to the fact that ADAM had sealed it and so no electricity or magnetic energy was getting in as to avoid further damage to the ship. He could feel the cold coming from outside, even with the I.M.F up and running. He could make out shards of the meteor lying in the passageway. They still ran the risk of de-pressuring this section of the ship if the shield dropped again, so it was imperative that they got the breach repaired as soon as possible.

"Flying millions of years through the unknown" Graves said staring blankly at the debris as he scratched the side of his head. "Floating past distant planets and breaking off of shooting stars. It could have seen a hundred different lives on a hundred different worlds."
Gilbey rubbed his finger over one of the asteroids holes. "Yet it turns out to be nothing more

than a big dead stone" he added as he banged the side of it and the two maintenance engineers could hear the sound echoing off somewhere within. "It's empty".

"Yes" ADAM's voice spoke out reminding Gilbey that they are never truly alone on board the Eden. "My exploitative analysis reveals that this object does not contain any contagious material or is otherwise hazardous to you or the colonists in any way".

"Yeah, thanks" Gilbey said in a way that was more to shut the computer up. He felt like the machine had started to repeat itself. He turned to Graves and began explaining the task at hand. "We'll need to saw through this section of the wall here. If the thing is stuck, we can lift it from the other end with a Carrier. We can't pass this rock back out through the way it came in..." he said as he rubbed his hand across the tear in the wall. "...as we could cause more damage. Better to take it down to the storage hold below us and cast it out there. We should be able to get it through the bulkhead door. If a Carrier can make it through then this piece of shit can". He went to kick it but decided against it. "We'll have to rivet a new sheet here and again on the outside. It won't look pretty, but it should do the job".

"Well maybe if there is nothing to do on the fourth cycle, I'll come back and paint this up" Graves laughed.

Gilbey wished that was true, but he was sure they would wake up to a new load of bullshit to deal with on the next cycle.

"Let's take a look at this thing from the other side".

The magnetic shield created almost an atmosphere inside everything within the field. The air is breathable and the gravity is set to whatever is on the ship, which is bottom deck of the Eden. The thing was that they still needed to suit up as the shields might drop at any moment, leaving them totally exposed to the vacuum of space. Although ADAM informed them that they had a three hundred and fifty seven point six two million chance of that happening, they did not want to take that chance, so it was of the utmost importance that they suited up before venturing out into the Sigma wing.

The suits themselves were clunky and old fashioned. Back on Earth, they had spent more time developing better thrusters and perfecting the EVE Earth-Forming technology, that they had pretty much forgotten about the spacesuits. It was the classic saying of 'if it ain't broke, then don't fix it. Humanity had used these thick bulky get-ups since the late 24th century and not changed their design once. With the constant threat of the Gloom, it was clear that they had more pressing matters to deal with.

Gilbey was used to their chunkiness. He felt safe and secure in them. That was only because of the Mag-Boots attached to their feet. Without them, if the shield generator failed, then they would be sucked out of the opening in the hull. Their artificiality grav detectors kick in the moment gravity is lost, magnetising the user to the floor. They were handy to have if you needed to make repairs outside, but inside they were annoying as hell to walk around with regardless. It reminded Gilbey of trying to wade through water.

He had seen, first hand, what would happen if the Mag-Boots were not in use. On one of his previous deep-space salvage missions, the ship he was working on suffered a bay door malfunction and one of the crew was sucked out into the dark unknown. He had not suited up properly and his boots were not yet secure. His helmet was not even on yet. The ship he was on at the time had searched for hours around the mineral deposit that they had previously been probing before they found his floating frozen corpse. Since then, he always ensured his Mag-Boots were secured before unsealing any location that had even the slightest risk of a vacuum being created. If they were sucked outside now, then they would be left to float around until they starved to death in their spacesuits, or alternatively, if the magnetic field had previously only gone down for about twelve seconds, then it might have rebooted by that time, catching them inside of it and breaking their bodies down into millions of microscopic pieces, burning them up; a fate no one wanted to suffer.

The two maintenance engineers approached the Sigma wing bulkhead door. Dietrich was watching through the window of the door of the stasis bay. She had a look of concern that she was trying to hide beneath her authoritative persona. He guessed that she thought that if she looked concerned, then her subordinates should be concerned. If she kept calm and focused on getting the job done, then no one would need to worry.

In the background they could see Reids examining the rock. He was on his hands and knees with a small torch trying to see through one of the holes. His tablet was resting on the floor beside him providing him diagnostic information on the debris.

"Hook us up" Gilbey asked as Graves lifted the helmet over his head and clipped it into place. As soon as Gilbey's head was completely submerged inside the helmet he could not even hear the noise of the helmet's locking mechanism clicking into place, sealing it to the suit. All that could be heard was the sound of his own breathing. It sounded almost exaggerated as if he was already about to breathe again before the sound of the previous exhale had dispersed from his ears. It echoed around inside his helmet. Right now, the constant sound of him breathing felt infinite.

There was something about being enclosed in a small area around your head before heading into a passageway leading out to endless space, which got the heart racing, making his breathing much more rapid than normal.

He looked over to Dietrich who mouthed something. Gilbey gave her a puzzled look before realising that he did not have his comms switched on. He brought his hand up to the switch on the side of his helmet. "Sorry" he said, almost embarrassed by his stupidity. "What's that?"

"Turn your camera on" she ordered as her name, rank and a small image of her voices sound wave appeared in the bottom right corner of his helmet's visor.

Gilbey complied. Another switch in the helmet and the image appeared on her data tablet. The word 'Recording' appeared in the top left corner. "Okay we're live" he told her.

"Can you give Graves a hand please?" she asked.

Graves gestured at the locking mechanism on his suit and Gilbey connected his helmet to it for him. "You good?" he asked.

Graves turned around and gave him a large gloved thumbs up before bringing his hand up and flicking on his comms. "Thanks man. I'm good".

"ADAM" Gilbey called out towards the panel and terminal beside the door. "Open Sigma wing doorway B".

"Unsealing Section C, Sigma wing" ADAM's voice said inside the helmet. The terminal display changed to green. "Door B is unlocked". Gilbey pressed the touch screen and the bulkhead door slid open almost instantaneously.

The passageway felt slightly colder than the others, even through the suits. It was clear that ADAM had reconnected the electronics for this area as the lights came on as soon as they had stepped inside. The heating had not had time to warm up this wing, and even if they did, most of it would have been drawn outside through the hull breach anyway, so ADAM had probably shut it down to conserve power.

On the ground lay the scattered meteoritic shards beside fragmented debris from the side of the ship. Gilbey gave a piece a kick, but his leg moved so slowly that the shard barely moved at all.

"Jesus" Graves exclaimed as he got a first glimpse at the damage the meteorite had caused. He stared at it in awe as he brought his hand up to scratch the side of his head again, only to realise that he could not possibly get to it.

Gilbey stepped over to the hole in the side of the ship and looked out. Beyond the Eden's hull breach, all that could be seen was a faint blue discolouring of the shield surrounding them in front of a backdrop of eternal darkness. The deep dark void of space swallowed everything. There were no stars, no nearby planets or satellites. All that could be seen was the colossal abyss that stretched on forever. He had never seen space look so empty. It truly was the furthest anyone had ever been from Earth.

The glimmering blue magnetic force-field looked like a thin almost see-through curtain that hung in front of it, shimmering like an ocean. It truly was beautiful to behold. Pulses of magnetised electricity shot through it like lightning bolts cutting through the sky.

Gilbey had forgotten what it was like to actually be outside. Seeing it through monitors or display units over the last few cycles did not do it justice and, in no way, showed how magnificent it truly was. For a moment he wished he could take his helmet off and take in a deep breath. Although the air outside here was breathable, the human body could only take so much and extended exposure could cause serious health concerns.

He took a look at the hole itself. The jagged inward tears in the Eden's hull did not look as bad as he had initially thought. A sheet on either side, held down with some rivets, might be enough to hold this section together. It would need to be welded around the edge so that it would be airtight in order to keep the passageway's pressure normal should the shield drop again, but he doubted it needed to be fully repaired, given the astronomical chance that another piece of space debris would hit exactly here, he thought that they would be okay until they reached the Delta.

The breach itself was only the size of a small car, and given how something had come onto the ship, rather than out, most of the work was needed to be done internally. So at least that was something. It was still a lot of work, but they would be spending most of their time inside the passageway, rather than hooked outside. Gilbey would leave that for Graves to do, since he was the most experienced at it.

"This isn't as bad as I originally thought" as he explained what they could do to repair it to the others.

"Gilbey, get me a close up of the burn marks" Dietrich asked. He leaned in rather awkwardly so that the camera on the helmet could see the rim of the tear. "I see…" she said discouragingly.

"What?" Gilbey questioned.

"No… I just thought it would have caused more scalding along the framework when it came through" she replied.

"You want more work for us?"

"Don't be a prick" Dietrich replied laughing. "I just thought it would have caused more damage is all".

"It does seem strange. I think maybe it was just moving at a slow speed, if not at all. Chances are we crashed into it" Gilbey replied.

"It could have just been floating there." Graves' voice called out. Gilbey looked back around to see Graves was now holding the piece of debris in his hands. "This little thing is as light as anything".

An idea popped into Gilbey's head "See how it looks out there" he said, pointing towards the hull breach.

Instantly a smile appeared on the young man's face. "Ah… Hell yeah" he said as he went over to the hole.

"Wait!" a voice called out abruptly over the comms, rendering the two men catatonic for a split-second. "Bring one of those shards in with you, will you" Reids said.

"Doctor" Dietrich chimed in. "We don't know anything about that rock. The sooner it is off this ship, the better".

"What happened to 'so long as it isn't melting through the hull, then you don't care'?" Graves laughed, but almost instantly regretted it as Dietrich's silence made everyone listening feel uncomfortable.

"Dietrich… what we have here is ancient fossil. It is millions of years old and has travelled an incomprehensible distance all over the universe. It could have come into contact with anything…"

"Exactly!" Gilbey heard Dietrich cut him off, almost as if the two of them were having this debate inside his space helmet. "It has already been on the ship for months, we need this thing off of here as soon as possible".

"Don't have to tell me twice..." and with that Graves threw the chunk of asteroid out of the hole.

"Oh for..." Reids irritatingly called out as the rock flew out towards the magnet field, before losing momentum and dropping suddenly. "God's sake" the Doctor said at the same time as releasing an enormous sigh of annoyance knowing that it was already too late for anything to be done.

As the asteroid fragment fell, the debris dropped past the centre of gravity on the ship, flung back up, hit against the hull on one of the lower decks and was knocked off into the shield. Instantly being erased from the cosmos. The shield glimmered like a diamond for a moment as ripples dispersed over it.

"Officer Dietrich" Reids said calmly, which came as a surprise to the rest of them as they had never heard him address Dietrich by her rank. "My lab is the most secure location on this ship". As he spoke, Graves was busy picking up the remaining meteorite fragments and was enjoying throwing them out of the hole, watching as they too took the same journey to their inevitable destruction as the previous piece had done. "I will take full responsibility if anything happens. Look, I will even take a piece off of here". Over the comm they heard the sound of a Beam-Saw light up once more. The faint glow of the intense blade could be seen through the cracks where the meteorite was lodged into the stasis bay wall. "I will cut myself off a piece now" Reids said.

"Don't you fucking touch that!" Dietrich barked at the Doctor. None of the maintenance crew had ever heard her speak like that to him. Today was truly a day of the unexpected for them all. "You cut that rock open, you don't know what is going to come out".

"My preliminary scans..." ADAM's voice softly said before Dietrich told him to be quiet.

"Quiet! We don't know enough about this damn thing..." she sighed.

"I understand. Really I do" Reids interrupted softly. "One of the shards from in the Sigma Wing might provide useful information into rocks from beyond our world. ADAM has a limited data based on what we had back on Earth. When we reach Delta Tauri, we do not know what we might face there. The planet could have changed over the hundred and thirty-seven years that it has taken us to get there". Everyone could tell the Doctor now had Dietrich's attention. "If we could learn more about the Solar System we are supposed to be making our new world within before we get there, then it could save years of studying and research".

ADAM's voice spoke out. "I have to agree with Doctor Reids. My calculations show that this meteorite could have passed through Delta Tauri eons ago, or even could have broken off one of the neighbouring planets or moons. If a piece is to be uploaded to my database then I could study it in-between cycles and provide relevant information before we reach our destination". The comms fell silent for a moment. Everyone waited, listening for how to proceed. Graves was eager to see another fragment of this alien rock thrown out and disintegrate in the magnet field.

"At the very least..." ADAM said after a few moments. "...it will give me something to do whilst you are in Stasis. It can be incredibly lonely between cycles".

After a short moment Dietrich had made up her mind. "Look... Doctor Reids" she said softly, and instantly Gilbey knew that she had weighed up her options in her head and allowing Reids a small piece was a small price to pay for getting him off her back and letting them get on with their job. "If you ensure the security door of the lab is sealed at all times, then I will sign off on you taking one of the smaller fragments for the purposes of helping us learn more about the new world once we reach the Delta".

He knew that Reids would be pleased with Dietrich's answer. If it was up to Gilbey, he would have thrown the whole thing off of the ship and be done with it, but scientists always seem to have to get their way with this sort of thing, and if it did help speed up studying rocks from another world, saving mankind years of research, then he didn't have a problem so long as it did not affect the rest of the flight.

"Thank you" he heard the Doctor say and with that the light of the Beam-Saw disappeared through the crack in the wall. "Graves... bring me one of those segments by the door, will you".

It wasn't so much a request as it was a demand and Graves knew not to question rank so he did as he was told. The piece he picked up was the largest one left in the passageway. It was not as big as the shard recently thrown out of the hull breach, but it was good enough for what the Doctor needed. Reids sealed the rock in a hazardous waste container and was gone before the rest of the crew could begin their work.

The next two and half weeks went by like clockwork and by the end of the cycle, they had managed to make all the repairs that they could to keep the Eden flying. The crew remained in high spirits despite all they had learned since they first woke up about the world behind them that was now lost.

Lane managed to pull herself together after a day or two. She did her job but there were days when Gilbey noticed her crying in her room. Eckhart was often there to comfort her and do what he could for her without Dietrich knowing. Dietrich made sure that they got enough downtime and Lane seemed to utilise this to the fullest, most likely to keep her mind off of things. Everyone was sure that she just needed some time, and within the last week of the cycle, she was back to her normal self.

Dietrich and Reids did not come to blows again about the asteroid. The Doctor focused on his research after he had finished attending to the health and well-being of the colonists still in stasis. He spent most of his time in the lab with the security door firmly locked behind him, as Dietrich ordered and Gilbey was sure that everyone preferred it that way. Rather than having him breathing down their necks, making little comments about how things should be done, and doing very little work in front of them, it was better that he was keeping himself busy locked away in his lab.

The Senior Officer asked Reids, from time to time, about his findings, but he always seemed to come back with the same answer; "It is too early to tell. I will know more once we awaken for the fourth cycle", or something similar.

As for the repairs themselves, half the team worked on getting the shield up and running whilst the other half needed to work on the breach itself. Dietrich, Eckhart and Carter worked on the I.M.F and the rest focused on the hole in the ship.

Graves did his thing from the outside as Gilbey and Lane worked on getting the inside panel riveted and welded shut. Thankfully this area of the Eden had a Rivet Gun already located here, so Gilbey didn't need to travel back to his own stasis bay to retrieve his.

When they had finished, it looked botched, but they knew it would hold. A lick of paint and no one would even notice. Repairing interplanetary crafts with limited resources was difficult back on Earth, let alone in the middle of uncharted space.

When the others had finished with the magnetic shield generator, it appeared to be functionality normally. The crew performed extensive testing after it had been fixed in hopes that they could stop it from dropping again over the course of the next twenty two years that they would be in Stasis. As far as ADAM could tell them, what they did should do the job, but some minor re-calibrations might need to be made when they next woke up. He had been reprogrammed so that he would wake them if the shields did drop again over the next two decades. It was not ideal, having to wake up early and waiting until the next time the maintenance team were able to re-enter stasis, but it was a lot better than waking up to find your pod floating through the endless darkness of the infinite.

It was Gilbey who Dietrich tasked with taking the meteorite to the Storage hold in the Carrier. It was an awkward task; trying to manoeuvre it through the passageways and down the Cargo lift, but he got it there in the end. He was the most experienced out of the lot of them to use the Carrier. Back on Earth he had been assigned to load supplies into the storage hold in the lower levels of Section D.

The Carrier Loader was a large mechanised exoskeleton used for lifting heavy materials and other type of objects around the ship. The Eden had one on every deck, and the idea was that once they reach their new world, the Carriers would be used to help build homes for the colonists once the EVE had finished making the planet's atmosphere liveable.

Unlike the P-5Ks, which were used in conjunction with your own body's movements, the P-7 series Carriers were driven from a seat at the back and used foot pedals to move the legs and analogue sticks for the arms. They were the lazy man's machine.

The contraption itself was a bit tricky to get the hang of, but Gilbey managed to get the job of moving the meteor without any hassle. Graves had previously dropped some machinery with it during the first cycle, so nobody wanted to risk him transporting the rock down to the Section C Hanger bay.

The only issue the crew had faced was that the Hanger airlocks are not intended to be opened whilst in flight, and so someone needs to be inside to open it in order to jettison the rock out of the ship. Thankfully the Mag-Boots of the spacesuits came in handy for that as well. They just needed to ensure that everything was strapped down or else all of the machinery the passengers of the Eden needed to build their new civilisation would be blown out when they opened the airlock.

They needed to turn off the I.M.F for a moment, which was ironic considering they had only just got the thing up and running earlier, but ADAM had ran a collision detection scan of the surrounding space beyond the ship and provided them with the best time to deactivate the shields. They needed to do this in order to create a vacuum strong enough to pull the meteor out of the Hanger and throw it as far away from the ship as possible, or else they ran the risk of the thing crashing into another part of the ship when it dropped past the centre of gravity within the shield and was pulled back upwards. Without the shield activated, the gravity remains exclusively inside the Eden and allowed the asteroid to return to the black abyss from where it came from.

When everything inside the Hanger was secured in place, it was time for the cause of the hull breach to leave. It had well and truly overstayed its welcome and caused enough damage for a life time. As Gilbey pulled down the switch of the Section C Hanger bay airlock, he felt the rush of air exiting the ship as his boot's sensors kicked in and he was locked in place. Even through his suit's helmet, he was able to hear the sound of the air rushing all around him. It must have been deafening to anyone not suited up in there.

The loose parts of large equipment flapped as the vacuum of space tried desperately to pull everything and anything it could out from within. A steel chair had clearly been forgotten about and shot across the bay. It crashed into the side of the bay door's frame, causing a soundless dent, before being dragged out into space, never to be seen again.

In a heartbeat, the meteorite flew out of the Eden with such force that it had vanished from view in a matter of moments. It all happened so quickly that Gilbey did not even really notice it had gone. It had followed the same route as the chair, crashing into a section of the frame, causing a much larger dent, but thankfully it didn't look as if it had done any real damage to the ship. A small shard broke off of it but that too was pulled out of the hanger bay door, disappearing as quickly as it had appeared.

And with that marked the last piece of work the crew needed to do this cycle. Inside the suit, Gilbey let out a sigh of relief knowing that their work was complete. He had worked so hard that he had barely taken in the sights of this part of space. He would never visit this place again and doubted that any human would ever again, unless of course they fucked up the new planet like they did the last one. But here, in this moment standing before the large opened hanger bay door, he was able to take it in. Without the shield up, he could see just how beautiful the universe around them was. The Eden was passing by some far off distant planet that glowed a rich green on the back drop of pitch-black. Thousands of stars could be seen spanning his entire view that shimmered like sequins.

He closed his eyes and listened for a moment and it made him feel as if, he too, was drifting off into the darkness alongside the meteor, which was now hundreds of miles from the ship. He felt his body relax and he found himself just standing there, in complete silence, taking a moment for himself.

After a few seconds, Lane could be heard over the comms asking about the I.M.F and suddenly the moment had passed. It snapped Gilbey out of his trance and he pulled the lever up, shutting the bay's door. As it started to close, the magnetic shield generator kicked in and the world around them slowly became encased in a translucent glimmering blue.

A few days later they went back into their stasis bays. They had spent this time cleaning and unwinding as their bodies reached the minimum time that they were physically allowed to re-enter stasis. It felt good to have this short time together. They had no idea what mess would need fixing when they next woke up. The thought that they might not even wake up at all lingered in their minds.

They said their goodbyes and joked about how they would see each other in only a few moments, however, in reality, decades would have passed before they saw one another again. To them, that time would pass like a hazy dream.

Gilbey climbed into his stasis tank as ADAM began to close and seal the door as he got himself into position.

"See you in twenty two point five years, Gilbey" ADAM told him.

"Good night ADAM" he replied. "Don't break the ship whilst we are asleep and kill all the colonists". The monitor switched on beside him and displayed a green light. It was then that the pod began to take a hold of him and he felt his existence fade away as the world around him began to slow down and disappear. Within seconds he was gone, unbeknown to him what horror awaited the next time the maintenance crew would be awakened.

"I won't Sir" ADAM told Gilbey's body suspended in time within the stasis tank. "I'll keep them safe".

4ᵀᴴ Cycle – ETA: 47.7 Yrs

Part One: Reawakening

"How... oh my god... holy shit... how... how many... how many are dead?" Gilbey asked the machine as his stomach clenched in anticipation of the horrific answer that was soon to follow.

ADAM fell silent for a moment, as if it was far too many to count. A few seconds later he answered and as soon as the words came out of the nearest speaker, the reality of the situation sunk in. "There has been Seven hundred and thirty-three casualties in Section C".

"Se..." Gilbey couldn't speak. He fell against the wall of the passageway and dropped down in disbelief. "I..." he tried to say something, anything, as if to rationalise what was going on, but the words caught in his throat. "Seventeen" he finally managed to say as the gears in his brain ground together in a desperate attempt to put everything into place in his mind. "There are Seventeen colonists left alive in that entire section of the ship". When his own words reached his ears, he felt a hit to the gut once more. He thought he was going to throw up, but the feeling was a hundred times worse than any Awakening Sickness he had ever felt.

"Are you okay Gilbey?" ADAM asked. "You have an increased heart-rate and irregular breathing patterns. I would suggest to the Senior Maintenance Officer that you schedule yourself in for a short medical examination".

"Am... I..." Gilbey tried to laugh but the smile dropped and he felt as if he was going to cry. "Carter..." he said as he tried to control his breathing following the AI's advice. "What happened to Carter?"

The last time he had seen Carter was when the mass of gore and black organic liquid seemed to reach out and grab hold of him. Everything happened so fast that no one had any idea how to react. Carter let out a cry of agony as something emerged out of it, like it was trying to defend itself. Carter's screams were dwarfed by the terrifying shriek that Gilbey could still hear ringing in his ears.

Graves, Lane and Eckhart had just run from the Sigma Stasis bay, but at that point, whatever had come out after them had blocked the way, causing Gilbey to become separated. He made a break for the passageway between Sigma and Tau bays when he noticed the same black root-like stems oozing outward through the ventilation next to the door. He turned down the corridor and just kept running as fast and as long as he could. He felt as if he had been running for hours before he finally stopped to catch his breath and everything he had just seen and experienced since first waking up less than an hour ago, had caught up with him.

"I am afraid I do not know what you mean. Technical Engineer Carter is currently..." ADAM went to say before Gilbey cut him off.

"No... no, what the fuck happened to him!" he yelled out as he brought his hands up to his head, clutching at his hair as he remembered Carter's tormented face as he was pulled beneath the depths. The black liquid pouring down his throat as he screamed. "Wha..." Gilbey went to ask again but the image was too much to bear. He swallowed hard and managed to force the question out.

"Is he dead?" he asked ADAM in hopes that the machine would be able to provide him with a straight answer.

"No" ADAM replied.

The news came unexpectedly causing Gilbey to stand upright once more. "What?!" he said with incredulity.

"He is currently residing in the Sigma Stasis bay, however, he may require medical attention as his vital signs are currently dangerously low".

Carter was alive, which meant whatever had grabbed hold of him still had him, or he had managed to escape and was wounded somewhere. Gilbey looked back towards the direction he had just ran from, as if to see if he could still see the Stasis bay, but he had taken every possible turning he could find to get here, so as to avoid being caught by whatever was now loose on the ship.

Was he going to go back for him? He didn't know. He had no idea if he could face whatever that thing was in there. There was no telling how big this thing was and how much of it had spread to the ship. If it has already killed over seventy-five percent of colonists in this section of the ship, then chances are it had either taken over here completely, or it had a way of transporting itself to slaughter more colonists elsewhere, meaning that every single person on board the Eden was now in mortal danger.

Gilbey did not want to go back in there alone. "Where are the others?"

"Senior Officer Dietrich is in Operations. Doctor Eckhart and Maintenance Engineer Lane are both at the Section C Tram Station, and Maintenance Engineer Graves is waiting for the Cargo lift to the Storage Hold of this section".

"What the hell is he doing over there?" Gilbey wondered, but he figured that Eckhart would have focused more on protecting Lane than Graves, and if he was separated from the rest of them, then maybe he was going down there to find a weapon of some kind. A few had been stockpiled in case of any threats once they reached the Delta. Of course there was no telling if this thing, or more of them, were hiding down there.

The other two should be fine so long as they get back to Operations. They had no issues when they first woke up until they saw the preliminary reports of the status of the colonists and headed over to this part of the ship.

The Maintenance crew could not believe what they saw on the holographic display. A sea of red blinking lights indicating the sheer number of fatalities. All of them were in the four Stasis bays of Section C, with three of the bays completely wiped out.

The first thing most of them had done when they woke up was check to see if they had received another message from back home, but there was nothing. No flashing little light, nothing. Everything else appeared to be functioning normally and even the corridors were warmer as per Gilbey's request. No one could have prepared them for seeing all those red lights.

Gilbey remembered looking over at the rest of the crew who were in complete stunned silence with their mouths wide open. Their reactions were far worse than when they learned the news of Earth the cycle before.

"Oh my god!" was the only thing he remembered anyone saying.

"Did we suffer another hull breach?" Graves asked but ADAM told them that they had not and that the Interplanetary magnetic shield Generator was operating at maximum capacity and had done so since the repairs were made twenty-two years earlier. There appeared to be only a few problems with the ship, such as the secondary engine's compressor appears to have failed and various cooling ducts all over the ship are not functioning. Neither task were large jobs, so the cycle would have been relatively simple as luck would have it, allowing them to just catch up on anything else that needed to be done left over from the previous cycles, however, it was clear that luck was definitely not on their side.

"What the hell caused this?!" Lane cried out as tears flooded down her face. "Why are they all dead?!"

ADAM told them some of the answers, but each one lead to more and more questions. According to the system, every single colonist in the affected areas had died as a result of heart failure. ADAM's protocols state that the teams are not to be woken up unless there is some kind of critical Stasis pod failure, a detectable pathogen, or a forced opening, such as a breach that will result in the death of a number colonists if not dealt with as soon as possible. Since heart failure was the most common cause of death for people in stasis, there would have been no reason to wake them up no matter how many died. It was an unfortunate loophole in the programming that had cost the lives of nearly eight-hundred colonists.

"What about Doctor Reids?" Eckhart had asked. "Where the hell is he?"

As everyone looked around for the Doctor, Carter informed them that during the second cycle, Reids had made sure that any death resulted in his awakening and he would tend to the well-being of the colonists on his own unless further complications occurred. According to ADAM, the Doctor had been brought out of Stasis nearly twenty years prior and had not returned since.

"Twenty years!" Eckhart replied almost rejecting the remark he had just heard. "My god. So he only returned back into Stasis for two years after we all went back in?"

Graves nervously laughed. "The guys got to be in his sixties now" he said as he frantically scratched the side of his head.

"You've got to be fucking kidding me" Dietrich added before asking ADAM to bring the feeds from the cameras in the Stasis bays up on the holographic display in the centre of the room, but when it did, all they could see was darkness. "ADAM" Dietrich asked. "What's going on? Bring up the feeds now!"

"My apologies Senior Maintenance Officer. I am having some difficulties finding a feed that's visual field has not been blocked".

After a short moment the computer managed to find one, but the angle was so obscure that it didn't show them anything.

"God dammit!" Dietrich shouted as she threw the coolant packet she had brought in with her from her Stasis bay across the room before turning around to the rest of the crew. "What... what is going on? Is there a virus or some kind of toxin in the air that has caused these deaths?"

"ADAM would have woken us up if there was anything like that" Carter added almost as if he was defending the A.I. he was in charge of.

"Shut up!" Dietrich barked at him before he could say another word. It was clear that she was feeling the pressure of being the highest ranking officer out of Stasis and having nearly every colonist in that section of the ship dying on her watch. "We..." she thought for a moment. "We need to know what is going on in there". Dietrich tried to control her breathing, as if she needed a moment to compile her thoughts.

"But... but ADAM, where the fuck is Reids?" Gilbey asked and the Operations room fell silent as they waited in anticipation for the computer's response.

"Doctor Reids is currently located at the scientific research and development wing of Section B".

"His lab? So he has just been sitting around working in his lab for the last twenty years while those people in Stasis have been dying?" questioned Graves before Dietrich broke in.

"Look!" she said firmly, as if she had compiled her thoughts and decided on the best course of action. "We can worry about the Doctor later. Our priority is the colonists. If there is something mechanical or viral that is causing this, then we need to stop it before it spreads to the rest of the ship. All of you get down there and take a look".

"Take a look?!" Gilbey added. "We don't know what is down there".

Eckhart had to agree. "If we go down there then we might infect ourselves, at which point there will be no one left to help the rest of the colonists".

"The air is breathable" ADAM explained. "There is nothing on my scanners that shows any kind of airborne pathogens or..."

"ADAM! Be quiet!" demanded Dietrich. It was clear that the team's trust in the most sophisticated and intelligent A.I. ever created by man had been shaken. "Get down there and find out what is wrong!"

"It might just be a technical glitch on ADAM's part" said Carter as he picked up his tablet, which allowed him remote control access to ADAM's mainframe beneath Section A's flight deck. "If it is then maybe everyone down there is fine".

Carter's out of place optimism seemed to get Lane's attention. "Really?" she said, her voice full of sorrowful hope as she wiped away the tears from her eyes.

"I don't know... maybe".

"Get down there and see what you can find out. I will try and gather more information from here and try to get in contact with Reids".

All but Dietrich left for the unknown fate that awaited them in the bowels of the Sigma Stasis bay, which was at the centre of the catastrophe. They headed for the Tram station as quickly as possible and sat in silence for nearly the entire journey. Everyone's mind must have been all over the place, thinking what the hell could have happened to the colonists. What could have caused that many deaths over the last two decades or was it just some kind of system glitch? If they'd have known what Gilbey knew now, then they would have never gone down there. Carter would still be alive and Gilbey would not have found himself lost and alone in some obscure part of the ship, feeling a million miles away from everybody else.

"ADAM..." Gilbey said but had no idea how to word his question in a way that the computer would understand as he stood in the passageway near the Rho Wing of the Eden. "What was that thing?"

"What are you referring to?" ADAM asked innocently, as if Gilbey hadn't just watched a man be pulled into some inhuman organism.

"You know what I mean! What the hell is that fucking thing that has taken over this section?!" he was starting to lose his patience with the computer. He took a deep breath and tried to speak more calmly. "What took Carter?"

"Doctor Reids has created a file on my database under the name of the Ouroboros in twenty-five zero-one. He has uploaded relevant data to the life-form that we acquired during the third maintenance cycle".

"What? What do you mean acquired? How the hell did we even..." but then the answer flashed in Gilbey's mind. He saw the asteroid as it drifted out of the open Hanger doorway followed by it lodged into the passageway wall. "That thing that breached the hull... the meteor thing? It was in that all along?"

"Correct" ADAM replied, almost like a school teacher that was proud Gilbey had managed to come to the conclusion on his own. "Although there was no life detected when the meteorite first came into contact with the Eden, however, I have concluded that it must have been carrying a type of microscopic life-form, which was unknown at the present time due to not having any relevant data on the subject matter. Based on limited information, I can only speculate as to how the entity's growth was accelerated, but I have hypothesised that when inside colonist one-five-seven-three's oxygen tube..."

Suddenly Gilbey's thoughts were of the small shard of the rock that Doctor Reids had accidentally sealed inside Jessica Kerrigan's Stasis tank. Reids had suggested cutting it out but ADAM had assured them that it would be destroyed as it was sucked into the recycle processor during air refining.

"...the organism may have unexpectedly reacted with the chemicals used for air purification, or possibly it was caused when it came into contact with the colonist inside following the resupply of oxygen to the tank".

"Is the colonist..." Gilbey stopped for a moment remembering Jessica's frozen face as it stared coldly out of her pod in what only seemed like a few days ago. "Is Jessica dead?"

ADAM answered almost instantaneously. "Yes. Miss Kerrigan was the first recorded casualty between cycles three and four to have died as a result of heart failure".

A noise drew Gilbey's attention back to the reality he was currently facing. It was a distant clank that sounded as if it had echoed its way through the corridors. It was not close, but close enough to worry him. He decided to get moving. He made his way down the passageway, past the Rho Airlock, and down to the cabins on this deck.

Each deck contained its own set of personal cabins for the colonists and the crew once they reach Delta Tauri. The idea was that they would live here until the EVE Earth-Forming system had finished its twelve year process. Then they would be free to start building settlements and colonies further outward away from the Eden.

Most of the cabins would be empty as nearly everyone's belongings were currently being held in the Luggage hold of Section D, as individual or family quarters are assigned to the colonists once they have been medically exterminated following their awakening from their hundred and thirty-seven year journey in Stasis, however, each cabin did have a comms link that would allow Gilbey to make contact with Dietrich in Operations. He hoped that she could see him on the surveillance system cameras. It was designed that from the Operations room, you should be able to see every part of the ship, but whatever had taken over the Sigma bay had blocked them all, so Gilbey had no idea what was even going on. For all he knew, it could have already gotten to them.

"Has anyone else been killed?" he asked as he rushed through a doorway knocking into the side of the frame.
"Yes" ADAM replied, which almost stopped Gilbey dead in his tracks. "Seven hundred and thirty-three colonists..."
"No! Are any of the Maintenance team dead?!"
"No" ADAM's voice spoke out from various nearby speakers which changed whenever Gilbey got close to one. "Other than Technical Engineer Carter, all maintenance crew members are alive and well. There are a few spikes in heart-rate and irregularly respiratory patterns, but other than that, all appears normal".
"So Dietrich should still be safe in Operations" he thought.

He approached the door to the first cabin and went to open it. It was locked.
"Dammit ADAM! Open up the door!" he yelled.
"I am afraid that cabins are to be assigned to colonists following..."
"Open this fucking door now!" and the machine did as it was told. The door slid away revealing the small quarter's interior.
It was a dull and unglamorous living accommodation with a single bunk above some storage space in the main central room, a door leading off to their own bathroom, a small area off to one side with built in kitchen appliances, and a holograph projector on the back wall. It was smaller than Gilbey's own Stasis bay. He was pretty sure that this must have been for one of the lower-class passengers on board, with the better cabins being found in the front two sections of the ship, however, he had no idea that people would be living here in places like this. They had much more space in the bunkered cities back on Earth, if it was not for the ever

adapting cyanogenic smog threat ever looming.

None of that mattered so long as the cabin had comms hub that connected to the rest of the Eden's communication network, which it did. A small display with an audio output port and a keypad sat attached to the side of the wall beside the door. Another button on the opposite side closed and locked the door. Gilbey hit that first before heading over to the comms hub.

The call ran for a moment before the Senior Officer's face appeared on screen. "Gilbey! Oh my god. Are you okay?"

He brushed it off "Yeah... yeah, I'm fine. Where is everyone else?"

"I've been trying to keep track of everyone from here, but it is near enough impossible. Graves went down to the cargo hold of Section C, but Lane and Eckhart were attacked at the tram station".

"Are they hurt?" he asked but Dietrich informed him that they were okay.

"They have locked themselves inside the Surgical Centre to get away from whatever that thing was. It chased them to the door but they managed to get inside before either of them suffered any injuries".

"Okay... okay" Gilbey sighed in relief as he realised that the noise moments earlier that spooked him must have been something else.

That was until Dietrich informed him that; "I think there's more of them". She was still trying to stay firm and decisive, but there was a hint of worry to her tone.

"What?!" he asked in complete shock.

"I need you to tell me what happened Gilbey. I could not see anything on the displays here and it looks as if Carter is dying! What was that thing?"

With the door securely shut, Gilbey felt safe, even if there might be more of those creatures on board. He sat on the bunk beside the hub and told her what happened.

They had arrived at the Section C tram station with the feelings of dread squeezing their insides tight. Neither of them wanted to believe that whilst they had been suspended in Stasis, nearly every colonist there had died. Each one dying under similar circumstances and resulting in ADAM not triggering their reawakening. They still had hope that Carter was right and that ADAM had suffered some kind of software glitch, which was terrifying in its own way as he was in control of every person on board's lives. So they were hoping that they would find the colonists alive and well, still asleep in Stasis, after which they would work on ADAM's

A.I. and try to figure out why he was showing a misreading.

Unfortunately it was not the case. As soon as they approached the Sigma bay's door, they could see black vine-like organic looking roots breaking through the ventilation ducts besides the door, spreading out across small sections of the wall. Right then they knew that whatever they found inside, just beyond this door, would be the personification of their worst nightmares.

"What is this?" Lane questioned as Eckhart moved cautiously closer to the root to get a better look at it. Gilbey stepped forward as well, but both Carter and Graves made sure they were staying well and truly back. Out of the way of any danger.

"Jesus Christ" Eckhart muttered watching the vine pulse as black fluid and deep red slime passed through the inner veins. "It's alive" he stated following witnessing this strange event unfold. "This thing is..."

"Growing" Gilbey interrupted as he noticed more of it stretching out across the ceiling, emerging from behind a warning sign that now hung by one corner.

Everyone followed it with their heads as they looked upward and back to the final point which was about a metre behind them.

"Fuck!" Graves gasped.

"The colonists!" insisted Lane. "We have to get in there and help them".

A few worried glances were exchanged, but if it was something they could deal with, then they needed to get in there.

"Okay" Carter stepped forward to the door. "ADAM... open it up" and before the sound had finished echoing off the walls in the corridor, the doors to the bay began to open.

It looked as if it was struggling. It appeared to be caught on more of the roots behind the door, but the mechanism was strong and managed to force its way open. Inside the previously white Stasis bay looked dark and foreboding. Usually the lights would have come on by now, but, like the cameras, these vine-like growths must have been blocking them.

Humidity oozed out of the room. It was thick and smelt like rotten meat that percolated their nostrils the moment it had seeped out of the doorway. A faint mist was obstructing the view up ahead. The light from the corridor behind them illuminated a small section of the room, but that was all that they could see.

All of them stood wondering disturbing thoughts of what was waiting for them inside. Eckhart took the first step forward. "Is the air harmful ADAM?"

"No. There are no hazardous airborne toxins inside" the machine responded. "According to my sensors, the air particles in the Sigma bay is made up of a mixture of oxygen, nitrogen, hydrogen, and argox, however, I am detecting microscopic traces of tellurium, but these are almost non-existent and will not cause any danger to your breathing".

Within the Stasis bay the air got worse. It felt as if the mist itself was all they were breathing in. Even though they had previously been cautious of ADAM's advice, since they hoped that he was wrong about the colonists, seeing inside proved at this point that the artificial intelligence was right and therefore correct about the lack of any dangers in the air.
The first step Gilbey took squelched as his foot pressed down into something wet and spongy beneath him. "What the..." he blurted out as he tried to put his foot somewhere else but found only the same type of floor below.
"It has spread all over the place" Carter informed them, moving further inside.
The whole team felt nervous as they pushed their way forward through the darkness and the mist.
"ADAM get some lights on in here, will you?" Graves asked, but ADAM replied that according to his readings, the lights here were currently on. "Great... that's just great".

The end Stasis pod of the first row appeared out of the shadows up ahead. The black roots here twisted themselves around the wires and tubes connected to the tank, with more deep red particles growing out of it. The red light from the screen could be partially seen underneath a layer of proteinaceous silk. Eckhart brushed this away with ease and the red light shone through, lit up a small section around them, as well as reflecting off the side of the glass section of the Stasis tank's casing. It was dark inside. There was too much condensation on the glass to see through completely, but from what they could make out, the colonist inside was gone.
"Where did they go?" Gilbey asked nervously as the ominous feelings began to develop.
"The tank is still sealed" Eckhart explained as he continued to check the details on the display.
"Lars Jansen. Died of myocardial infarction in twenty-five seventeen. According to the computer he is still in there".
"There's no one in there" Gilbey told him rubbing the silk away to try and get a better look inside. He could see that the roots had spread all over the inside of the tank. His eyes were

drawn down towards the bottom where a pile of pulp and mush resided. It was too dark to see exactly what it was, but it was probably what was left of Lars inside. "There's something strange at the..."

A noise cut him off. Everyone turned towards the source of it. It had come from the centre of the bay, but with the large area, high ceiling, and with the entire place being littered with metallic objects, the sound was impossible to pinpoint.
"We should get out of here" suggested Graves and the look on nearly everyone's face said that they agreed.
"Come on. Let's check it out" Eckhart said, ignoring Graves' idea. He switched off the display and the area fell back into the twilight shadows that the bay had been before.

As they continued on, every Stasis pod that they passed contained no occupant. Each one they saw showed the same red light and warning messages on the terminals beside them covered beneath more translucent silk.
The further they got in, the worse the roots and the vines became. Some of the tanks were completely covered in them and grew upwards, interconnecting with vines that hung from the ceiling. The walls and floor were completely covered and everyone felt as if they were a good foot off of the ground. It became difficult to walk normally as they travelled deeper into the depths. Lane stumbled and Graves fell to his hands and knees, before quickly picking himself up in a panic and trying to brush away the black and red slime from his hands and trousers. "What is this shit?" he asked, but no one responded. Mainly because no one had a real answer for him.

Eventually they reached the middle of the anomaly. In the centre of it all was an enormous unnatural darkened shape. It was so large that it covered six of the Stasis pods with its mass. The roots they had seen all around them seemed to be coming out of it. It glimmered in what little light remained in the bay.
When Eckhart first saw it he looked as if he was going to throw up. "Oh my god!" he uttered bringing his hand up to his mouth.
It was only when the rest of them had caught up that they actually managed to see what it was in front of them. The mass was pulsating and rippling like twitching muscle, and that's exactly what it was. They realised that liquid like mush that coated the entire entity was also

covered with thick red gore. The gore looked like a combination of blood and sludge made up from pulped up human remains. There was no physical characteristics of any manlike body parts, but everyone came to the same conclusion that this was what was left of the colonists.

Everything happened so fast after that. Carter must have gotten too close to it and something awoken from within. Suddenly the mass began to move sporadically causing a panicked hysteria amongst the maintenance team. More organic black vines flew out of the body and grabbed hold of Carter. He cried out for help, but unarmed and ill-prepared, the crew could do nothing as he was quickly pulled into the centre of it, pushing through the mass' tissue, where Carter disappeared beneath the oozing black liquid pouring out of the opening. His gargled cry became distant as he sunk further into it.

Gilbey had been so knocked out by what had transpired over the last few moments that he did not even notice Lane scream out in horror at what she was witnessing. When he did manage to compose himself, the mass opened up and then he heard that shrieking noise that seemed to pierce through his very soul. A monstrous form emerged out of it, two huge black gore covered appendages dragged the rest of its grotesque body forward. Gilbey caught sight of the section of body where its face might have been, but he was not sure. All that he knew was that it had no eyes despite appearing to stare right at him.

It had managed to get in between Gilbey and the others, and as soon as they started to run, he knew he had to as well. It didn't matter where, and it didn't matter how far, all that was important was that he got the hell out of there as soon as he possibly could, but staggering over the roots, feeling as if he was going to tie his legs up with all that was over the ground. It made it even more hard work than it already was in such a state of fear. His fight-or-flight response kicked in and he had to move. Somehow he got out of the Sigma bay, with the feeling like whatever that thing was had been right behind him, gnawing at his heels.

Gilbey had thought that explaining what had happened to Dietrich would help put it into some strange perspective. His head had been all over the place, and as he huddled on the side of the bunk in the empty cabin, having retold the events out loud, his head was more foggy now than it had ever been.

"The fucking thing came in with the rock..." he tried to explain but Dietrich was focused too much on trying to take control with the situation.

"That doesn't matter now" she said in an authoritative tone. "We can't let it get to the rest of the colonists".

"There has only been one cardiac arrest related death in another Section of the ship, which appears to be unrelated" ADAM added.

Gilbey sighed with comfort knowing that the rest of the Eden was safe. "That means it has not spread to the other sections of the ship". All he needed to do was get to one of them and he would be okay.

"I had to lock down the tram tunnel" Dietrich's voice shattered that plan in a heartbeat.

"You... wh... what?!" he was floored. He was trapped with it unless he could get to one of the Service Docks connecting the various sections of the ship to one another. It was possible to travel the Eden without the use of the Tram system, but it was not advised.

"I had to" she informed him, trying to justify herself. "It was right at the station when Eckhart and Lane were attacked. It could have gotten to B without any trouble and slaughtered the colonists there.

"So what?!" His outburst had taken his Senior Officer aback. It was clear that tensions were at an all-time maximum, and this was the action that had brought it to boiling point. "Are we just fucking trapped in here?!"

"No... I..." she tried to explain, but it was futile. Gilbey was not accepting anything that she was saying.

"Unlock the tunnel! Let us get the hell out of here!" His demand was met with silence. After a short moment he called out and finally she responded. "Dietrich?!"

"I can't risk it. The only connecting areas between sections are those Tram tunnels and the Service Docks. With them sealed, it is stuck in there".

"Yeah, with us stuck in here with it!"

"I am sorry" she sighed. "But the colonists are the most important part of this mission. You know what is at stake. This is the last hope for our species and if the Eden fails, then there will be no one left. You heard the message from Earth twenty-two years ago!" Her voice began to grow more determined and passionate with each word. "I will not let anything else happen to them. Those people are our future... our salvation".

"Oh fuck you!" He slammed his hand into the wall beside the comms hub. "You've trapped us in here and now we are all going to end up like Carter!"

"Carter is still alive!" she tried to reassure him, but Gilbey had seen first-hand what had happened to him. He knew that Carter's fate was the same as what had befallen the other seven hundred plus people that this thing had killed.

"Look..." Dietrich sounded conflicted. "I don't want anything to happen to you guys either. I will do whatever I can from here to help you guys. You can either stay locked up in there..."

"And stay awake for another forty-four years in this small cabin" Gilbey thought to himself as he glanced around the grey dimly lit quarters.

"...or you can get to the Service Docks. So long as that thing isn't nearby then I will open them up. That is all I can do. I'm sorry Gilbey." and with that the image of her disappeared. The comms display turned to the Eden mission's logo.

"Dammit!" he shouted out as he slammed his hand into the screen and the Cabin returned to silence.

He sat there for a moment in the dark cabin thinking about the gravity of the situation. He was alone, unarmed, trapped, hunted, and had no idea exactly what it was he was up against. If he had any hope of getting off of this section of the ship then he needed to get to the Service Dock between C and B. If he went any further back to section D, then he would be cornered.

Eckhart, Lane and Graves were all still trapped here alongside him, but it was anyone's guess if they knew it.

"ADAM..." his voice was almost a whisper. "Are the others still okay?"

"I am afraid that Technical Engineer Carter's life-signs are at a record low. However, the other members of your team appear to be in perfect health".

"Okay" Gilbey said trying to get his mind into order. "I have to get to the others. If they try and get to the Tram station then they will be sitting ducks. Which means I've got to get past the Sigma bay again. I need a weapon".

"I am afraid that there are no firearms permitted on the Eden. All weapons are secured in the Storage hold..."

"No... I need a Maintenance Tool Kit" he insisted.

It took him the better part of thirty minutes before he was ready to venture beyond the small cabin. He had figured out what he was going to do within the first few minutes following Dietrich's call, but the rest of the time he had spent standing in front of the cabin door trying to prepare himself for whatever might have been outside.

"Open it up" he told ADAM and the door slid open. In front of him was the quiet well lit corridor. The lights were almost blinding. He had spent quite some time in the dark in the few hours since his awakening, and it had not helped him adjust to being out of stasis. Thankfully he did not have A.S. as being stuck in this situation with the need to throw up every few moments would have made this a thousand times worse than it already was.

The passageways to the Rho bay were silent. All he could hear was the sound of his own footsteps echoing off into the distance behind him, and the sound of door mechanisms kicking in whenever he approached one.

The Rho bay was his first stop. Every stasis bay had a Tool Kit in and he needed something to defend himself with. He was unsure if the creature was even able to be hurt by such things, but having it and not needing it was much better than the other way around. At the moment he was defenceless. The thought that this thing could be waiting around any corner filled him with terror unlike any he had ever felt before.

"ADAM?" he asked softly. "Do you know where those things are?"

"What 'things' are you referencing Gilbey?"

"The fuc..." he took a moment and collected himself. "Whatever those organisms were that came out of the bigger one in the Sigma stasis bay. Do you know where they are?"

"My previous readings has unknown movement registered outside the Surgical centre, and another near the Tau Wing. I am afraid that I cannot give you a live update of these unknown movements as it takes approximately eleven minutes to run a detection scan for the entire section".

"And by then they would have been long gone" Gilbey concluded. "When did you run your last scan?"

"Previous scan was time stamped at two minutes previous" said ADAM. His voice felt as if he was inside his head, but the truth was that it was coming out of the speakers and could be heard by anyone nearby, which meant the A.I. was giving away his position every time he spoke to it. "Would you like me to update you when the next scan is available?"

"Yeah, yeah sure" he quickly said, in an attempt to keep it quiet.

The Rho bay appeared to be the one that had the seventeen survivors inside of it. The door to it looked normal and there was no signs of any black and red vines or roots anywhere nearby, which was a good thing, but he already knew that the other one hundred and eighty-three colonists inside there had been killed.

When the door opened, the faint familiar thick rotten smell returned. It was nowhere near as strong as it had been in the Sigma bay, nor was there the strange layer of mist.

Stepping inside he saw that most of the lights stayed off, but the ones that did come on showed more than he wanted to see. At the far end of the bay, he could see most of the monstrosity that had managed to spread itself all the way from the Sigma bay and its point of origin at Jessica Kerrigan's stasis pod. It must have completely taken over the entirety of the passageways on that side of the ship in order to have managed to make it all the way over here.

Although the black unnatural roots were not as prominent as they had been in the other Stasis bay, they had still taken control of a large section of the room.

The far door could be seen in a small section of light that had not been completely blocked up yet at its source, and from this Gilbey could see that there was no exit out of here other than the way he had entered. From what he could make out, each root had a number of smaller roots that fed out and were coiled around the various tanks here. The roots that had grown upwards and along the ceiling above them had vines that dangled down, sliding into any opening that they could find, such as the drainage port or the small filtration vents on the back of the tanks. Each one he could see looked different. Some were completely covered by the black and gore like muscles of the vines, which appeared pulsing slightly as if sucking the life out of anything within, whereas others Gilbey could see in, and it was these that he realised exactly what it was doing to the colonists inside.

As he looked over the row in front of him, he could see, in the glow of the bright red light monitors beside the tanks not obstructed by any of the roots, the people held in stasis were in various states of, what could only be described as, decomposition. It looked as if the closer the pods got to the source of the roots, the worse they became. In the one on the far right, Gilbey saw that the colonist just looked dead. It was similar to the one who had died in the previous cycle, his cold lifeless eyes staring out, however, unlike the other person, the one here's skin looked withered and twisted. Further along it had done just that as more grotesque corpses could be seen. Their muscles and tissue had almost completely melted away as they stood ankle deep in a puddle of mush. What little skin remained on their faces seemed as if it could fall off the bone at any moment. Some of them still had eyes in the sockets, where as others had been liquefied, slowly seeping down through the gaps in the skull.

It started becoming too much to witness. Further and further along the row of tanks just became too horrific to look at. After one that looked as if the body's very bones were melting, and they were now slumped up against the glass, with blood and other unknown organic liquids smeared over it from where the cadaver was slowly sinking into the pulp below. The faces here, almost completely skeletal, looked contorted as their mouths hung open at their decaying jaws.

The vines that had managed to creep into the several openings had wrapped themselves around different parts of the body. They too looked as if they were draining nourishment from them.

It was clear-cut that the enormous mass in the Sigma bay had been breaking down the bodies, over the last few decades, little-by-little, until they were nothing more than a puddle of slop at the bottom of the tank. Either it was the stuff it had not managed to consume, or it was saving it for later. Maybe once it had run out of fresh meat to feed upon. All of the colonists were suspended in stasis and would not have put up a fight at all against their bodies being slowly liquidised and devoured, feeding back to whatever had taken over this section of the ship from within.

The red bodily fluid that was present in small congealed pools were all being fed throughout the roots and vines, giving them a disgusting gore like appearance in amongst the slithery black colouring, which must have made up the thing's original organic structure.

It was dissolving the colonists and sending nutrients back through this network of roots that were now everywhere here. It would have been during this process that their heart would have begun to shut down, resulting in them appearing to have suffered heart failure, which meant ADAM would not have woken the maintenance team up in order to investigate.

If only ADAM knew what had been truly taking place within the supposed safety of the stasis tank.

Gilbey felt like he was going to be sick, so he found himself turning away in disgust, swallowing hard to try and push it back down and resist. All he had to eat or drink was a sachet of coolant when he first woke up, but he was sure that seeing any more would cause his stomach to find something for him to throw up.

Thoughts were racing through his head of what those poor people had suffered as their bodies were broken down and digested amongst their family members and future neighbours;

a future that was now no longer possible. They had left the dying world of Earth and went on a one-way mission across the cosmos to find a new place for humanity to carry on, but instead they had been consumed by some intergalactic organism which had mutated as a result of a fortuity that no one could have predicted.

He went over to the first pod which had a yellow screen beside it. The light emitting from the terminal stood out among the ocean of red that covered the rest of the bay. Four of these tanks in this section, closest to the exit and the other side of the ship, were all showing yellow. Gilbey could see that only a few roots had managed to reach these ones, with a couple of vines forcing their way inside. It did not look like it was a fast operation. It could have taken the thing years to get inside enough to begin the devouring process.
He wiped away the small layer of silk from the glass and took a look inside. Here he could see the black growth spreading all over, with some of the vines starting to attach themselves to the body.
He was unsure if it had started to liquefy them yet. According to the terminal nearby, the colonist was still alive.
"Isaac Price" Gilbey said aloud, but as he did it suddenly humanised the man inside the tank even more and now he felt compelled to help the man. His stomach was in knots and he felt physically drained and fatigued by everything he had observed. He looked over and saw that the furthest tanks away were still displaying green lights, meaning that they were completely unaffected by the organism.
"ADAM" he called out. His voice bounced off of the walls of the huge empty room. "Awaken colonist Isaac Price..." He squinted as he struggled to read the man's identification number beneath a thick glob of black secretion that had dripped off one of the roots above. "...three, um... three, two, nine". He waited there for a few moments in silence, eagerly waiting for the machine's response. "ADAM?"
"I must apologise Gilbey, but I am afraid I cannot do what you have requested of me" he replied taking Gilbey by surprise.
"What? What are you talking about? Open colonist tank; three..."
"There is a parameter in place that prevents me from opening any personal tanks without direct authorisation from the Senior Officer in charge".
"Dietrich!" Gilbey hissed as he clenched his fists, looking around for something to throw or break as the rage was now beginning to grow rapidly inside of him. "Fuck sake! Can you not

override it?"

"I am afraid that is impossible. I am unable to remove Senior Officer Dietrich from her position either, as I calculated that this would be your next question. In order to do this, I would need to process an evaluation of her mental and physical state before conducting any changes in the chain of command. That is unless she was dying or had already died, at which point Doctor Reids would become the next in charge".

"Reids?" Gilbey thought imagining how much worse that would probably be. Although his priorities were the safety of the colonists, which might mean that he would be willing to awaken the remaining seventeen still alive in Section C. He would need to get to Reids and convince him to open them up, that was if something was to happen to their superior officer.

"Alternatively, if Admiral Walker, or any of the flight crew was to awaken, then they would be assigned as the highest level of authority on the Eden" ADAM informed him.

"But I can't wake him up without Dietrich's say so?"

"Correct".

Gilbey turned back to look at the surviving colonists. He knew that it took the creature a long time to turn their bodies into mush, so maybe it took a long time before they suffered a heart attack. This meant that he could worry about this later. His first priority was getting out of this Section of the ship. His own life needed to come first since the maintenance crew were the biggest threat to this thing's stationary food source. Whatever it had released, one of which had attacked Eckhart and Lane at the Tram station, must have been a countermeasure to protect itself.

"Gilbey?" ADAM asked unexpectedly causing Gilbey's heart to thump against his ribcage vigorously. "The next scan for any unregistered movement is now available. Would you like to proceed?"

"What? Oh, right. Yeah, sure. Knock yourself out kiddo".

"Scanning..." ADAM called out before the entire room fell back to total silence.

Gilbey headed over to where the maintenance kit was located at the northern wall of the stasis bay. He passed by more disfigured and deceased colonists the closer he got to it. At one point he had to turn away so as to avoid actually seeing the foul remains inside one of the more devoured tanks.

"My scan is complete" ADAM proudly declared.

Gilbey stopped walking. He stood there for a moment, in amongst the rows of stasis pods that were now thankfully wrapped almost entirely in the black roots, shielding the contents inside from view, before finally asking the machine: "Well... where are they?"

"I have detected two unknown movement patterns over the last few moments. One was located near the Cargo lift of Section C..."

"Graves" Gilbey realised. One of those things must have known he was there somehow. "Is Graves okay?" he hesitantly asked.

"Yes. Maintenance Engineer Graves vital signs show he is well. As of this moment, I have not received any communication from him and..."

All of a sudden Gilbey's attention was drawn to a faint noise from somewhere nearby. "Whoa, hold up" he told ADAM and the machine went quiet.

Gilbey waited for a moment and listened. It was difficult to make out at first. It sounded like something scraping across the smooth metal flooring of the passageway outside. At first he thought he must have been imagining it, but soon the distant shrieking cry of something inhuman blasted its way down the corridor, his head began to feel faint as his chest tightened around his organs, suffocating him from the inside. The screech lasted only a few seconds, but the noise lingered around his ears infecting his mind with thoughts of dread as to the source of it.

Soon the noises were growing louder. He could hear a squelching splatters of some unknown living material that became more apparent the closer it got. The noise seemed to coexist with the clawing of metal to form a horrifying orchestra from the bowels of hell.

"Shit!" he uttered softly as he crouched down sinking one foot into the side of the nearby root. He moved away from it and over towards the closest stasis tank, resting his hand on the exposed metal frame, and nervously peered out towards the door. It was closed. Thankfully it had shut shortly after Gilbey had entered. The only way to open it was to either ask ADAM, or press the buttons on the panel beside it, neither of which Gilbey expected these things capable of. That meant that so long as he did not draw any attention to himself, he should be fine in here until that thing had left the area.

In the completely silent bay and the passageways, with its metal walls and floors, steel stairs and catwalks, any kind of noise was magnified a hundred times over. Even though Gilbey had been fearful that the creatures could have been anywhere, he had been pretty sure that he was safe due to the fact that any kind of noise would have hopefully alerted him first. Now that his theory had been proven, he thought to himself that he would have done anything to return the stasis bay back to silence.

The sounds were coming from just behind the door now, as far as he could tell. A scraping could be heard running past the entire width of it. It was then that he began to hear the blood-curdling gurgles and snarls that the creature was making nearby. His mind raced with images of whatever he had seen back in Sigma, as it crawled itself out of the huge black gore-covered mass in the centre of it.

After a couple of moments of nightmarishly waiting for the sounds to pass, paralysed in daunting dread that it would find him, Gilbey felt a small amount of comforting relief that it was getting quiet, indicating it was heading away from him.

He realised that he had not blinked the entire time and now his eyes were filled with water. He brushed them away alongside an exhale of alleviation as his muscles released their grip on his inner organs.

"Would you like to know the location of the other unregistered movement Gilbey?" ADAM's voice was like a supernova exploding in the middle of the silent solar system of the Rho stasis bay.

It may have been the fact that moments before, Gilbey had been almost holding his breath in unnerving anticipation in order to remain as quiet as possible, but when ADAM spoke, it sounded as if his volume had been turned up to the highest possible setting.

Gilbey tried to quietly shush him halfway through talking, but the machine had either not understood or not even heard him say anything, and continued talking.

"I have detected that it is..."

His heart sank and he felt the tight squeeze of his insides take hold once more, however, Gilbey managed to utter a single word; "Quiet!" and the world around him returned to just such a state, if only for a brief moment.

At first he had hoped that whatever had been beyond the stasis bay door was too far to have heard. It seemed like it for a couple of seconds, allowing Gilbey to begin to think that everyone was okay, but that was before another haunting shriek erupted, somewhat louder than the previous, returning the formidable feelings of petrifying horror to every inch of his body.

The scraping noises grew faster as everything became louder. It knew Gilbey was in there. He could feel his eyes widening further than they had ever done before. His mouth went instantly dry and he found it impossible to swallow. He felt as if he couldn't breath as frequent metal clanging could be heard at the other side of the door.

Another shriek broke out once more, only this time it gurgled, like its voice was being ripped out, and was suddenly replaced with a roar that made every hair on Gilbey's body stand on end. Dents started to form on the door as the creature smashed against it.

"It can't get in here" he thought, trying to calm himself down as he ducked down behind the tank as low as he could go.

He noticed that the roots and vines all around him were now pulsing and twitching. Everything felt like it was trying to grab hold of him and keep him there to be ripped apart by the thing trying to break its way in. He tried to make a break for the maintenance tool kit nearby, but was immediately caught up by his own legs and stumbled into the computer screen. His hand slid on the silk membrane covering it and the red light flashed into his eyes. The contrast burned for a second, causing him to fall completely over. He put his hand out to support himself, but it soaked into a small pool of liquefied human remains that had seeped out of the bottom of the stasis pod and that apparently had not yet been absorbed by the root, causing him to land on the floor in mess. His arm smashed against the ground and, in a panic, Gilbey awkwardly picked himself up and carried on across the bay.

All the noises had unexpectedly stopped at this point. There was nothing that could be heard other than the sound of Gilbey's own heart pounding in his chest as the blood pumped frantically through his temples and into his brain, giving birth to his own terrifying thoughts. The thumping on the door had ceased. "Was it gone?" he wondered, looking back towards the direction where the sounds had come from, but all he could see was the shadows of the towering roots lingering all around amidst the stasis tanks.

He wasted no time and went over to the maintenance tool kit, which was attached to the wall in a plastic case. Trying to get his breathing under control, he took the kit out of the case and opened it up, revealing the contents inside. The bay was unnaturally quiet now. Nothing could be heard coming from the corridor either. It was almost as if the creature had stopped doing anything entirely and was now standing in front of the door, waiting for him to come out. With the roots covering the door to the other wing, the door it had been at moments earlier was the only way out of here.

Gilbey grabbed hold of the Beam-Saw and the cold metal frame in his hand made him feel instantly better. It was probably not enough to take on whatever those things were, as a rivet gun would have been better, but it was an improvement over his previously unarmed state. Other than a Weld-Pen and a screwdriver, which he shoved through his belt, there was nothing else of use.

The kit had been designed as a backup if a repair was to be made and either the maintenance crew was not around, or their portable tool boxes were not present. It had not been designed to harbour self-defence items capable to killing an extra-terrestrial life-form.

Now, feeling marginally more protected, Gilbey had to figure out how he was going to get out of the room. The creature could have easily moved on, maybe drawn by one of the other crew members, or it could have been summoned back to the mass in the Sigma bay.

Speaking to ADAM was a risk, as it could have alerted that thing back to him, but, without the AI, Gilbey was pretty much blind.

"ADAM" he whispered softly, in hopes that the machine would reply in kind.

"How can I be of service, Gilbey?" He did not. His voice seemed to come from all around, but after a moment of silence, there was no other noises that could be heard.

Still speaking low, Gilbey asked him if the movement scanning was available, although it had been ADAM letting him know the results which had lured it here in the first place.

"I am afraid that it is not operational for another three minutes and fifty-seven seconds"

"Okay... until then just make sure the door stays closed"

"Would you like me to close it now?" ADAM asked and his words caused a sudden alarming realisation hit.

"The doors open?" he gasped hearing the worst thing he could possibly imagine. Had it broken through? Or had Dietrich opened it remotely in an attempted to trap it inside here with him?

"Yes. Technical Engineer Carter requested the door to be opened a few minutes ago".

ADAM's words confused Gilbey, as if he had just spoken in a completely different language.

"Carter?" he repeated befuddled. He tried to put everything together in his head, but he kept seeing images of Carter being pulled into that thing. Surely he did not get out of it and his first instinct was to come all the way to this end of the Eden. Gilbey had only come here because he had been cornered by whatever had attacked them, so if Carter had managed to somehow escape, he would have gone the same way as the others and tried to get back to Operations. "It can't be". Carter was alive?

He moved to the end of the row of stasis tanks he was near and peered around it. The bay's door was in fact open, just like the computer had said it was. He could see the intensely bright lights of the passageway shining in like some kind of beacon guiding his way.
But did that mean that thing was in here with him? He couldn't hear anything nearby. When it had been in the corridor, he had heard it from quite a distance. He assured himself that he would have heard it if that was the case. With that small glimmer of hope, he climbed to his feet and began heading towards the door.

He stayed close to the wall as he moved down so that only one side of him was exposed. He was not running, as he wanted to create as little noise as possible. Luckily the roots had not managed to reach this far back of the stasis bay entirely, instead there were only a few of them sticking out a couple of feet from the row of tanks beside him. But the fact that he wasn't running didn't mean he was moving slow. He was trying to put as little pressure in his steps as possible in hopes that it would make his journey more silent, and by doing this, it meant that he was able to move a little bit quicker.
It wasn't until about halfway when Gilbey started to think that this was all going a little too well and slowed down. It would have been easy to now make a break for the door, keep running as fast as possible, and get into one of the other parts of this section of the ship with the others, but something in his gut was telling him different.

He was walking now, as slow and with as much caution as possible. At one point it was almost like he was moving in slow motion the closer he got to the door, until something in the corner of his eye made him stop moving completely. He looked over towards the backs of the stasis tanks beside him and searched for whatever his brain had subconsciously warned him about, but he couldn't see it. All he could see was the back of pods in the row. Nearly all of them here had been swallowed up in the roots and vines, which had wrapped themselves around each one and were busy feeding on the poor souls inside, however, all of them showed signs of what was underneath; an oxygen tube here, a drainage port on that one, and the metal ringed base at the bottom of the other. None of them were completely covered up, except for the one in the middle, with all that could been seen was the black and red gore coloured tissue casing over it.

And that's when he noticed that it was closer to one of the tanks either side of it than it was the other, not only that was the only one in that row that fell into the column. In all the other rows, this section of the bay was a pathway through, but right here was another stasis pod slap bang in the middle of it all.

The tissue on it began to throb rapidly as the tank began to grow slowly upwards, until it felt as if it was towering over him. Gilbey's heart must have stopped dead when the sides of the supposed stasis tank slid apart to reveal the creature's face, what had previously been hiding behind the enormous appendages it used to pull itself out of the mass earlier. It must have been what it had been using to create the dents in the door. Now it had used them to lure Gilbey into an ambush.

The organism's featureless face stared at him in a strange moment that transpired between Gilbey and the beast. The few milliseconds that passed felt like they went on for hours. It was almost calming, until its huge muscular arms crashed down into the ground beside it, lifting its central form off of the ground. A section of the head detached itself from the rest, which must have been its lower jaw. As it slid down, a warming vapour emitted out between splits in the thick black sludge revealing an abyssal pit of a mouth. There was no teeth that he could see, but the very sight of it sent images in his mind of being ingested and dissolved like the colonists.

The creature let out a gargle which suddenly evolved into shrieking screams before an almighty bone crushing roar that felt as if it shook the entire ship.

Gilbey had to run. He turned and sprinted as fast as he could through the door. Meanwhile he could hear the phantasmal monstrosity charging through the row of tanks, knocking one out of its metal ringed base with ease. He looked back to see a spray of watery human remains discharge from it as it toppled on its side into the pile of blackened roots that had previously been feeding off of it. He saw the silk covered terminal beside it flash from yellow to red as it severed its connection with the pod in a similar fashion to how the person inside was severed from life itself.

The creature gave chase as Gilbey grabbed hold of the stasis bay's door frame and pulled himself out of the room and around the corner.

Another cry exploded behind him, where it had lost sight of him for a moment, but as much as it was determined to get him, Gilbey was determined to get away.

"ADAM!" he shouted at the top of his lungs whilst trying to move as quickly down the corridor as he could. "Close the stasis bay doors now! Do it now!"

ADAM's voice was that of god's. "Right away Sir".

The bay's door slammed shut, blocking the creature's path. Gilbey heard it crash into it, screeching out horrific noises, before the sound of it trying to break through thumped all down the passageway.

Gilbey ran up the corridor for a few moments more before stopping to catch his breath. The sudden and unexpected run had taken it out of him. He rested his arm on the portcullis, displaying whatever sector of godforsaken space they were currently residing in, and turned back towards the stasis bay, where he could still hear the thing trying desperately to get to him, before slowly stopping until there was no sound once again.

"Fuck you" he uttered under his breath, his heart still pounding frantically in his chest. He went to turn and head off when a distant voice spoke out from somewhere he had just come from. The sound stood every hair on his body on end.

The voice was distorted and hoarse when it spoke in a gurgled sound that was somewhat surprisingly recognisable, but Gilbey could hear it clear as day. "ADAM... Open... the door" Carter grunted inhumanly.

"Of course Carter" ADAM responded and the stasis bay's door began to open.

Before the door had even slid halfway, one of the creature's towering black appendages pushed its way out, spilling secreted slop onto the metal floor. A hiss rattled out of the bay as more and more of the thing began to emerge.

Gilbey ran. He did not look back at all as he made his way forward, haunted by the ghastly revelation that these beings were able to mimic whatever they consumed. With access to ADAM; the most sophisticated artificial intelligence mankind had ever created, nowhere on the Eden was safe.

4ᵀᴴ Cycle – ETA: 47.7 Yrs

Part Two: Into the Infinite

Even with the changes made to ADAM's pre-heating protocols before the start of a new Maintenance cycle, the Eden felt as cold as the frozen expanse beyond its steel walls. Gilbey's hands were numbingly painful and his entire body felt tighter with each step as he made his way to the Cargo lift. His whole body felt tight and every step was agony, but he had to keep going. He was unsure if the ship was really cold, or the sheer terrifying realisation of what he had witnessed earlier had given him a chill that he could not shake off.
He had made his way passed the Sigma bay by going the longest route possible. It had been a tense journey as any more of those things could be waiting around the next corner, or it could have even been hiding in plain sight for all he knew. The creature's ability to adapt to its surroundings, like it had done pretending to be a stasis pod back in the Rho bay, as well as the fact it could impersonate Carter, or anyone else it had ingested, meant that he had to be on his guard at all times. He gripped the frame of the unlit Beam-Saw so tight that his knuckles were white, fuelling the numbing pain of the surrounding cold.

Along his route, Gilbey had managed to find a small lavatory near the observation lounge on this deck to speak to ADAM. He figured that the smaller the room, the less noise the A.I. would make when answering him. Back in the stasis bay, ADAM's voice felt as if it was coming from all around, and he did not want to give his location away to anything that might have been pursuing him.

Enough time had passed to run another movement scan of the ship, so this was Gilbey's first question. He needed to know if the creature was following him, and also where the location of the other one was, because the last he heard it was outside the entrance to the Cargo lift, and that was exactly where he was heading. He needed to pass it in order to get to the Tram station and the Surgical centre where the others were, but Graves might have been trapped down there, not to mention that the man might have acquired something to actually fight these beings with, so heading down to the Storage Hold wouldn't be such a bad idea.

ADAM told him that unregistered movement had been detected south of the Rho bay near the water treatment centre, which meant that the one that had imitated Carter's voice had headed in a completely different direction to where Gilbey had ran to, which was the good news, but nothing of the sort could be presented without a side of bad news. In this case it had come in the fact that ADAM could not detect any other movement from anything that was not one of the crew members assigned to the Eden. So either the creature had returned to its hive in Sigma bay to sleep off its eventful day, or was perfectly still in whatever room it was in, which meant that it was most likely waiting to jump out and surprise anyone who came near it.

ADAM's answer had not filled him with the confidence he needed in order to proceed. Part of him wanted to just wait it out inside the observation lounge. He had a comfy place to rest as he watched the universe go by, not to mention clean water from the taps, although there was no telling how long that would last. He could starve to death in a lot worse places on board.

His other question to the computer was what Dietrich was up to. Her choice to lock down the entire section and trap them inside it with these things made Gilbey feel uneasy about what she was going to do next.

"I am afraid that Senior Officer Dietrich has activated a level 2 security clearance and as such I am not at liberty to provide you any additional information" ADAM told him. "Please accept my sincere apologies".

"Dammit" Gilbey snapped as he wondered to himself what she might have been up to.

It was sure enough that she wasn't planning on letting them die, only to keep this thing sealed up inside Section C until they reached the Delta in just under fifty years' time. He did not believe that she would have the confidence to wake Admiral Walker up from stasis. She was trying too hard to ensure that Earth had picked the right person for the job, so she needed to deal with this situation on her own.

Armed with what little information he had managed to get out of ADAM, it was time he got moving.

When he reached the entrance to the Cargo lift, he could see through the bulkhead door window that the lights were off. The world beyond the door looked as if it had been painted black.

"ADAM, turn on the lights in the Section C Cargo lift" he requested, leaning around the corner of the passageway, trying to make himself as hidden as possible.

"There has been a severe lighting failure reported in this area and a call has been logged with the maintenance crew".

Gilbey would have laughed if he was not so worried that ADAM's voice might have alerted one of those things. The noise did not seem to disturb anything, so it was so far so good.

He imagined Dietrich receiving the notification from one of the terminals in Operations advising her of this mundane task in amongst the chaos and death that had been unravelling since they came out of stasis when this cycle began.

"That's great..." he said. "I'll get straight on it".

Moving up to the door, he felt his finger hover over the on switch for the Beam-Saw. He wanted to be ready if anything was going to jump out in front of him, but even armed, he still felt the despair building up inside of him with every step that he took. The foreboding feeling of his own death haunted his every thought. He stared aimlessly at the panel displaying the black void beyond the bulkhead door.

If it was still in there, the darkness would only help the creature hide somewhere within. Avoiding the area completely meant that he needed to go through the Sigma bay to the other side of the ship in order to reach Eckhart and Lane, leaving Graves to his fate. He had to go through.

He pressed the panel, changing the light on it from red to green, and the door slid open. A cool air was there to greet him, making him feel even colder than he already did. He thought of how hot and humid the stasis bay had been. The central mass there must produce so much heat into the area. No matter how cold he was, he would rather suffer that than be anywhere near that thing.

He stepped inside, the beam of light from his saw illuminated a section around him like a torch in a darkened cave. The sections that were lit up from it glowed a deep purple. The nearby row of steel lockers reflected the light all around the room, highlighting various parts of the area that filled Gilbey with a sense of uneasiness, as he felt eyes watching him from the shadows.

Something moved in the corner of his eye and, in a flash, he spun around with his saw up high, as if to defend himself from whatever had moved. After a moment nothing came. He looked and noticed one of the damaged light fixtures he had seen. It hung from wires above him, with four tremendously daunting gouges slashing through it and the ceiling where it had once sat in place. The claw marks seemed to stretch right across the whole world above him, from the bulkhead door, all the way around the next corner.

He moved past the line of lockers and peered around the corner. The Cargo lift entrance appeared normal. The terminal beside it showed no damage, meaning he shouldn't have a problem getting down into the Storage hold below. The only issue was that the lift was already down there.

"Shit" he thought, trying desperately not to breathe, let alone speak.

If the lift was down there, then it would take a minute or two for it to come back up. Other than the pipe works beside it, there was no obvious place to hide whilst he waited. He would be totally exposed if he activated the lift from the terminal.

Gilbey went to ask for ADAM's assistance but managed to hold his tongue at the last moment. He didn't want the A.I. to shout out here, so he decided to handle this on his own and as quietly as possible.

Each step he took closer to the lift door felt like it had been mere millimetres away from the last. The passage extended further and further away, but he was determined to get there, and as quietly as possible.

Just before activating the terminal, his finger lingering in the air just a few centimetres in front of it, Gilbey glanced all around him for anything that might have been the creature using the darkness to camouflage himself. Without the cover of the enormous roots here, he wondered if it was possible for it to hide as well as it had done in the Rho stasis bay, as it was able to use the nearby entrapped pods to mask its own skin.

Everywhere looked normal. There was no obvious hiding spots for it to be waiting. The fact that ADAM had told him earlier that he had lost the movement signal of the other made him on edge. It could have been anywhere, and it had been a while since it was last recorded as being in this area, so the organism could have easily moved on, hopefully not down below.

As soon as he made contact with the terminal the Cargo lift rumbled with power as gears and mechanisms began to turn, pulling the platform up from the depths. The large orange warning light began to flash as its beam began to circulate around the room. Gilbey had completely forgotten about it. The warning light had just been there in the past, so he had not even noticed it before.

If the light was not enough of a signal to his location, the tremendous racket the lift was making as it slowly ascended had to have been.

His heart began to bang in time with the clanking sound of machinery and a faint metal scraping.

"No..." Gilbey thought. "That's not the lift".

The scraping grew louder as he realised it was coming from behind him, back towards the intersection linking the various corridors to the other side of Section C. In amongst the noise of the lift mechanics, he could pin-point the same distinctive bone scratching sound he had heard back in the Rho wing of the ship, when that thing had been moving past the bay's door. It was coming.

Looking down the lift shaft, he could see it coming up, but it was going at an incredibly slow pace. The lift never seemed to move this slowly when there wasn't a flesh hungry alien lifeform hunting him down, but maybe it was down to the fact that he wanted to be inside the elevator right this second with the door firmly shut behind him.

He flicked the switch on the Beam-Saw and turned it off in an attempt to not draw it to him, although he feared it was far too late for that. As soon as the purple light vanished, he saw the great hulking shadow lingering beside the line of cabinets. The bulkhead door was still open and the light shining in from the passageway he had come from, was now painting a picture of the monstrous entity on the wall.

Gilbey's eyes drew wide at the sight and his heart began to race faster than before. With still time to wait until the lift arrived, he slid into the pipes to his left, huddled in the darkness, and tried to hold his breath.

A soft hissing became audible as the light from the door had nearly completely disappeared behind the creature's body. It moved into the room on its muscular frontal appendages, pulling the rest of itself into Cargo lift entrance.

He could not see it, but Gilbey knew that it was now only a few metres away, just on the other side of the lockers. Over the top of them, in the dim lighting, he could just about make out the tops of its crooked elbows that seemed to hunch over the top of the rest of its body. The sight of it made his vision blur and he frantically blinked in an attempt to wipe it away. When it had cleared, the thing was now at the far end of the cabinets. An unnatural hand, with jagged hooks driving their way into the end locker. The metal bent as if it was made of aluminium foil under the sheer brute strength of it pulling itself around the corner.

The hissing suddenly became deafening as the featureless face glanced around the bend. The sound became so bad that Gilbey wanted to cover his eyes, but he was too panic-stricken to move. All he could do was watch in horror as it scanned the shadows, searching for him.

Gilbey tried to get a good look at the creature, as it looked around completely stationary, but the darkness and the pipes in front of him made that difficult. Before, trying to work out what he had been looking at when it was revealing itself from hiding in the Rho bay was all but impossible, but now, with the nearby orange warning light still flashing, it illuminated the monstrosity for a second at a time, revealing some of its exterior details.

He could see that the two red and black towering arms were massive bulks of meat it used as its main way of getting around. It had no legs, instead the thing's main body, where the arms connected to, stretched downward and curved like some deformed giant snake, but rather than slick and scaly, this section of its body was just like the rest. It looked as if it was made entirely of this black solidified liquid moulded together with human muscles and organs meshed together in a grotesque display that covered its entire body. The tail section itself had spines of all sizes sporadically scattered on it. At the very tip there were three hooked blade-like claws.

"Those must have been what was scraping along the metal flooring" Gilbey thought.

The hissing went on and a terrifying thought kept calling from the deepest niche of his brain. "Sonar" he realised. It was using some kind of sonar to find him.

It appeared to know that someone was in this area, but it didn't seem to be able to locate him exactly. Thankfully the rumbling of the Cargo lift must have been making it hard for it to find, but that was not going to last. At that moment the lift slotted into place, the orange light switched off, and the room began to fall into silence as the last echoes faded away.

If it was using the hissing in the way that he thought, then he had moments to act before it would find him. The Cargo lift door was not open. He would need to activate the terminal at the opposite side of the door to where he was in order to access it, but it was only the touch of a button. It used the same mechanisms as the ones in the bulkhead, and this meant that it can open and close in seconds, so long as nothing was blocking it.

The final clang of the lift drew the creature's attention towards it for a moment, before it turned and began hissing once more. This gave Gilbey a sudden idea that he had no choice but to act upon instantly. He grabbed hold of the screwdriver, he had shoved into his belt, and in one quick motion tossed it out of the pipe work recess and over the top of the lockers. It clipped the top of one, and for a second, he thought it was going to land on this side of it, resulting in just pulling the organism closer towards him, but he released a sigh of relief, which he felt he had been holding onto for the whole time he had been crouched down here, as the screwdriver flew over the locker and crashed onto the floor. The sound of it hitting the top sparked a jittery motion to occur in the creature, which would have drawn it towards it, Gilbey had no doubt, but thankfully the second clanking sound of the screwdriver crashing onto the metal floor on the other side of the room, moments later, created enough of a distraction.

Another gigantic shriek broke out as he saw the thing's lower jaw detach as the other one had done, giving more shape to its face. It pulled itself back around the corner, and once most of it had disappeared to investigate the noise, Gilbey made his move.

With adrenaline now taking over him, he climbed out from behind the pipes and rushed over to the door, slamming his hand on the open button. As the Cargo lift door shifted, the creature let out a booming cry as it must have figured out what was actually going on.

Stepping inside, Gilbey could hear the thing crashing around the lockers as it gave chase. He turned around to see it charging towards him, clawing at the ground in an attempt to pull its body faster than normal. It was slower than he expected, but it still moved quickly enough that it would close the distance between them in seconds.

With his clenched fist, still clutching the frame of the Beam-Saw, he smashed the side of his hand into the panel on this side of the elevator, and the Cargo lift door sealed shut. The monstrous hulk crashed into it, as parts of its body seeped through the bars. Black liquid oozed off of it and dropped in pools on the floor, with more flooding out of its open mouth. Vapour was steaming out of it and Gilbey could see silvery teeth inside, sharp as razors, gnashing at the bars as it tried desperately to get through.

The noises it made, as it was so close to capturing its prey, and at this distance, was soul destroying. He felt it ripping him apart from the inside without even touching him. He pushed himself to the back wall of the lift as the orange light in the entrance area flashed on again and began to spin.

The eyeless face kept its focus on him when the machinery started up the lift started to slowly descend. It must have sensed that it was about to lose him, so that was when it did something drastic. The middle of the face seemed to push forward, through the bars, as two thin tubes began to appear out of it. At first they were straight, but after a second they wiggled and stretched out. Without warning they were halfway across the platform, pulling themselves towards Gilbey. They looked like thin versions of the vines that hung from the ceiling in the stasis bays.

As they drew in closer to their target, Gilbey flicked the switch of the Beam-Saw, brightening the entire Cargo lift in a purple haze, and without even thinking he swung it at the tentacles coming for him.

The concentrated beam of high intensive lasers sliced through them with no resistance what-so-ever, and the tentacles dropped to the ground, but not before spraying Gilbey with a splatter of black liquid blood.

The thing cried out in a mixture of rage and agony as it recoiled from the bars, disappearing on the level above him as the lift continued to travel downward. The noise could be heard for a while on his descent.

Gilbey looked down to see that the vine-like tentacles had instantly started to dissolve into small pools of black mush.

"Jesus Christ" he stammered, slumping down into the corner of the lift for the rest of its journey.

When the Cargo lift finally reached the bottom of the elevator shaft, any trace of the creature's attack was gone. The cries could no longer be heard, and the tentacles had all but turned into a black smear on the steel floor.
As the door behind him slid opened, Gilbey spun around and was immediately greeted by Graves, armed with an Industrial Rivet gun pointing the barrel straight to Gilbey's face.
"Whoa! Whoa!" was all Gilbey managed to say, stepping back and throwing his arms up in an attempt to defend himself.
Graves' face had been locked in a state of frozen panic that vanished when his brain managed to process what he was seeing. He recoiled the gun back. "Shit man" he sighed before bringing up his hand to scratch violently at the side of his head. "I was just about to bolt you to the fucking wall".
Gilbey stepped out, over the black slush, and into the hold. "Well I appreciate that you didn't".

He looked at Graves and realised that it was good to see him. The last time he had seen the man, those things had just emerged from the central mass in the Sigma bay, and Carter had been screaming in horror as he was pulled into it.
"Glad you made it" he said, but by doing so, he could tell that Graves' thoughts were of Carter.

His face and his shoulders dropped. "Yeah… good to see that they didn't get you. What happened to the others?"
"Have you not spoken to anyone?" Gilbey asked.
"Nah man. I got out of there with Eckhart and Lane, but that thing was after us. I was lagging behind so I ducked out into here. Thought I could get something of use". He tapped the side of the Rivet gun. "I wanted something a little more… heavy duty, but the crates with the weapons are stored right at the back. I've been using the Loader to shuffle things around and try to get to them".
Gilbey remembered his own Rivet gun stored away in his stasis bay back in Section A. He wished that he had grabbed it before all this had happened. But at least one of them was well armed.

He looked out across the Storage hold. It was a mess. There were various containers scattered all around, most of which looked as if they had just been thrown. One of the crates had been pried open and some of its contents, of canned processed food and cans of purified water, were laying nearby. Even a couple of the spacesuits, which should have been locked into their docks on the wall, were laying in heaps on the floor.

"It's a god-damn mess down here" he joked, trying to block out the haunting images of that thing upstairs' face trying to get to him through the bars.

Graves laughed nervously. "I... emm..."

Gilbey realised that he thought he was being serious, so he quickly moved the conversation forward. "Have you managed to get to the guns?"

"No not yet" Graves replied. "I can see it, but I just can't get to it yet. I've disconnected the row it is in, so we should be able to get to them quicker with two of us".

"Graves..." Gilbey was hesitant about breaking the news to the young engineer. "We need to get back to Operations as soon as possible. Dietrich has sealed the Tram tunnel and..."

Before he could finish, Graves broke in. "What?! What the hell man?!"

"She is trying to contain this thing to stop it from spreading to the stasis bays in the other sections of the ship" he tried to explain but Graves' face still had the look of stunned worry on his face.

"She's fucking trapped us in here?! That bitch!"

"She said if we get to the Service Dock to Section B then she'll open it up".

"She's shut the Service Docks as well?! Oh fuck me" Graves' face was a mixture of anger, frustration, anxiety, and every other negative emotion all rolled into one.

Gilbey put his hand on his shoulder to try and get him to focus. Graves was his subordinate, and so he hoped that he would listen. "So long as those things ain't standing next to us, she'll open up the Service Dock. All we got to do is get there".

"Well... let's get the guns then"

Graves went to turn around but Gilbey kept his hand on his shoulder, holding him back. "There's no time. Dietrich is trying to handle the situation by herself and there is no telling what she is going to do. We need to get out of this section of the ship as fast as possible".

"Wha... what about the other colonists? Is it just Sigma that is affected right? We can just seal that bay and..."

Gilbey's thoughts were on the remaining colonists still alive in the Rho stasis bay at the other end of this section of the Eden. Their tanks infected with the thin vines entering through whatever gap they could find in their tanks. Soon they too would be melted down into a liquefied form and digested. There could be a few that they could save from such a fate, but they needed to get to Operations and override access to the pods to open them up, and the reality of it was that they needed to get as far away from the thing in the Sigma bay as possible.

He swallowed hard and told Graves how many colonists here were left alive. He then proceeded to tell him exactly how the creature had come aboard their ship as some kind of microscopic organism on the meteorite, before it mutated with the chemicals in the air recycling system, causing it to grow. This was all ADAM's educated guess work based on Dr. Reids' Ouroboros files, but it was the only explanation that he had. When he finally got to what had happened to the colonists, he realised the look of horror on Graves' face as he stood there in total silence.

"What about Carter?" he asked and Gilbey's stomach sunk. "Is that what happened to him?" Gilbey did not know how he was going to respond. He did not know what was worse. Did he tell him that Carter; a man they had all gotten to know over the course of this mission, had died, or did he tell him what he had witnessed escaping from the Rho bay?

"Carter... the colonists" Gilbey stuttered and paused to think between each word in an attempt to explain it all to him. "Those things..."

All of a sudden the lift control terminal lit up. An upward pointing arrow appeared on the screen, stating that someone on the upper deck was calling the lift to them.

"The others" Graves announced hopefully. "They here".

A smile broke out on his face, but Gilbey knew what it really was. "No!" he yelled, rushing back to the doorway of the lift in an effort to block it.

"Hey! What the hell are you doing?"

"ADAM!" Gilbey shouted out. "Give me another unregistered movement scan on the entire ship".

"One moment" ADAM's voice called out.

"Let them down!" Graves demanded. He was starting to get angry.

"They can copy us... whoever those things capture, eat, or whatever they did to the colonists and Carter, they are able to... mimic them". The words sounded insane coming out of his mouth.

Graves' expression made it all seem crazier than it already was. "What the fuck are you saying? Gilbey, you ain't making any sense!"

"One of them used Carter's voice to interface with ADAM's voice recognition software after I locked in one of the stasis bays. I heard it speak... it was just like Carter. It told ADAM to open the door and he did, thinking it was Carter".

"It... it... this is madness" Graves replied turning his head upward through the lift shaft. "What if it is not one of those things? What if it is Lane or someone trying to get away from them?"

"ADAM?" Gilbey called out once again.

"I have detected two distinctive movement patterns that are not registered on the Eden flight crew and colony manifest. One is located in the Sigma wing, star-port side, and the other is in the Cargo lift entrance of Section C".

"Shit" Graves realised stepping back off the lift platform. "It's up there".

"ADAM shut down this lift".

"My apologies Gilbey, but a level 2 security clearance is required to activate such actions".

"We'll have to block the doorway" Gilbey told him. "We can stop the lift from going up there". But then he had a sudden realisation that there was no other way out of the Storage hold. Being an unessential location during flight, only the Cargo lift had been designed to get here, as, when they landed at their destination, there were multiple ways down to this level from other areas, which would take them outside the ship and through the large hanger door. The idea was that they could keep important or dangerous items and equipment, or even food storage, down here locked up tight. It was a great plan for once they reached the Delta, but being stuck down here with a flesh-devouring beast blocking their only way out, it was problematic to say the least.

Looking around for inspiration, some kind of way to get out of this situation, he could see Graves clutching the rivet gun like a baby. He released his grip for a moment to scratch his head once again as he stared up to where the creature was most likely standing, as it waited for the lift to come and bring it down to them. He could see absolute terror in his eyes. It was then that Gilbey got an idea. His eyes locked onto the spacesuits and memories of the asteroid; the Trojan horse that had brought this plague to the last hope of mankind, as it was sucked out of the hanger and fired off out into the infinite.

"Get that suit on!" he barked at Graves.

"What?"

"Suit up god damn it!"

Gilbey stayed in the doorway of the Cargo lift, stopping it from going up, as Graves did as he was told. He put the Rivet gun on a nearby crate and climbed inside the suit. As usual, Gilbey had to connect the latches on his helmet.

Once he was ready, it was Gilbey turn. He ordered Graves to stand in the doorway. "Don't move from that spot" he ordered, but Graves only stared at him with a perplexed looked of confusion whilst Gilbey got the spacesuit on.

As soon as the helmet went on, the world turned silent. In that moment, it was almost as if all the troubles vanished and Gilbey felt a euphoric minute of bliss in this calm and secluded place. His breathing was all he managed to hear, making him feel as if he was the only person in the entire universe.

It was short lived when Graves called out over the comms "Are we going out there?!" Gilbey looked over to see him pointing his huge gloved finger towards the hanger door. "You're fucking nuts! We can't walk all the way to the airlock in Operations!"

It was a good idea, but Graves was right. It would have taken them hours to get all the way to the far end of Section A. Besides the interconnecting joints between the four different sections of the ship were a jungle of external short-range engines and other contraptions for if that section needed to fly independently, which makes crossing over from section to section hazardous.

"No" Gilbey replied. "They're going out there" his hand pointing to the lift shaft and to the location of where the creature sits.

He could see the gears in Graves' mind working as he tried to process the information. He could imagine hundreds of questions racing past until one finally clicked into place and everything made sense, as his face changed and he nodded. "Right. What do you need me to do?"

The Cargo lift had left and was already on its way back down by the time they had gotten into position. The entire lift process lasted only a few minutes, so they had very little time to get ready, and manoeuvring in the suits made it take even longer.

Since first waking up, about four hours ago, the maintenance crew had been on the back foot, caught off guard, but now, as Gilbey watched the lift slowly descending towards them, he felt that confident that he knew a way to fight back against the epidemic that had infected the Eden.

The flashing orange light, at the top of the Cargo lift doorway, shone through the spacesuit's visor, making visibility difficult every few moments. He looked over to Graves, who was now hiding behind some crates near the hanger door. Gilbey was closer to the lift, wedge between two containers, but he was close enough to where he needed to be when the time was right.

The Cargo lift locked into place on their level with a thunderous clang as the machine slotted into place. It was so loud that it could be heard through the thick hide of the helmet. The orange warning light switched off and the mechanisms for the door began to open.
The visor of Gilbey's helmet began to fog up slightly before his eyes. He realised that he was now breathing frantically. He could hear his own heart in his ears as his blood pumped through his temples and into his head. He felt his entire body throbbing as he watched in agonising anticipation at the Cargo lift door opening and revealing the horror inside.

Tall, slick and covered in human gore, the creature grabbed hold of the top of the door frame to pull itself out. Its featureless face twitched and jerked, searching for its prey, as it moved out into the Storage hold. The back end of it appeared to hold up its central form. The three hooked claws at the end of its spike covered tail scraped over the grated flooring.
Gilbey could hear the thing's hissing noise in his head as he watched it lower its huge arms appendages to support itself. He knew that he should not be able to hear it through the suit, but he remembered the dire sounds these things had made earlier, and the memory caused the noise to ring out in his ears, echoing around the inside of the helmet. Soon enough his own breathing was dwarfed by the insensate hiss.

After the thing had pulled itself past where Gilbey was hiding, he slowly peered around the side of the container in front of him. He made sure to move as slowly as possible, since he would not hear any noise he was making as his suit squeezed through the gap. It was a large enough gap to fit through without the spacesuit, but given how the outfit added an extra couple of inches to his size, Gilbey knew that if he moved too fast then it would have ruffled and scratched against the side of the containers, possibly alerting the creature to his presence.

From this angle, the creature; known as an Ouroboros, as per Doctor Reids' files on ADAM's server, could be seen in all of its horrifying glory. Its grotesque back had similar spikes to those that covered the majority of its tail, only here they were more haphazardly protruding through its soulless black skin. Its flesh, the non-human looking parts, were a shimmering black that looked wet to the touch. In this light, Gilbey could see that it was not actual flesh at all, but the same liquid that had formed from the detached vines in the Cargo lift earlier, only this was more solidified. He wondered if these things were just made up of a solid variant of the same black slime, and if it lost connection from the rest of its body, such as having a Beam-Saw cut off an arm or the tail, would the separated limb revert back into its liquid form?

There was so much that they did not know about these things. He would need to study Reids' notes, if he ever got the chance, to learn what the Doctor had discovered during his twenty years awake with it evolving over that time.

For all he knew, the behemoth could turn into nothing but the black fluid that coated its body, leaving behind the human remains it was wearing, and disappear through the floor grates, in order to flee from danger, and reform itself elsewhere when it was safe again. Everything that was solid, or gave the indication that the thing did indeed have bones, did not appear to be naturally part of it, and it felt as if it could easily discard it in order to escape.

But then again, for all he knew, this might not have been the case. Once separated from whatever might be the core of these creatures, it might not be able to survive and just simply disintegrate, as the tentacles did in the Cargo lift. Detaching its arms might be the only way to defeat it, so long as they got close enough to it to do so, or managed to get into the crate of weapons down here.

Although the head section clearly was a central point that the creature used to, somehow, see and hear its target, despite the fact it had no eyes or ears, the rest of the body looked frail and almost useless. The arms were the biggest part of the body, other than the long clawed tail, which looked as if they contained most of the thing's important organs, given how they pulsed with every slightest movement. Their connection to the middle section was thick, but nowhere near as thick as the arm-like appendages themselves. If these were severed, the creature might become immobilised.

Destroying the connection of the arms would be riskier than Gilbey's plan, so unless this thing sprouted wings and managed to escape what was coming, severing its external body parts would have to be a backup plan.

The Ouroboros knew they were down here. Other than the vent at the far end of the hold, there was no way out of here. It had them completely trapped, and unless its victims were planning on fighting back, it was only a matter of time before it found them.

Gilbey could not remember if someone else could hear any talking inside the suit from the outside, but he needed to make sure that Graves was ready and in position.

"Graves... I'm going to start making my way over to the switch". When the final word had left his mouth, he waited anxiously for the thing to turn around and come charging at him, but it never did.

"Okay" Graves' voice came through the comms, echoing inside of his helmet and dissolving the hissing noise in his head. "Just give me a sec..."

Suddenly Gilbey caught sight of one of the smaller metal crates near to Graves' position topple over. It fell in slow motion before soundlessly crashing onto the ground.

"Shit!" Graves shouted as he could be seen moving about, trying to get his entire suit hidden behind one of the other crates, still standing.

Of course the crate had not been soundless for the creature, who, after hearing it, immediately lifted itself upwards, facing towards the source of the noise, standing almost upright on the claws at the end of its tail. It towered over the top of everything, with its head almost touching the ceiling. It peered over the containers and crates, as its arms throbbed and twitched.

Everything was still silent before the thing's head spasmed and the lower jaw pulled itself way, more black muck oozed out of the opening and dripped onto the floor, as it screamed out, almost in excitement, as it had discovered exactly what it was looking for. Even through the helmet, the noise pierced through their ears.

"ADAM" Gilbey asked as quietly as possible. "Switch off the I.M.F".

Turning off the Interplanetary Magnetic Field would leave the Eden defenceless for a few moments, but it should create enough of a vacuum to blast that thing out of the ship.

"Are you sure Gilbey?" ADAM's voice spoke out inside the helmet.

"Yes! Do it... do it now". Gilbey had expected ADAM to respond with something about not having the correct clearance, but he figured that Dietrich had not changed the clearance levels on the I.M.F. Thankfully he was right.

"As you wish".

He caught sight of Graves, but the nearby lights, shining on his visor, were hiding his face, but he knew that Graves must have been terrified. The monstrous abomination was screaming out for him, now knowing exactly where he was.

Graves had not properly seen it in the light before. The first and only time he saw this thing was in the Sigma stasis bay, but the lights had been damaged or covered, causing bad visibility, but here, in the brightly lit Storage hold, the young mechanical engineer could see clearly now, staring at one another in a moment that stretched on for as long as the space beyond the Eden.

But in a heartbeat that moment had passed without any of them realising, and now the creature was pulling itself, charging towards Graves. He tried to move out of the way as fast as he could, but the spacesuit slowed his movements and he could not get away quickly enough. He was knocked over by the container as the thing crashed into the side of it, recklessly travelling the shortest possible distance towards him, not caring about anything in its way. Graves pulled himself up in the few seconds where the Ouroboros lost sight of its prey and frantically searched about for it in the carnage around it.

During this time, Gilbey had already managed to make his way across the Storage hold to the hanger door control panel. He looked back to see Graves move into the centre of the room, right in front of the door, as the creature, now with his sights back on the fleeing target, was moving up behind him.

"Do it!" his voice called out over the comms, and with that he did.

He pulled the lever down and instantly felt the rush of air being pulled out of the hanger door. Smaller objects began to rush past him and out through the opening door.

Another shriek broke out, causing Gilbey to spin round. At the same moment, ADAM announced that the anti-gravity detectors had been activated, and the Mag-boots of the suits secured him to the floor. He knew Graves' had as well, as he stopped moving as fast as he had been, but still had his back to everything else that was happening.

The creature managed to get within a couple of metres of Graves before the hanger bay was completely open and the pull was becoming too much for it. Crates and containers, that were no longer secure, were pulled out of the hanger door and flew off into the black void of space. He saw the crate that had drawn the creature to where Graves was hiding, was thrown from the Eden and was gone in an instant.

It was then that he suddenly noticed the crate of firearms was now scraping across the floor towards the door.

"Shit!" he thought as he watched their only weaponry moving closer and closer to the exit. He now had a choice; either he let them be lost in the endless expanse, in hopes that it would pull the creature out, or he shut the hanger door, putting them into an even worse situation than they had been before. The choice was obvious.

As the weapon case crashed into the frame of the hanger door, the impact caused it to open and all of a sudden there was a stream of guns and ammunition flying out into space.

Gilbey felt powerless to see their main defence against these horrors, disappearing right before his eyes.

It was not in vain, however, as the thing became powerless to resist the vacuum that had been created. It screamed out once more after being pulled backward towards the door. It slashed desperately at the grating with its tail claws, but it was not enough.

Graves was shouting out all kinds of profanity over the comms, but his voice was muted in the shadow of the chaos every where.

Another crate crashed into Graves, which would have dropped him to the floor if it had not been for the boots, before it careered across the Storage hold and hit the side of the creature, knocking it off balance. The thing was lifted off of the floor and flew towards the door. It frantically reached out for something to grab hold of, but it was futile. The thing smashed into the top of the door frame, denting it worse than the asteroid had done on the previous cycle, and was just about to be pulled out into the dark abyss, when suddenly the world outside turned a translucent blue.

"Wha..." Gilbey gazed in affright as the gravity inside the Magnetic field centralised and the creature dropped from the air. Using one of its massive arms, it stopped itself from falling out of the open doorway. The Mag-boots deactivated.

"What the hell is going on?! Disable the shield!" he called out to ADAM.

Graves dropped to his hands and knees, finding it impossible to stand on his own two feet after being hit with the crate.

"I must apologise Gilbey" ADAM's voice spoke out. "But Senior Office Dietrich has reactivated the I.M.F and changed the security clearance on it. My hands are tied".

"Dietrich... you bitch!"

The creature, now hanging out of the doorway with its back end completely suspended outside the ship, reached out with its other arm and something began to happen.

The thing cried out, reaching outwards with its half metre long facial vines, as a mass began to form beneath the skin at the end of the appendage. An object began to push its way out and slither across the floor. It was difficult to make out at first from this distance, but Gilbey soon realised that it was some sort of tentacle, sliding its way across the hold towards Graves as he tried to get himself back onto his feet.

"Graves!" Gilbey called out, but the thing had started to wrap itself around his leg. By the time Graves had realised, it had a tight hold on him.

His cry bellowed over the comms. "Get this thing off of me!" It pulled him off his feet and began dragging him towards the hanger door. His scream rang out inside of Gilbey's space helmet. "Gilbey!" he cried. "Help me! Help me!" He managed to grab hold of one of the handles of a container which was still strapped into place.

The creature began to lift itself up, pulling itself out.

"No!" he thought, turning back to the control panel and lifting the lever back up.

"There appears to be an obstruction, stopping the Section C Storage hold from closing" ADAM told him. "Please remove the blockage and I will be able to close the door".

He cursed as he began to run over towards Graves, at this point looking like a flag tied to the side of the container. Gilbey flicked on the switch and fired up the Beam-Saw. He could feel the heat emitting off of it, even through his suit.

Just like he had done to the creature's facial tentacles in the Cargo lift, Gilbey went to slice through Graves' binds in one swipe, when the thing must have sensed the threat. It had learned what that bright purple light could do to it, and it knew it would lose the fight if it allowed him to cut the tentacle off.

The organism released its grip on the hanger door frame and another tentacle formed from the centre of where its hand should be. It poured out of the opening like a worm, slithering and twitching as it raced out and across the hold floor. The creature itself, now lost its grasp, began to fall back out of the open hanger door from the weight of its shoulders and tail end. The tentacle moved faster than the previous one, and just as Gilbey was about to cut the one wrapped around Graves' leg, the newly arrived appendage cut through the chest section of his spacesuit, slicing Gilbey's skin and the muscle beneath.

Each tentacle appeared to have smaller variants of the spikes and spines running along the tail of the creature.

An excruciating pain shot through his entire body, knocking him to the ground on his back. His head smacked into the back of the helmet. He could feel his warm blood running all over his chest, as the stinging sensation from the open wound felt as if the laceration itself was on fire.

His helmet latch must have disconnected in the fall, as the entire thing detached from the rest of the suit as he somehow managed to lift his head a few seconds later. The noises around him returned and he was able to hear the true horrific nature of what was going on. Graves' screams blasted out of the speaker in the helmet next to him, whilst the creature; the Ouroboros, fearfully roared, falling from the Eden, and pulling Graves back with it. The two of them disappeared from sight as they fell down inside the I.M.F.

Gilbey stared out of the opening in hopes of seeing Graves emerge back inside somehow, but he didn't. Instead both he and the behemoth dropped below the centre of gravity inside the shield, and were flung back up into the air. The creature shrieked and roared as it came into contact with the Magnetic field. Its cry was even worse than any other noise the organisms had made. Even from this distance the shriek was deafening as its entire body was broken down and disintegrated within seconds, into millions of tiny specks which were instantly destroyed ejecting back out into the inside of the shield, small traces of its remains like a small explosion of dust.

Graves, being pulled into the same fate by the thing's tentacle wrapped around his leg, was powerless to resist the collision course he was now on.

"Oh god, no! Please!" his voice yelled out over the helmet's speakers, and by the time Gilbey had even a moment to process what he was seeing, it was over. He was gone.

The hanger door shut almost instantly after the event, almost as if ADAM was trying his best to save face being partially responsible for what had just transpired. The Storage hold became so silent that Gilbey thought he had his helmet on still.

Still stunned at seeing his subordinate, co-worker, and friend, being completely erased from existence, he remembered the feeling in his chest and the pain began to set in. He looked down to see his suit's chest piece and the blood soaked tear in the centre of it.

It took him nearly half an hour to get out of it. The torturous pain was almost too much to bear when he needed to stretch his arms up to get the suit off over his head. By the end of it, he lay in a heap on the floor like the clothes he had just stripped. He shook and rocked himself until the feeling subsided. It wasn't gone completely, but it had become so much more bearable, so he sat up and checked out the damage.

The wound went from his right pectoral and down across his ribcage and stopped at the start of his stomach on the left hand side of his body. It was only a few millimetres deep, but that was enough. The suit had taken most of the impact, completely ruining it and tearing the entire chest-plate in half, but his muscles still felt torn open and exposed, as blood was running down the rest of his body. The tissue surrounding the injury hung like slithers of processed meat, pink and wet, which flapped about as he moved around to check the injury. The sight of it brought the painful sensations back. He went to clutch at his chest, but the thought of touching it made the feeling even worse. It took Gilbey a few moments of enduring the agony before he could do anything else, during that time he was almost completely motionless.

He pulled the top down and climbed into the Cargo lift. As he rode it back up, his thoughts were of Graves and how he had been alive the last time he had been in this lift less than an hour ago. Now there was nothing left of him. He had been obliterated by the force field surrounding the Eden and with no body, there was nothing to bury when they reached the new world.

"When we reach the new world?" Gilbey muttered as he realised that there was now an increasingly high chance that they would not actually get to Delta Tauri and find the new home for humanity.

These things had killed so many of the colonists already, and now it was taking down the maintenance crew one by one, if they did not fight back, then there was a hundred percent chance that they would not make it, and man-kind would disappear. But fighting back, in part, had been what had caused Graves to die. If Gilbey hadn't thought of opening the hanger door to blast the creature out of the ship, then he might have still been alive. There might have been another way, but there was so little time to think.

"We were trapped" Gilbey said, trying desperately to reassure himself that he was not responsible for Graves' death, but it did not work. The feelings of guilt hurt almost as much as the slice across his chest.

"Graves... I'm sorry". His words were but a whisper as he covered his face in shame and slumped against the lift controls.

There was never a doubt in his mind that the entire crew would reach the Eden's destination. He knew that some of the colonists would not make it, especially after the first cycle when they witnessed the first deaths from heart failure, and there was always the fear that it could happen to any one of them as they re-entered stasis, but that was just a niggling voice in some distant place in his mind. He never thought that it could actually become a reality. He had imagined one another as neighbours living and working together in the shadow of the EVE Earth-forming system, growing crops in the newly rejuvenated soil, exploring the uncharted world, and just living out their days in the beautiful sunlight and clean air, free from the cyanogenic smog that had plagued the Earth they had departed from. It was something none of them had truly done in their lifetimes, and the very idea of it was what had drawn most of them to this experimental mission.

Now it was looking less and less likely that they would get there. Graves disappeared from the image in his mind of what the new world would have been like and all he could think about was the threat that they faced.

Heart failure during stasis, engine failure or loss of fuel, or something enormous colliding with the ship and killing them all, even the smog somehow getting on the ship and contaminating their oxygen; these were the things that had scared him during their flight. These were what Gilbey had thought was going to kill them before they got to where they were going, but the truth of it was that there was something far worse hiding on board, hunting them, that had a far greater chance of killing them than anything else.

When the lift reached the Cargo entrance, the pain had returned. It became almost impossible to stand and Gilbey collapsed into the side of the row of lockers, creating an enormous clang which echoed throughout this section of the ship. He waited for a moment in silence for any indication that the other creature was nearby, but there was nothing.

"ADAM" he spoke out, and as he did, each word felt like it was ripping its way out of his open wound. He couldn't bear it. He gripped his chest and, whilst suffering the torment, clenched his hand in an attempt to close the injury. His shirt was now soaked in his own blood.

"Yes sir" the machine replied. "How can I be of service?"

"Do a scan for unregistered movement"

"Scanning..." ADAM announced before stating that the only movement he had detected was located near the Sigma stasis bay.

Gilbey sighed in relief as he dropped down to the floor, resting his back against the lockers and sitting in the dim light. His whole chest felt as if it was on fire.

"ADAM... where is the nearest medical equipment?" he said softly, trying to maintain his strength.

"There is a first aid kit located in the Observation Lounge" Which was back the way he had just come, and he didn't want to be anywhere near the Sigma wing. "Alternatively the Surgical centre is the next closest location".

"The Surgical centre?" Gilbey repeated, remembering that it was where Eckhart and Lane were hiding out, at least the last time he asked ADAM.

"Are the others there?"

"Yes. Doctor Eckhart and Maintenance Engineer Lane are both at that location" ADAM replied.

If he made it there then Eckhart could help him. He could stitch him up and stop him from bleeding out, if he didn't do so before he got there.

Gilbey tried to stand but the pain shot through him like a bolt of lightning and he fell back to the floor with a shout. His hand slammed against the locker and he felt the tools in his belt dislodge and hit the ground. The Saw-Blade frame crashed onto his foot before scudding across the metal grated flooring.

"Shit" he grunted dropping to one knee. His blood dripped from his clothes and fell between his fingers as his hand supported his entire pain stricken body. "I... I can't make it" he knew. He would die before he got anywhere near the Surgical centre.

Just then something rolled across the floor and tapped him gently on the fingertip. He opened his eyes, horrified for a brief moment at the blood pool forming beneath him. He then noticed the Weld-Pen lying beside it. It had come away along with the Saw-Blade frame and the second he locked eyes onto it, he knew what he had to do to survive.

Harnessing some unknown power, he pushed himself back up against the lockers, grabbing the Weld-Pen in the process. Slumping back and lifting his shirt, he asked the A.I. to provide him with data on the best way to close his gaping chest wound with the welding tool.

"I would not recommend doing..." ADAM went to inform him, but Gilbey was not interested.

He knew that he was going to die if he did not get it done. "In that case Gilbey, I would suggest that you hold the pen at a thirty degree angle. You do not want the flame to make contact with your skin, but instead you want the heat surrounding the flame to do so. As it burns at over three thousand degrees Fahrenheit, it would melt the very skin from your bones.

"I..." Gilbey went to make a joking remark along the lines of "I'll bear that in mind" or "I don't need that skin anyway" but he felt something in his throat that caused him to cough violently. Each cough felt like another stab in the chest that pierced through his ribcage and struck at his lungs. He could taste blood, which he swallowed to try and get rid of it.

"Do be careful sir" ADAM pleaded in an almost life-like sympathetic tone of voice. It was at times like this that Gilbey forgot that the voice all around him was not that of another human being.

When he turned on the Weld-Pen, the instant heat from the end of it reached out around three inches. He had used these for fixing small issues in pipework in hard to reach places, but for the larger jobs he had an industrial weld tool to mould huge sheets of steel together. He had never imagined using it on himself, but the second he had seen it on the floor, he knew that it was all he had at hand to close his injury and potentially save his life. If not, he was going to make his last moments of existence agonisingly horrendous.

"Good luck Gilbey. I will inform the others of your actions, in case they can offer any advice or assistance".

"Thanks ADAM..." he told him and then he went to work on himself with the Weld-Pen.

4ᵀᴴ Cycle – ETA: 47.7 Yrs

Part Three: Beneath the Surface

"Gilbey" a voice called out from the darkness. At first it sounded almost angelic, like he had died and finally left the hell that now overrun the Eden. It was a soft gentle voice that spoke to him from somewhere in the distance.
The sound stirred him from his slumber and the sudden rush of pain came flooding back in his chest. His mind flashed with images of his botched operation, sealing his own skin back together with the intense flame of the Weld-Pen. Before he could even open his eyes, his head began to pound intensely. He remembered being only millimetres away from closing the wound completely when he felt as if he was going to pass out from the pain. It seems that he finally did.
"Gilbey, wake up!" they echoed again, with each word bringing him back to reality, and the familiar voice of Lane became more apparent.

Gilbey opened his eyes and all he could see was a white light that scarred his eyes the second he made contact with it. He tried to recoil, but the sensations of pain were too much. All he could do was close his eyes and pray the agony away.
"He's awake!" Lane announced and suddenly Eckhart could be heard.
"Gilb, are you okay?" His voice grew loud as he approached. As Gilbey tried to open his eyes again, he could see the silhouettes of his colleagues standing over him. "What the fuck did you do to yourself? ADAM, decrease the lighting here by thirty percent".

After a few moments, his eyes began adjusting. He could see the young Doctor looking over his chest, as Gilbey lay in a heap on the Cargo lift entranceway. He saw Eckhart's confused and horrified expression, but there was something else he could see in his eyes; curiosity.
"What is it?" Gilbey asked.
Eckhart laughed. "Did you... did you seal this yourself with one of those pens? My god".
Looking at the injury, Gilbey could see the charred scar running over the entirety of his chest. Blood covered him, but it looked as if it had done the job. The wound was closed.
"How long was I out?"
Lane stepped into his view. Her eyes looked darkened, like she had been crying non-stop since she first came out of Stasis, and given how she had reacted to the deaths on the last cycle and how many more there had been this time around, she most probably had been.
"We got a call from ADAM about forty minutes ago. It took us nearly that long to get from the Surgical Centre over here" she told him.
"Did you run into any of those things?" Gilbey asked, touching his scar, before Eckhart grabbed his hand and pulled it away.
"No" he told him. "We were attacked by one at the Tram Station... but that..."
Lane cut in. "But that bitch Dietrich shut the station down and trapped us". Her voice was full of rage at the very thought of her senior officer.
"I take it you haven't spoken to her?" Gilbey said as he tried to lift himself up off the ground but the pain became too much.
"Here" Eckhart opened a small satchel beside him and pulled out a needle inside a sealed packet. "This will help".
"We spoke to her when we first got away from that thing at the station" Lane explained. "She told us to make our way to the Service Dock, but that would take too long. The longer we wait, the more colonists those things are slaughtering".

Eckhart opened the packet and wiped away some dried blood from Gilbey's arm before injecting the needle into him. "This is an intracardiac shot of epinephrine and an analgesic that should help take the edge off. You'll feel a little hazy, but it should get you on your feet again".
"Thanks Doc" Gilbey gratefully answered, however, in doing so, every muscle in his chest tightened up. Thankfully this disguised the feeling of the needle going in.
Eckhart flicked the switch on the side of the needle casing and within seconds Gilbey started to feel a warm sensation all over his body. The pain seemed to subside and he felt as if he could breathe normally once more.
"It will take you a couple of minutes before you can function normally, so just try and rest. Once we get back to Operations and away from these fucking monsters, then I can take a better look at you".
"We ain't getting anywhere Eckhart. Not unless you can convince ADAM to unlock the Tram station".
Gilbey already started feeling better at this point, sitting upright and touching his flesh caused

no pain. His head felt a little fuzzy, but it had done so since first waking up a few moments ago, so any side-effects of the adrenaline shot were non-existent at this time.

"I've been working on bypassing the lock-down from a terminal in the Surgical Centre. I have done all I can, but I need to do the finishing touches at one of terminals at the station for it to take effect".

"A bypass? You can't bypass ADAM" Gilbey exclaimed as he managed to pull his shirt over his head and covered his injury back up. The entire thing was now a blood soaked rag, but it was all he had. Lane watched as his wound disappeared behind the deep crimson material.

"Carter showed me a few things in the last cycle and I think I might be able to convince..." he stopped and looked around, as if the A.I. was literally watching over them, and Eckhart was making sure that ADAM was not listening. "...him that I have level 2 security clearance. It won't hold up for anything else she has locked unless there is another terminal I can get into, but I should be able to get the Tram station up and running long enough for us to get back to Section A".

"Wow" Gilbey replied. "Carter actually showed you how to work ADAM's coding?"

"Well..." Eckhart was hesitant. "That's if it works" he sighed. "We could have done with Carter. If he was here he could have told ADAM to just open the door. I'm a Doctor, not a technical engineer".

"Carter was a good man" Lane added. "He didn't deserve to die like that".

Gilbey was unsure if he should tell them that Carter was still alive, however was suffering a fate worse than hell as he was, most likely, being slowly broken down and consumed by the central core of the horror in the Sigma stasis bay. How it was slowly digesting him and was mimicking him for, whatever the organisms that came out of it, could use to try and trick the rest of them.

The look on Lane's face told him that he shouldn't. He was not sure if she would be able to take it. The idea that the colonists had suffered this same miserable end was bad enough, let alone someone that she had become quite attached to.

"Yeah" was all that he could muster.

After an awkward moment where the three of them reminded themselves what had actually happened to Carter, Eckhart broke the tension. "Let's get you up" he said as he grabbed hold of Gilbey's arm and carefully pulled him up to his feet.

It was difficult, as he felt his legs had never actually been used before, but he got there. He rested his arm on the row of lockers. "Thanks Doctor".

The word 'Doctor' suddenly made Gilbey think about the other medical officer in the team. He had been absent from their entire endeavour. Having possibly aged by twenty years.

"Have you heard anything from Reids?" he asked.

"Not a thing" Eckhart responded unsettlingly. "We have only spoken once to Dietrich and other than that, we have been talking to ADAM to find out where you guys were".

"What... what happened down there?" Lane stuttered, knowing she didn't want to ask her next question. She swallowed the fear in her throat and managed to push through. "What happened to Graves?" The look in her eye told Gilbey that she already knew, but she just had to hear it.

"I..." he struggled, looking for the right way to word that Graves had been disintegrated into millions of specks by the I.M.F, but he knew whatever he said was going to upset her.

He reached down and picked up the framework for the Beam-Saw, slotting in back into his belt and took a deep breath. "We opened up the hanger door to blast one of them out. Dietrich never imagined that we would shut down the shield generator, especially not after what happened the last time the shield went down, but we did, in an attempt to blow it out into space. We were in our suits so the Mag-Boots stopped us from getting sucked out, but..."

He knew that by telling them the next part, it would have been the final nail in Dietrich's coffin. There would be no coming back from this. Whatever hatred Lane and Eckhart had for her for locking down the entire section of the Eden and trapping them along with those things, was only going to get worse once he told them that she was responsible for Graves' death.

"The shield came back on" he recounted. "Our boots deactivated and that creature had Graves round the leg. It pulled him out with it".

"Oh my god..." Lane turned away, as if she was going to cry again. Gilbey knew that the image of him hitting the I.M.F was now running through her mind.

"Jesus..." Eckhart looked over towards Lane as she leant against the pipework on the opposite wall, trying so hard to keep her emotions in check, whilst tears flooded down her face. "Lane" he moved in to comfort her, grabbed her by the shoulders and pulled her into his embrace. "He would have felt nothing" he said as she broke down, pushing her face into his chest.

It was a some comfort in knowing Graves wouldn't have felt anything as he was erased, but Gilbey had seen it first hand, and he had heard him pleading for rescue as he was slowly dragged out of the hanger door. These thoughts, Gilbey knew, would stay with him until his dying day.

It had taken some time for Lane to pull herself together and for them to head off. Thankfully that had given the intracardiac shot time to take effect. It had numbed the slash across Gilbey's chest almost completely. A strange tingly feeling could still be felt, but it did not hurt, not even when he touched it. It had caused his vision to blur but, as they carefully moved through the halls, Gilbey kept wiping it away in an attempt to get his eyes to focus.

His legs had been weak in a similar fashion to the times he had reawakened from stasis at the beginning of each cycle. After a few cautiously trodden passageways, the feeling began to return to normal and they could move at a faster and steadier pace.

The three remaining maintenance crew members, still trapped within Section C of the ship, had made the decision to go ahead with Eckhart's plan to bypass the security lock-down their superior officer had placed on it as the quickest way of getting out of this nightmare. Getting to the Service Dock would have taken them far too long, leaving them exposed for the majority of the journey. The sooner they got off of this Section of the Eden, the sooner they could try and save the lives of the remaining colonists. There was still another twenty-four thousand remaining in stasis that slept on completely unaware that a large amount of their travelling companions had been liquefied and ingested into a grotesque inhuman anomaly that had stowed away on their ship.

Gilbey had told Lane and Eckhart about a way for them to track the creature's spawn by their movement, but when he tried it, ADAM could find nothing.
"What does that mean?" Lane questioned in hopes that maybe whatever had consumed Carter was now gone.
But Gilbey knew that the fact ADAM could not detect it meant that it was just not moving. Previously the A.I. could only pinpoint one of the two monstrosities that had emerged from the central mass in the Sigma bay, but the other one was still out there somewhere, which was much more terrifying as it could have been anywhere.
"I don't know" he tried to lie, but he didn't want to give her hope that the threat was over. "Maybe ADAM can't detect them".
"They could be gone right?" Lane asked with only a slightest hint that she believed her own words.
Gilbey remained silent. Thankfully Eckhart interrupted the moment by informing them that the Tram Station was just beyond the next door.

Looking through the small glass port in the bulkhead door, they could see the large platform with the Tram Station at the far end of it. It was a wide open space filled with benches, tables and food stalls covered over in tarpaulins, in hopes that little cleaning was required once everyone re-awake from stasis. The idea of these places were to act in the same way as that of the train stations of the old world, once they reached the Delta and the Eden would act as their living accommodation during the time that it took for the EVE Earth-Forming system to make the planet's atmosphere habitable.
Passing through here during past cycles, Gilbey imagined the place busy with crowds of colonists travelling all around the landed ship to their various work assignments, or meeting one another for a drink or just to talk during some of their free time, but now he couldn't picture it. The entire place looked deserted, and that was the way he imagined it would remain; a quiet and lifeless place.
The lights were still functioning here, but the enormous shutter door, which allowed the Tram access to the tunnels connecting the various sections of the ship, was closed, blocking their path back to safety, and was now casting a huge shadow over a large portion of the platform. In the darkness Gilbey could see the covered over stalls, making him wonder what was lying just on the other side.

Large pillars had been built in the centre section of the area in an attempt to give these places a more unique feeling, as oppose to the cold steel grated flooring and white walls. The floor of the Tram Stations were stone tiles, still white, but they stood out dramatically to the rest of the ship. Although its design was to appear cultural, the designs themselves were based on ancient civilisations from Earth's past just to act as a contrast to the vast amount of technology found all around the Eden, but without the colonists and crew members populating it, the whole area felt cold and dead.

The pillars themselves obstructed a lot of the central section of the station, which was where most of the covered stalls were located. They could just about see the Tram parked on the blocked track, and it was here that they would find the terminal that they needed.

"It looks clear" Eckhart told them. Being the most senior member of the crew at present, Eckhart had taken on the role of the team leader and made it his duty to ensure that the three of them unlocked the shutter and got back to Operations. "Let's go".

Just as he pressed the door's control panel and the door slid open, Gilbey grabbed hold of the young Doctor's shoulder. He clenched up and stopped dead in his tracks. "What?" he said almost in a whisper.

"They hide in the shadows" Gilbey informed him ominously remembering back. "In the Rho bay... one of them was pretending to be a Stasis pod standing still amongst the rest. It adapted to its environment and tried to hide in plain sight. That was the last time ADAM had not detected any movement".

"Wh...what?!" Lane stammered as she searched desperately around the platform in hopes of spotting one. "It could be anything?"

"It was not perfectly camouflaged. If I wasn't paying attention and noticed something weird, then it would have got me, but I could have easily walked right past it. The whole place was covered in the same vine stuff that had taken over the entire Sigma bay, so it was easier for it to hide". Gilbey tried to remember how many stalls there had been from the numerous times he had come through here, but it was no use. All of them looked the same in the shadow of the shutter. "It used the darkness. If it is here, then it would be there". He knew that he had made them all feel instantly more frightened of potentially nothing, but Gilbey had more experience with these things than Eckhart and Lane. Both of them had previously been attacked here at the station and fled to the Surgical Centre, whereas Gilbey had already been trapped inside both a stasis bay and the Cargo hold with one, witnessed Graves be pulled off the ship, and he himself had been chased down various corridors with one in pursuit of him, so he thought he had better share his experiences with the others in case they thought that the area was clear just because one of those thing was not standing atop one of the central pillars. The station could have been clear for all they knew and this had done nothing but cause them more stress, but it was better to be cautious than end up being digested by some interplanetary abomination.

All of them moved carefully further into the Tram Station, keeping in mind what Gilbey had just said, taking care to stay clear of any of the larger structures here. The pillars made it difficult to see the food stalls properly in the dim lighting, but everything appeared normal. Gilbey kept his Beam-Saw gripped firmly in his hand with his finger hovering over the 'on' switch. He was concerned that the light and the small humming noise, which emitted from the tool's activation, could alert one of those things to their presence, but he wanted to be prepared, so that at the first sight of danger, he could try and defend himself.

Closer to the central pillared circle, they could see the aftermath of the creatures previous attack here. There were broken benches, claw marks on the side of pillars, and black secreted slime left in its wake. The door leading to the Surgical Centre, where Eckhart and Lane had escaped to, looked as if it had taken a beating. Half of the shutter seemed like it would never function properly again. It was clear that the two of them had not come back this way, but possibly one of the interconnecting passageways that ran like veins all over this section of the ship.

"What was that?" Lane suddenly stopped moving and started to glance around. "Did you hear that?" Gilbey and Eckhart stopped and listened, but there was nothing.
"I don't hear anything" Gilbey told her.
Eckhart took her by the hand. "Come on" he said as he tried to gesture her towards the terminal near the Tram, but Lane refused.
"No... I heard something" she exclaimed desperately trying to hear whatever she had heard once again.
They tried to listen once more and once again there was nothing that could be heard. Eckhart sighed and cautiously moved past the pillar circle and stepped up onto the Tram Station, moving closer to the terminal.
Gilbey waited for a moment, trying to give her the benefit of the doubt that she had actually heard a noise, but the Eden was a tremendously large spacecraft currently travelling through the cosmos at a ridiculous speed, so there were constant noises occurring on board at all times. The engines never ceased functioning during the entire hundred and thirty-seven year trip, but Lane should have been used to that by now, especially after spending months awake and alone on the ship with only the other members of the maintenance crew as company, so the fact she could now suddenly hear something strange did make the hairs on the back of Gilbey's neck stand.
He wanted to tell her that she had probably not heard anything at all, but Lane appeared adamant that she had heard something that he knew it would be futile. "Just... stay close" he advised before turning and heading towards the Doctor.

Eckhart was busy linking his data table up to the Tram Station terminal in an attempt to run a bypass.
"I am not sure that this is going to work Doctor" ADAM told him as the connection between the two devices was made.
"A threat?" Eckhart asked giving the computer a scalding glance, at which point you could tell that if ADAM was capable of finding something funny and physically laughing, this would have been one of those times.
"No, of course not Doctor Eckhart. I am just advising that attempting to override the security measures in place, set by Senior Maintenance Officer Dietrich, clearance security level two,

could result in your user functions being locked out of the server".

Eckhart, who was able to laugh, did so. "As if I care about that" he told the A.I. as he began swiping through the various folders and into the coded scripture of the Tram Station's service controls, both on his tablet and on the terminal itself. "If we get this opened, then I'll get Dietrich to cancel the security clearance, okay? Then we can just focus on the fucking monsters on this ship".

"I think what he means…" Gilbey added, peering over his shoulder to get a better look at the bypass in action. "Is that we only have the one shot at this. You are only able to do this because your clearance level is higher than the rest of us, bar Reids or Dietrich, so if you get locked out of the server, we ain't going to have another shot at this. Carter isn't around to unlock you".

He felt as if his words fell onto deaf ears as Eckhart continued working on the terminal.

Just then a foreign noise in the air broke his trail of thought. Gilbey's mind flashed with memories of Lane and what she had heard. He turned to where she was previously standing, but she was no longer there.

"Lane?" he uttered softly under his breath, too quietly for even Eckhart to hear it working beside him, and he began to search the area around him with his eyes in hopes of seeing her, but she was gone. "Lane!" he repeated, much louder than before, causing the young Doctor to stop what he was doing and turn around. His face dropped as he frantically looked around for her.

"Where the hell…?"

"I thought… she was just there" Gilbey explained, but Eckhart did not even acknowledge what he had just heard. Instead he stepped away from the terminal and walked back across the platform, past Gilbey, and in the direction of the central pillars. He went to shout, but stopped himself a split-second before doing so and turned to Gilbey.

"All you got to do is select the shutter from the control panel, and then click execute on the pad. It will start running then, and once it is done, the shutter will open".

"Well where the fuck are you going?" Gilbey asked him, knowing full well the answer he Eckhart was about to give moments before he saw movement in the corner of his eye. Without even properly taking in what he had just seen, he said "There" pointing in the direction of where Lane was now cautiously moving towards one of the other passageway entrances.

There was no door here, but with the total darkness beyond it, it looked as if the entrance was a black painted wall. The lights there must not have been functioning, which suited whatever lay in wait there just fine.

"Oh my god" Eckhart spat as he began to move faster across the platform in Lane's direction. By now she was only a couple of metres away from the total abyss up ahead. Gilbey wondered what she could have possibly been doing, but another noise in the air, this one much clearer than before, rushed by.

"Help… me… please…" it said in a familiar voice.

Eckhart must have heard it too as at this point he started to sprint and shouted out her name as loud as he could.

"It's Carter!" Lane yelled back as she turned away from the entrance. "It's Carter!" she called again in hopeful excitement, just as the trap was sprung.

There had been a faint scratching sound which had gone unnoticed until now. As soon as it became apparent, Gilbey's thoughts were suddenly of earlier, when the creature had mimicked Carter's voice before to get itself out of the room he had trapped it in. He remembered how horrified he had felt when the voice of his former friend, twisted and distorted, reached him, and now that feeling had once again taken over.

He watched as Lane slowly turned back towards the darkness. "No! Don't!..." was all he could scream at the top of his lungs, his own shrill freezing him in place as the cry echoed all around them, but it was too late.

It was just a movement in the darkness beyond the doorway at first. Blink and you would have thought that your mind was playing tricks on you, but if you watched it all unfold, then you would have thought that the very darkness itself had come alive.

One of the enormous gore covered arms clawed its way out of the shadows just as Lane turned back to see it all unfold. The faint scratching noise grew louder as the creature's scraping tail on the metal passageway flooring suddenly filled the quiet hall, closely followed by its horrendous shriek as the central mass emerged out of the shadows before her.

Eckhart tried to call out again as he stood there with one hand clutching his own hair in frustration, feeling powerless to do nothing but watch everything unfold. He started to move towards her, in some futile attempt to make it across the entire hall before anything could happen, shouting at her to move, run, or get out of there, but his voice was dwarfed by the murderous roar as the creature's other arm reached out and grabbed hold of Lane.

It was not in the traditional way that a normal human being would hold something with their fingers and thumb, but instead it pushed the thick wall of the black slime and deep red gore covered appendage into her, entrapping her as black vines quickly moved all over to hold her into place. She went to scream as one of the vines forced its way into her mouth and began to drive its way into her throat.

Out of nowhere, the monstrosity stepped out of the darkness entirely and came fully into view, stopping Eckhart in his tracks. Even from this distance, he could see Lane's face of tormented horror, as the black bile began to consume her. Even with the vines running into her mouth, she looked as if she was trying to scream, almost anticipating what was coming next.

Bone coloured spikes erupted from the arm and thrust their way through Lane's entire body sending a mist of blood and chunks of flesh and muscle raining down in front of her and her captor. They could see as she drew her last breath, her eyes becoming bloodshot before rolling back into her head, and her body falling limp.

Whilst watching in stunned repulsion, unable to turn away from it all, Gilbey remembered what Eckhart had asked of him. He twisted around and selected the Tram tunnel shutter from the list of files on screen, and then clicked the large green execute button on the tablet. The glass screen of it reflected back, not only Gilbey's own terrified face, but also the events transpiring behind him.

In the few seconds that it took for the shutter command to take effect, Lane was starting to be absorbed into the Ouroboros' skin. The black sludge began pooling over her more rapidly, as her lifeless body started to be swallowed into its depths.

Eckhart stared on, still frozen in terror by what he was witnessing, as the woman he had become attached to over the course of this interplanetary journey, was now nothing but a pulsating black bulge on the surface of some inhuman atrocity, which must have now been feeding off her for sustenance.

"An error has occurred" ADAM's voice said, drawing Gilbey's attention once more to the terminal. On the screen the words; 'Security clearance – level two required' appeared, but on the tablet, a loading bar had begun to fill with a percentage amount sitting beside that. As far as he could tell, the bypass was working. Once the loading bar had reached one hundred percent, the tablet would override the security settings and the Tram door should have just opened. In theory, the tram itself would be able to take them back to Section A.

But of course this was if they could survive long enough for the bar to fill. If they met the same ill-fated destiny as poor defenceless Lane, then they had just given the abomination full run of the entire ship by opening the front door. From there, it could spread and feast upon the rest of the colonists in the other stasis bays elsewhere, in which case, Dietrich's plan would have been the right move, except for the part of locking her co-workers in a nightmarish domain.

With that in mind, Gilbey felt determined to get there and make it out of this. He could not wait to see Dietrich's face when he stepped into Operations and confronted her. Lane, Carter, and Graves, all of those deaths were on her.

Another horrific roar brought him back into the moment. The Ouroboros dropped down off of the walkway and landed just before the central pillared area, where Eckhart had now retreated to.

As he tried to make his way back to the tram station platform, the creature picked up speed, smashing into one of them with such force that cracks formed all across it from top to bottom. The pillar shook and wobbled, looking like it could topple over at the brute strength that had smashed into it. The Ouroboros, appearing to have expected to smash through it with ease, pushed itself around the pillar, grabbing hold of another on the other side of its body, and pulled itself back into the chase. Eckhart had used this time to get some distance between him and the pursuing monstrosity.

Gilbey left the tablet beside the terminal and ran across the platform to help. He flicked the switch on the Beam-Saw and charged as fast as he could towards the young Doctor. From here he could see the tentacle-like vines emerging from the depths of the black abyss of its skin and then weave between the pillars to get close to the fleeing Eckhart.

"Watch out!" Gilbey cried out, causing an enormous sharp pain to stab him in his chest. He body went cold as the agonising sparks flickered outwards from the wound he had sustained there. It would have normally caused him to fall to his knees. He felt his legs go weak beneath him, but he was determined to push through it and get to Eckhart. He struggled but he managed to shout out "It's coming!" in an attempt to warn the Doctor of the approaching horrors.

Eckhart looked backward and noticed the vines just in time, causing him to move between the last few pillars, obstructing the tentacles completely. Outraged, the Ouroboros shrieked out, climbing up to onto the platform the pillars held up, towering over the entire Tram Station.

Gilbey could tell that was the first time that Eckhart has seen one of these in all of its wonder, judging by his face locked in an expression of stunned perplexity as he watched for a moment the creature push itself up with its two large arm appendages, lifting its three clawed tail off of the ground, and roar.

"Oh... my..." was all the young Doctor had to say as he stared at the indescribable atrocity before him.

They could see the protruding lump in its arm that was Lane only a few moments ago. Now she was slowly being slowly digested just beneath the creature's skin, as the black soulless muscles twitched frantically, more so as the abomination lifted its central mass higher, as if it was attempting to spot its prey across the other side of the platform.

Gilbey grabbed Eckhart by the shoulder, pulling him behind him. He had the only weapon at their disposal, and the Doctor's life was a far more important than his own. He was the second most technologically skilled person to work with ADAM after Carter had met Lane's ill-fated ending to her travels to their new world. All of the maintenance crew members knew how to make repairs to the ship, but they were not all trained Doctors with the knowledge of how to bypass ADAM's security measures. It was in that moment that Gilbey realised that he needed to get Eckhart out of this Section of the Eden.

He stepped forward with the Beam-Saw glowing beside him. There was a moment of stillness, when all that could be heard was the humming of the beam of energy, when Gilbey and the Ouroboros stared at one another. For a brief moment he felt as if he was truly staring into the beast's eyes, and it just looked right back at him.
The moment seemed to stretch on and on, until Eckhart pulled him back towards the Tram. "It's done! It's open!" he called out and once the last word left his lips, the chaos resumed.

Gilbey blinked and the world returned to its normal speed. Staring at the creature, he felt as if he had not been inside his body, as if he was being drawn to it and his very consciousness had left his physical body and was being sucked into it. He turned and the two men sprinted as fast as they could for the tram.
An orange warning light began to flash all around them as the colossal shutter door of the tram's track tunnel began to open. The rumbling sound did a good job of masking the noise of the brute as it charged itself across and pushed itself off the roof platform. When it crashed into the ground below, where they had both been standing, watching it, moments earlier, it felt as if the entire spaceship began to shake.
Eckhart fell into the tram carriage door frame, but Gilbey collected him as he moved inside. "No! The tablet!" the Doctor called out, but there was no time.
As the Ouroboros rapidly approached the tram, moving faster and more frantically than either of them had ever seen, Gilbey pressed the manual door lock control and called out "ADAM! Get us to Section A! Now!"

The creature smashed into the side of the tram beside them. Both of the maintenance crew members moved to the other side of the carriage, but they were only a couple of meters away from certain doom.
At this distance, Gilbey could see the Ouroboros in such fine detail. He could see that the gore covered black secretion that was its skin was actually translucent, and that the dark midnight colouring was actually the result of its internal workings that appeared to be the same liquid black slime that had become of the colonists inside the stasis pods in the Sigma and Rho bays. He could see that beneath this skin, deep purple veins, barely visible within the black slime

inside it, were pulsing, all appearing to lead to the middle torso section of the central mass of the creature. Chunks of red organic material fluttered around and moved as and when the veins began to twitch.

As it went to smash into the side of the tram once more, moving its body around and bringing one of its massive arms forward, both Eckhart and Gilbey's jaws almost dropped as, in this position, they could see Lane's lifeless body floating beneath the surface. Her face looked frozen in her last moments of agony before she was swallowed into the depths of the beast. They could see that the black goo was imbibing sustenance from her skin, as sections of it were being pulled slightly in different directions. Her eyes were white, not in the sense that they rolled back into her head or anything, as a small imprint of her iris looked diluted, appearing as if her digestion had already begun from the inside out.

"L... Lane" Eckhart whimpered. He went to bring his arm up, as if to reach out and take her hand and pull her out, but the reality of it set in and he slowly dropped it back to his side.

All of this happened in a matter of seconds. Just as the creature went to crash into the side of the carriage, Gilbey called out ADAM's name once more and suddenly the machine kicked into action.

"Destination; Section A" ADAM's voice spoke out over the speakers all around them. "Please remain seated" and the tram began to move.

This caused the abomination to recoil, most likely having never seen anything this large, and inorganic, move like this before. It pushed itself backward on the platform and watched as the tram pulled away from the station and began heading through the recently opened tunnel.

"Shut the tunnel!" Gilbey called out, but when he looked around he saw Eckhart staring off into the direction Lane had been moments earlier. "Eckhart! Eckhart!" he called and the man snapped out of whatever terrifying thought was running through his head. He looked over to Gilbey.

"Wh..." he tried to utter, but Gilbey cut him off.

"Shut the fucking tunnel so that thing can't follow us!"

"I... I can't" he confessed. "I left the tablet there".

Gilbey slammed his fist into the trams control panel. "Fuck!"

Without the tunnel being re-sealed, the creature was now free to go anywhere it liked on board. It was then that Gilbey began to think that maybe Dietrich was right, and that sealing it inside one section of the Eden was the best course of action, even if it did mean leaving her co-workers and the remaining colonists to their fate.

Even so, Gilbey sighed a breath of relief that they had escaped the Tram Station. If Eckhart had not managed to run the bypass, then they would have had to trek to the Service Dock, which meant they would have been trapped in there with it for longer, but then again, Lane might not have been caught.

He turned around and saw the young Doctor sitting on the seat with his head in his hands. He was visibly damaged from what he had witnessed. He and Lane had gotten close over the course of the maintenance cycles. He had comforted her after learning the doomed outcome of the Earth after they had left, as well as even going against standard procedures and Dietrich's orders to give her medication to calm her nerves.

The two of them would spend nearly every free moment together, and often talked over their tablet's comms when they were not at each other's side. When Gilbey thought about it, the two of them had been inseparable during their time on board the Eden, and her gruesome death, right before his eyes, must have hit him hard.

He stood there, powerless and not knowing what to say, just simply staring at the man, before Eckhart took his head out of his hands and looked upward at the tram's ceiling.

"Are you... okay?" Gilbey managed to ask, but something grew inside of him and he couldn't help himself but add afterwards: "I am sorry about Lane. I know the two of you were close".

The Doctor looked over to him and nodded. It was a quick moment, but Gilbey knew that he appreciated his sympathies.

"I... we were close" Eckhart explained. "When we first met, we talked of our past lives and the things we would miss back on Earth. She had left her mother behind, but she had pushed Lane into this flight, as if she knew what was coming". The Doctor climbed to his feet and walked over to the front window of the tram. "When we learned what had happened back there after we left... it was just too much for her to bear. Her mother had most likely died years before that, having suffered from respiratory issues from living on the surface when she was a little girl. But her mother was all Lane had in the whole universe. I just wanted her to know that she wasn't alone. That the new world was a new beginning for her, for all of us". His face dropped as he fell back into one of the passenger seats. "But it's not... she'll never get to see".

Gilbey went to say something, something to just normalise this moment. It was calm and, for a second, if you forgot the pandemonium that they had just experienced, then it almost felt like everything was normal, although Gilbey did not know what to say. He knew that Eckhart's thoughts were of Lane, and maybe it was best to leave him to them for the moment, and just enjoy this quiet and safe moment before they reached their destination.

All that could be heard was the rubbing sound of the tram as it raced through the tunnel towards the light in the distance.

Gilbey turned to the front window. "We have opened the shutter" He eventually said. "It can go anywhere".

Eckhart took a deep breath and climbed to his feet once again. The quiet moment of reflection appeared to be what he needed. "I can seal the tunnel from the terminal once we reach the platform. The security measures shouldn't be in place there" he replied.

That made Gilbey feel a little bit better, and better still, if they managed trap the beast in the actual tunnel then that would be the best possible outcome for this situation.

"Okay, good. We should make sure that..."

Just as he was about to speak, ADAM's voice called out and broke his train of thought. "We are now approaching Section B".

It wasn't their stop, they still had a little while to go, but thankfully the tram felt safe, despite the fact that it was reasonably slow going. They knew that it was still a while before they reached Section A, but at least here they were on the move and covering far more ground then they ever could have if they were on foot, running and hiding for their lives against some cosmic horror that stalked them.

As they got closer to the end of the tunnel, leading to the platform of Section B, a bloodcurdling cry exploded from the subway behind them startling both Gilbey and Eckhart as they felt their chests tighten at the noise. The two of them turned and stared down through the empty tram, out of the back window, which showed nothing but the dark tunnel that they had just traversed.

"Oh no... oh shit!" Eckhart gasped as out of the darkness, he caught a glimpse of their worst fears.

The Ouroboros was, somehow, pulling itself along the tram tracks at rapid speed to catch up to them. The gaping hole in its face was hanging open and all of its silver coloured fangs were exposed. If being absorbed into the skin of the creature and slowly digested wasn't bad enough, being torn into by those teeth looked much worse.

"Can't this thing go any faster?" Eckhart asked, rushing over to the control panel in hopes that a button marked 'speed' with an upwards arrow would miraculously appear. "ADAM! Make this thing go faster!"

Gilbey knew that there was no changing it. He had worked on the tram briefly in a previous cycle and remembered seeing on the data file of his tablet that it only had the one speed, otherwise he would have made the thing go as quickly as possible the moment they first stepped onto it.

"I apologies Doctor Eckhart" ADAM's voice spoke out.

It was clear that Eckhart knew that this was going to be the machine's response and paid it no mind. Instead he turned to Gilbey. "What the fuck are we going to do?!"

Gilbey glanced back to the creature, which was now hot on their tails. He was currently only using one of his grotesque arms to pull himself along the track whilst the other reached out for the back of the tram, its tentacles seeping out of the enormous mass on the end, where a hand or a foot should have been, and closed the gap between the hunter and its prey. His tail must have been contributing to his stability as the hooked blades at the end of it scraped along behind him, sending an ear-splitting scratching sound ringing off down into the tunnel and the darkness within it.

"We need to seal the tunnel!" Gilbey yelled. "It couldn't get into the other sections of the ship when the shutter was down. We might be able to trap it..."

Just then the vine-like tentacles made contact with the tram, grabbing hold of bars on the back. As soon as it did, it must have used that as leverage to pull itself forward, but by doing so, it caused the entire tram to pull backwards sharply, as if it was going to rip them straight off the tracks.

"Jesus!" Gilbey shouted. "Grab on to something!"

But it was too late. Another sharp pull abruptly occurred seconds later and Eckhart was thrown off his feet and back towards the end of the tram. He managed to grab hold of one of the seats that stopped him from crashing into the back panel, just feet away from where the thing, that was giving chase, had nearly pulled itself up to.

In an instant of panic, the Doctor looked back and out of the window at the beast. He could see its monstrous bulking appendage as it clenched and contorted as it held on. It was then that he suddenly realised that it was the same arm that had absorbed Lane, and by being this close to it, he could see that the darkened skin was more translucent, allowing him to see the gore beneath once again, and the large cluster with what appeared to be rib bones sticking out of it that must have been what remained of Lane. It seemed that the creature had continued to digest and breakdown her body as it had followed them through the tram tunnel. For all they knew, having that sustenance to feed upon is what might have given it the strength to catch up to them.

Tears began to form in Eckhart's eyes at the very sight of the gore mass, but he couldn't let himself become overburdened by his grief, that would have to come later. For now, he needed to get as far away from the window as possible. Thankfully by this time Gilbey hand maneuvered down the carriage, using the seats like a safety rail, to get as close to the Doctor as possible. It had been quite difficult as since the abomination was now holding onto the tram, it had caused the whole thing to shake violently as it barely managed to stay locked onto the tracks.
"Eckhart!" he called out with his hand stretched out.
As he took it, Gilbey pulled him up and the two of them attempted to climb back up towards the control panel. As they did, they could see the end of the tunnel as the platform for Section B began to come into view.
"This is going to have to be our stop" he told him, and Eckhart knew that Gilbey had managed to figure out some sort of plan. "ADAM!" Gilbey called out. "Open the tram doors but don't stop!"

Just then the tram shook again as the Ouroboros lifted its arm off the track, now able to support itself with the arm holding onto the back of the tram, and sent it smashing through the window. Glass shards flew inside before being sucked back out, some even driving themselves into the flesh of the creature.
With the window now exposing the world outside, the sound of the tram desperately trying to stay on its track rushed inside, accompanied by the scraping of the organism's tail and the

strange noises emitting from the abyssal hole in its face as it continued to climb inside. ADAM's voice could still be heard over all of this. "Are you sure Gilbey? I must advise that..." "Do it now!" he shouted as loud as his lungs would allow, and the machine did as he was commanded. The nearby exit opened up as the platform for Section B began to speed past and Gilbey grabbed hold of Eckhart's clothes. "Go!" he commanded.

Right as they started to move, he looked back and saw the central mass of the creature, as well as the top parts of one of the arms, had managed to push its way inside through the broken window with total disregard for the jagged glass shards that remained. These sliced through the skin and black liquid oozed out of them.

The two men did not care. They were too focused on getting off this death trap. As the tram shook, they maladroitly stumbled for the exit. Eckhart leapt off first, hitting the ground hard. Gilbey followed and just as he jumped, he saw in the corner of his eye that one of the thing's entire arm was now inside and was reaching out for him. A long tentacle snaked through the air in a frantic attempt to catch him.

When Gilbey smacked onto the floor of the platform. He felt the wound in his chest rip open as his back smashed into the ground. It hurt, but he knew he had no time to waste. He sat up, ignoring the stabbing pain in his chest and the warm liquid that was now running down from it, and watched as the tram rode past. The creature was now hanging out of the back of it, its tail swinging wildly, as it attempted to try and pull itself back out of the broken window it had only just half climbed to a few moments earlier.

Movement in his peripheral vision drew Gilbey's gaze over to Eckhart, who was currently climbing to his feet.

"Seal the tunnels!" he ordered and without even second guessing him, the Doctor ran over to the control panel on the platform.

The creature had now nearly pulled itself free, but its last sudden jolt managed to rip the tram off the tracks. As it did so, the tram twisted and wedged itself inside the entrance to the tunnel connection Sections A and B, but in that moment, the momentum of the beast being pulled along by the contraption caused him to crash into it. Chunks of metal drove into the creature's flesh as it moved wildly in an attempt to escape, but it seemed like it was only making it worse throughout the duration of the crash.

It reached out again, almost as a last attempt to grab hold of its target as Eckhart engaged the tunnel shutter. The rumbling sound of machinery blasted out all around as they watched the shutter descend. As it drew to a close, inches away from the beast's arm, three tentacles shot out of it towards them. Deep red chunks of flesh splattered all around as they exited the skin, like the thing was giving everything that it could to catch them.

Gilbey and Eckhart watched as the creature roared out in agony whilst the shutter sliced through its arm before coming to a close, sealing the tunnel and trapping it inside in its injured state. Black liquid stained the bottom corner of the door, where it had severed the appendage, which was now lying motionless as it slowly began to melt into a puddle on the track amongst the debris of the tram itself.

Gilbey managed to climb to his feet. He could feel the wound in his chest worsen, causing him to bring his hand up to it, only to be met with the warm sensation of fresh blood. Now was not the time for this he knew. Instead he focused his attention on making his way over to Eckhart at the control panel.

"It's trapped in there" he explained, knowing that the Doctor already knew this. He looked back at the tunnel that they had just come from and saw that the shutter here was also down.

"With this down, hopefully this should stop it from spreading to the other sections of the ship" Eckhart said. "It is just a shame that we still have to get across the entirety of Section B without the tram now".

"At least we don't have to worry about those things" Gilbey replied.

It was a nice idea that Section B was completely unaffected by the organisms that had managed to get on board the Eden. Logically thinking, ADAM had informed them that only Section C had been affected by it, and that all of the colonists elsewhere remained unharmed. It was comforting to think that it was a nice easy and safe stroll back to Operations from here, albeit a bit time consuming, but after what they had just encountered, Gilbey didn't want to think that something horrific was waiting for them just around the corner.

Just then a loud thud could be heard on the other side of the shutter where the creature was.

"It's trying to get out" Eckhart declared.

"I wouldn't worry about it" Gilbey responded. "It won't be in there for long". His comment had confused the Doctor, who looked over to him with concern. "The internal fuel lines run along the length of the Eden through the tram tunnels". He directed Eckhart's gaze up to the ceiling where various large pipes fed across from above the shutter of one tunnel to the other. "That's so if there is a leak, then the fire would be contained to the sides of the vessel, allowing them to be easily vented out. Which is why exhausts were built throughout them to help suck out everything inside so long as the shutters are down".

"You mean we can blast that fucking thing out of here?" Hopefulness began to appear on Eckhart's face as the words left his lips and were heard by his own ears.

"ADAM" Gilbey called out turning round towards the control panel. "Vent the starboard tram tunnel connecting Sections A and B".

"Of course Gilbey" ADAM replied. "One moment".

Within moments mechanical sounds could be heard on the other side of the shutter, followed by the sound of metal fluttering around. This must have been parts of the destroyed tram. As they listened Gilbey thought for a moment that he could hear the crying shriek of the creature as it was ripped from the tunnel and forced out into the manufactured atmosphere within the I.M.F, only to meet the same fate as the other one and be disintegrated into a billion small particles.

They left the vent open for a while, standing there in silence listening to the metal debris as it rattled around inside the tunnel as if basking in their victory over the terrifying entity that had slaughtered Lane and nearly killed them both earlier.

As they did, Gilbey could feel the pain in his chest getting worse, causing him to grab hold of the platform's railing to help him stand. Eckhart noticed this.

"Are you okay?" he enquired, but as Gilbey was about to answer him, ADAM's voice spoke out.

"There has been some damage caused to the exhaust in the tunnel connecting Sections A and B of the Eden. It is recommended that the shutters are not opened at this time and that the tram remains off until the exhaust has been repaired via the tunnel access in the Kappa Wing. Would you like me to log a repair with the maintenance team?"

Gilbey looked at Eckhart. "I'll get right on that" he said as a small smile appeared.

The young Doctor laughed and as Gilbey went to do the same, he felt a sudden and agonising stab in his chest that almost knocked him to his knees. He gripped the railing to hold himself up as tight as he could, but he could not hide the excruciating pain he was feeling.

"Jesus Gilbey. Are you okay?" Eckhart asked. "Is your injury acting up? I thought you had

welded that thing shut. Let me take a look". He gestured to a nearby bench on the platform and helped Gilbey over to it. Once there he managed to get Gilbey on his back and lifted up his blood soaked shirt. "Looks like you may have opened up your wound when you fell".
"Ah... It hurts like hell" Gilbey told him as he went to sit up. "I'll be alright". But Eckhart stopped him from getting up. When he looked at the Doctor's face, he could see something in his eyes; it was a terrifying realisation of something horrific that he was currently witnessing. Gilbey didn't want to look down. "What is it?" He asked him, but Eckhart did not answer. "What the fuck is wrong?" and as soon as he said it, he realising that the burning sensation discharging from the wound was now causing him pain all over his torso, and down his arms, all the way to his fingertips.

Eckhart tried to speak, but he could not find the words. It was clear that he had no idea what he was even looking at, let alone begin to comprehend how to explain it.

Gilbey took a deep and painstakingly agonising breath before he slowly got the courage to glance down at his wound. When they saw it, they stared at it with disgusting and horrifying curiosity to figure out what was happened.

The wound was still closed shut thanks to Gilbey's earlier efforts with the Weld-Pen, but the skin surrounding the gouge had become transparent, allowing visual access to what was occurring beneath it. Here a dark black form lay dormant beneath the welded slash, which appeared solidus in form. It looked as if various black coloured veins were now leading off from it all over Gilbey's chest, slinking off into the depths of his body beneath the sore, yet human looking, skin surrounding the area of infection.

He was speechless. He touched it softly and when he did, a small spore oozed out a clear liquid that contained small traces of blood coloured substances within them. It had been this that had leaked out of him after his fall, which he had mistaken for blood. He wished that it was just his wound that had opened up and was now bleeding, as this was far, far worse.

"Wh... wh... What is happening?" Gilbey stammered. He glanced up at the Doctor who stared at him with sorrowful dread in his eyes.

"I don't know" Eckhart replied, not taking his eyes off the inhuman infection that appeared to be spreading over Gilbey's chest with each passing second. "I don't know".

4ᵀᴴ Cycle – ETA: 47.7 Yrs

Part Four: Impending Doom

The journey to the first aid station in the Epsilon Wing of Section B had been as quiet as it had been on the previous maintenance cycles. Here, the Eden was unaffected by the gruesome monstrosities that had laid wasted to the other parts of the ship. The soft humming of the life support systems, air filtration units, and the distant and muted sounds of the ship's thrusters blasting them through the unknown, was all that could be heard, but you never really did hear these sounds. Spending so long on-board during the Eden's voyage, these noises became as normal as the sound of your own breathing, so, without the racket of flickering electricity from destroyed lights, machinery and other equipment, or the unexpected roaring and alarming shrieks of an unknown abomination hungering for your blood, it was almost comforting to think that some kind of normality had returned in this part of the ship.

The maintenance crew had only been awake for a few hours, but it felt as if they had been trapped with the interplanetary horrors in Section C for days and only now had just managed to escape it all for good. At least that was what they had hoped.
The Operations computer had told them that there had been no other casualties anywhere else on-board, at least not to the magnitude of what had awaited them in the Sigma Bay, which meant that Dietrich was right and that the entity could not have managed to travel between the four sections of the Eden. And now with the tram tunnels resealed, there was no way that anything in Section C could get them, as far as they knew, but Eckhart and Gilbey had still remained cautious as the young Doctor helped carry the maintenance engineer from the

tram platform, through the empty passageways, and onto the bed of the first aid station.

"Hold on, I can give you something for the pain" Eckhart said as he slid open one of the cupboards on the opposite side of the room. He took out a capsule of something, grabbed hold of a jet injector from the side and loaded the two together.
Gilbey lay in agony on the bed. The pain felt less intense now that he was off his feet, but it still hurt like someone was driving a knife slowly through him. As he glanced down at his chest, his blood and clear mucus soaked shirt crumpled in a heap on the floor beside him, he could see the surreal infection buried beneath the welded scar tissue in all of its glory.
The clear parts of his chest, forming a near perfect circle around the scar in the centre, looked as if it was now made of a see-through plastic, exposing his muscles below it, most of which was obscured by the strange black form. This solidus looking sludge-like form was almost completely hidden beneath the scar tissue created from the Weld-Pen. If it had not been for this, then it would have been easy to imagine that the entire area would have been as transparent as the surrounding area. What could be seen of the black form reminded him of a fragmented chunk from one of the creatures, or even part of the central mass in the Sigma Bay. The very thought of it filled Gilbey's mind with unimaginable fear.
Long and thin black veins stretched out from it and ran off further into the depths of his insides. There was no telling what these were doing to him. For the time being, other than being in unbearable pain from the sour flesh all around the entirety of the wound, and the stabbing sensation he felt right in the centre of his chest, where the unknown black object was located inside of him, then Gilbey felt normal, so there was not even a hint as to what was going on elsewhere.

"This should make things easier" Eckhart told him as he approached the bed with the jet injector now ready to administer something to help fight against the pain. He took Gilbey's right arm and held the tip of the barrel to his vein. "Just hold still".
When the jet injector fired, Gilbey felt another stab that cut into his soft flesh. "Fuck!" he grunted as that brief moment seemed to dull the sensation in his chest, but unfortunately this only lasted for a short while and as soon as the barrel of the injector left his arm, leaving behind a small puncture where a single droplet of blood trickled downward, the throbbing agony, from whatever was happening to his chest, returned.
"ADAM, increase the lights by fifteen percent" and the A.I. did as the Doctor asked.
The bright lights caused discomfort to them both, but Gilbey, who was facing up towards it, had to cover his face to stop the feeling that his retinas were on fire. As he brought his arm up to do so, he noticed that the movement in his shoulder and pectoral muscles caused no additional pain to his chest wound. The painkillers were working at least.
"I feel better" Gilbey told the Doctor, but Eckhart's face did not change, instead he stared at the exposed chest with morbid curiosity.
"With the epinephrine and analgesics from the intracardiac shot earlier, and the Neo-Hydromorphone just now, it's amazing that your heart hasn't exploded".
Now that Eckhart mentioned it, Gilbey did notice that his heart was beating excessively, but

he thought that it was somehow related to the sight of his own insides through a recently discovered window in his chest.

He sniggered. "It will take more than that to put me down".

Eckhart gave the comment no mind. "Well... I have got to be honest with you Gilbey. I have no idea what this thing is".

"Could it have been something that broke off the end of one of those things when it attacked me?" Gilbey asked. It was horrible to think of, but at least there was an easy solution. "Can you just cut it out?"

Eckhart studied the soft translucent skin. His face already told Gilbey that it was not as simple as he had hoped. The Doctor went to speak, but as he did he was taken aback when he touched the skin causing more clear liquid to ooze out of some unknown puncture in the area. "I...err... I don't know that we can".

Gilbey had expected that response, but not as to the reason why. "How come?" he asked.

"We have no idea what these veins are doing" Eckhart replied hovering his hand over one of the black trails and tracing it along. "These could be contaminating your with some kind of inhuman toxin, or even keeping you alive at this present moment in time. Cutting it out could kill you, but leaving it in could do just the same, given what it has already done to the skin surrounding where you got hit".

Gilbey couldn't help but laugh at the Doctor's bluntness. "Jesus. Give it to me straight aye doc. I think you might need to work on your bedside manner.

"Oh... shit. I'm sorry" Eckhart responded. "I forget that this is actually happening and I guess I just got caught up in it all. I'm sorry".

"Don't worry about it... just worry about what we can do about this thing".

"I don't think there is anything we can do" he said. His voice was full of sincere regret. "We'd need to get you to the Surgical Centre and get you into one of the Med-Pods for a diagnostics, but..."

"But we just came from the fucking Surgical Centre" Gilbey finished, and the idea of going back to Section C was inconceivable.

"Even if we did scan you, there is no saying that it would even be able to pick up anything. ADAM couldn't compute what that thing in the Sigma Bay was, and he has knowledge of every single element and lifeform that ever lived back on Earth. The Med-Pod would have the same information".

At least that helped Gilbey feel better about not returning to Section C. "What about if I was to be put back into Stasis?" he asked. "Maybe we could figure out what is wrong with me once everyone is awake when we reach the Delta... could always use a second opinion".

The Doctor looked away. "I... I don't think so. We have no idea the effect that this could have on the ship over the next few decades we have left to travel, not to mention if stasis has any effect on these things. After all, they were inside the Stasis pods in the bays, and they were still able to breakdown and digest the colonists inside". A moment of silence occurred before Eckhart finally added: "I'm sorry. I don't mean to be so doom and gloom. I just know the ship's protocols and Dietrich would never go for it, not after the stunt she pulled locking down

Section C".

"No... you are right" Gilbey added. "I just thought that..." he couldn't find the words to finish, and Eckhart never attempted to try and complete his sentence for him.

The two of them stayed silent. Gilbey was feeling better now, physically at least. He managed to sit up without much assistance from Eckhart, most likely thanks to the drugs the Doctor had just pumped into him. "Hand me my shirt, will you" he asked.

Eckhart grabbed the dripping wet clothing off the floor. "You sure you want to put this thing back on?" Suddenly it was clear that he had thought of something as his face changed to that of realisation. "Hang on a tick" he said, dropping the shirt back onto the floor and heading out of the room.

In his moment of solitude, Gilbey reflected on the prospect that whatever was festering inside of him could kill him, or, seeing what these things had done to the other colonists over the last twenty-two years, something much worse.

He thought of what his plans had been for when he reached the Delta. Gilbey had planned to just work on maintaining the Eden once they touched down on the new world. Once the EVE Earth-Forming system had completed its twelve year task of making the planet inhabitable, then he was going to help build homes for the colonists. He envisaged Eden being the central hub of their planet, and the buildings he would work on becoming the foundations for the first city, only a more economically friendly one so as to not repeat the tragedy of Earth's past. Even though he knew he would not be around to see it, he still took comfort in knowing that his work would be the first step at continuing the human race's civilisation.

Now that they had managed to escape the infestation that had spread all over Section C, the idea that the Eden itself would not make it to Delta Tauri had dwindled, but now it had been replaced with the thought that he, himself, would be the one not to make it there.

When Eckhart had returned, he carried a dark navy blue jacket. "I think this should be your size". He tossed it to Gilbey who managed to grab it awkwardly and slipped it on. Fortunately it was, near enough, his size. As he zipped it up, the young Doctor watched the strange black thing in Gilbey's chest disappear behind the material. Like this, he looked almost normal. "Just need to do something about your face now" he mocked, his welcoming smile had returned.

Gilbey climbed to his feet and walked over to the mirror. His face looked battered and bruised from his struggle to survive the various encounters with those creatures. His lip was cut, along with a small slash on the side of his gaunt face. The blood that had once dripped out of it had now dried upon his skin and in small clumps that were found in Gilbey's beard. Dark rings surrounded his eyes, one of which looked a little bruised, all of which stood out dramatically on his pale flesh.

He ran his hand through his hair in a sluggish attempt to neaten it. "It looks fine to me". Eckhart chuckled. "How are you feeling?"

There was a pause while Gilbey thought about the truth of what he had been thinking the last

few minutes, but he decided against discussing the impending doom metastasizing within.
"I'm fine... I feel good" he told him unconvincingly.
"That is probably the meds taking effect" Eckhart replied before asking him; "So what are we going to do now that the trams done for?" perhaps in a futile attempt to take Gilbey's mind off the previous subject.
"Without those things stalking us throughout the section, we should be able to get to the Service Dock at the far end" answered Gilbey. "The tram station is about halfway through Section B, so it wouldn't take too long to walk it".
"Would it be unlocked?"
"Dietrich has no reason to seal it if she believes that those things are contained in Section C. Just a quick flick of the control pad beside the door and we should be able to get in, so long as she doesn't shut it down".
"She did say she would open the Service Dock between B and C if we could get there" Eckhart remembered. "So she wouldn't lock us in this part of the ship for no reason".
Gilbey wasn't so sure. Her past actions were not ones that he thought Dietrich would do, such as leaving people, she had known for the last eight plus years, trapped to die in the most inconceivable ways imaginable. "If she has locked it then we are fucked. We'd need to find some sort of..."

Just then something in the mirror caught Gilbey's attention. On the jacket Eckhart had just gotten for him, Gilbey could see the words 'Security Officer – Section B' embroidered on the front left pocket. He turned to see 'Security' written on the back in large white letters.
Facing the Doctor he asked "Where did you get this from?"
He knew that these jackets were made for colonists who would be assigned jobs once they landed on the new world. There were various different uniforms hanging up in their specific working locations, and if this one had the word 'Security' on it that meant that there must have been a security office for this section of the ship nearby.
"From the office down the hall" Eckhart told him, not realising what it was that Gilbey knew. "There should be a Comms Hub in there".
The Comms Hubs were connected to the Eden's communication network, which allowed the ship's crew to keep in contact with each other.
"We can call Dietrich and make sure she doesn't lock down the Service Dock" Eckhart realised. "We will have to be careful though" he added. "She won't let us through if she knows that you are infected with something. For all we know that thing could just burst right out of you and spread itself here like it did in the Sigma Bay". Gilbey stood there for a moment just staring at him with an expressionless face, horrified at Gilbey's situation. Eckhart must have grasp what it was he had just said and how it must have come across. "Oh... sorry" he added. "We'll make sure she doesn't know".

Just as they went to leave, Eckhart stopped and turned back to face Gilbey. "I've been thinking..." he said in a positive sounding tone of voice. "If we were able to seal your own personal Stasis Bay, like shut off the water and stuff, then maybe we could contain any

outbreaks that might or might not occur if we were to put you back into stasis".
Gilbey considered the idea.
"It's not ideal" Eckhart went on. "But it might be your only chance of getting help".
Gilbey gave him a nod. "It could work... but then again we might just end up infecting the entire colony on the new world".
Eckhart remained silent as he pondered the very thought.
"Come on. Let's go".

The young Doctor escorted Gilbey to where the security office was located. Although the maintenance crew did have extensive knowledge of the entire ship, they were not expected to know what each and every little office actually was. Thankfully they did not have to travel far. It was located just left of the first aid station and a bit further down for the Epsilon Stasis Bay. When they got there they could see the Comms Hub on the security desk. Eckhart helped Gilbey into the chair.
"I'm fine, dammit" he told the Doctor, but he knew Eckhart was only trying to help.
"Listen" Eckhart said. "If it was not for her, then we could have gotten out earlier and Lane..." he fell silent for a moment.
Gilbey knew exactly where Eckhart was going with this. He did not want to hear the voice of the person who had indirectly slaughtered someone the young Doctor had developed feelings for. "You know, we passed a canteen on the way here. I didn't get a chance to eat when I first woke up, and who knows when we will get another chance of some grub".
"Yeah... okay" Eckhart replied and went to head out the door before stopping and turning back. "Just don't say anything about that... umm... you know" and with that he left, the door sliding shut behind him.

The Comms Hub display started to connect to Operations. He sat patiently waiting for Dietrich but the call just kept ringing. After the twentieth ring, he disconnected and tried again but was met with the same outcome. He didn't wait anywhere near as long the second time before trying it a third.
"Is she not there?" he wondered and soon his mind began to fill with horrors of the Ouroboros somehow making its way to Section A. Perhaps it had found a way to traverse the ship without their knowledge; something they had missed. Maybe she had finally decided to bite the bullet and pull Admiral Walker out of stasis.
Suddenly the Comms Hub froze. The words "Section B – Security Office - Connecting to; Operations – Section A", which had been previously moving slowly around the centre of the screen with each ring, had stopped completely still. The ringing sound that had been at intervals every few seconds had also ceased.
Just as Gilbey was about to look into troubleshooting it, ADAM's voice called out. "Gilbey. I apologise for interrupting your call, but Senior Maintenance Officer Dietrich is no longer stationed in Operations".
ADAM's words were almost foreign to him. "ADAM? What the hell are you saying? What's going on?"

"Office Dietrich has left Operations" the A.I. replied.

"What the fuck do you mean 'left'? Where?"

"She is currently heading towards my Mainframe beneath the Flight Deck of Section A".

"What is s…" Gilbey went to ask but the machine interrupted him.

"I must apologise again" ADAM went on "but for a different matter this time. I am afraid that I have been rather quiet whilst you were dealing with your current threat, only providing minimal capacity, for you see I have been running extensive diagnostics relating to data recovered from Senior Office Dietrich's terminal".

"What sort of data?"

"During the last few hours, the Senior Office has been looking into ways to contain, remove, or destroy the organism currently residing in the Sigma Stasis Bay. Whilst I was able to provide her with my limited understanding on the entity from Dr. Reid's research, in an attempt to assure her that with the Tram tunnels locked down, it would have no way to spread to the other Sections of the Eden, which Dietrich understood and followed my instructions, it was not enough to sway her from the idea that we still do not know enough about these beings and that they could still, somehow, find a way to infect and eliminate the other colonists held in stasis in supplementary bays located in the other Sections of the ship".

Right then Gilbey made a terrifying realisation that ADAM had in fact given Dietrich the idea to lock the tunnels, effectively trapping the maintenance crew in Section C.

"You told her to lock us in there with it?" Gilbey asked, fire beginning to grow somewhere deep inside of him. "ADAM… did you convince Dietrich that shutting down the tram tunnels, with us stuck with those fucking things, was the best thing to do?"

ADAM gave no response for a time. It was clear that the A.I. was analysing the situation to figure out the best reply, having moments ago given away the fact that some of their co-workers and friends had been killed as a result of his advice.

"ADAM?!" Gilbey called out, demanding a response.

"It was Sir" the machine finally admitted. The Senior Officer had ask what would be the best way to continue to contain the organism within Section C, so that it would not spread to the other Stasis Bays, and I merely provided a logical and an analytical answer, not based on the fact that you and your fellow maintenance crew colleagues were inside at the time".

"Shit" Gilbey sighed as he knew that the stupid computer was not really to blame. As much as he would have liked to have shouted at ADAM, he had only really been doing his job. It was Dietrich who had given the order and locked them in. She was not code and binary, but of flesh and blood, she should have known better. Not that the machine was not partly to blame in all of this, but it was like being mad at a toaster if it had burnt the bread.

"I apologise Gilbey for any advice that was provided to the Senior Officer which may had resulted in a death or…"

Gilbey interjected "Forget it. Tell me why Dietrich is heading to your Mainframe?" he inquired in an attempt to get ADAM back on point.

"Well, as I said, the Senior Officer was looking into ways to quarantine the entity completely, or destroy it, and she discovered; Fail-Safe Executive Order Twenty-Eight".

It was not the maintenance crew's duty to know the protocols of the higher ranking flight officers on board the Eden, but Gilbey did know a few of them. He knew that if there was a contamination of food in a Section, then that Section would have its supply cut off from the rest and investigated. It was the same with basically anything regarding to the different Sections, which was why it was built the way it was, but he had never heard of this 'Fail-Safe Order Twenty-Eight' or any 'Fail-Safe Orders' for that matter.

"This states…" ADAM continued "…that in the event that some form of outbreak has occurred in a Section of the ship, then the Admiral may give the order for that Section to be disconnected from the rest of the Eden".

"Disconnected?" Gilbey echoed, slumping back into the Security office desk chair. "What do you mean disconnected?"

Every Section of the Eden is effectively towing one another along, providing additional thrusters to compensate for the size and weight. Section A is the single most important part of the ship, and contains everything the human race needs to survive when they reach the Delta, except for the majority of the colonists themselves. Without this Section, the rest of the ship is nothing more than a glorified floating tin can.

"Senior Officer Dietrich plans to disconnect Section C from the rest of the ship in order to save the lives of the remaining uninfected people in stasis".

Gilbey sneered at the AI's comment. "She can't" he told him. "She'd have to…" and it was then that his eyes went wide as he pondered the disturbing thought he had just realised.

"Yes" ADAM added. "She plans to disconnect Section C, which would…"

"Still be connected to Section D" a voice from the other side of the room cried.

Gilbey glanced over to see Eckhart standing in the doorway. He had not heard the security office door slide open, as he had been too involved in the conversation with ADAM, nor could he tell how much the young Doctor had actually heard.

"She's going to kill every colonist in Section D?" Gilbey announced.

"My god… that's eight hundred colonists still in stasis" Eckhart covered his face in disbelief.

"Those people… they'll be left in stasis until the power runs out"

"At which point" ADAM added. "They will awaken from the Pods and be stranded until their oxygen supplies run out thirty-three days later".

"Not to mention any remaining survivors in Section C" Gilbey said as he pulled himself up to his feet. "They'll all be left to be digested by those things".

Eckhart removed his hands and looked up towards where he could hear ADAM's voice coming from "We can't let her do this" he declared. "You've got to stop this order".

"I am sorry" ADAM went on. "But I am unable to disregard any command that has been inputted at my Mainframe, which is why I have come to speak to you directly regarding this matter".

"What do you mean?" Gilbey asked.

"Due to the extreme nature of Fail-Safe Executive Order Twenty-Eight, it can only be authorised by the Admiral, but by accessing my Mainframe, it is possible for Senior Officer Dietrich to override the parameters required to execute this order and authorise it herself".
"Where is she now?"

A split-second after asking the question, the Comms Hub screen came to life and switched over to a camera feed from the passageway outside the Flight Deck. Here they could see Dietrich kneeling beside a sealed bulkhead door. She held a data tablet in her hand with the door control wiring hanging out of it and a single lead connecting it to the tablet. The light above the door was displaying red, indicating that it was locked.
"I have done all that I can from keeping her from reaching my Mainframe. I have sealed both this door and the entrance to the mainframe, but I cannot do anything more. She will be able to bypass the security locks within the hour, and it would take significantly less time for her to access the mainframe".
"Cut the oxygen in that hallway!" Eckhart called out.
"I am afraid that I cannot. I must not do anything that directly harms the Senior Officer, as it goes against my programming".
"Fuck" Eckhart shouted as he punched the wall beside him.
Gilbey went to get up to try and calm him down but he was too wrapped up in the very idea that Dietrich was going to jettison over eight hundred people to their deaths. "What is it you are asking of us exactly ADAM?"

A moment of silence passed before the machine spoke. Once again it was clear that he was processing the best response. "My sole purpose in this existence is to ensure that the lives of the crew on board the USC Eden during its flight to Delta Tauri are protected and to preserve the lives of mankind during its colonisation mission. Due to unforeseen circumstances, a large number of personnel have died because of gaps in my programming. I cannot allow any further loss of life and must attempt everything that I can in order to avoid the Senior Officer from disconnecting, and essentially murdering everyone in Section D. So even though I am unable to assist you in directly stopping her, and without the Senior Officer's interference from Operations, I am opening up every single doorway from your current location to my Mainframe, including the Service Dock connecting Sections A and B, located past the Epsilon Stasis Bay, in hopes that you are able to get to the mainframe before the Senior Officer does".

It was strange hearing ADAM's drive to preserve human life, despite the fact his mathematical algorithm of a brain had resulted in them being trapped and hunted by an interplanetary mutated species of bacterial space dusts, but the machine's ability to be sympathetic to people under his control, yet whom still held control against him.
"What do you want us to do when we get there? Kill her?" Eckhart asked bluntly.
"Perhaps nothing that extreme Doctor Eckhart" ADAM quickly pointed out. "But perhaps she could be returned to stasis, until the crisis is over, and awoken once we reach Delta Tauri".
"Mutiny it is" Gilbey mocked as he flicked the switch of the Weld-Pen, his only remaining

weapon, and watched for a moment as the orange glow burned before his eyes.
As he switched it off, Eckhart asked; "What about the creature in the Sigma Bay? What do you propose we do with that to avoid it spreading to the other Sections?"
"Sealing the entire Section would cut the organism off" ADAM replied. "Section D would be segregated from the rest of the ship, but it would still be able to function enough to keep the colonists there alive and in stasis until we landed. Afterwards a more permanent solution might be found for the entity".
"Or it could infect our new world before we have even settled it" Gilbey pointed out, putting his Weld-Pen back into his pocket. "And I don't like the idea of going back into stasis knowing that thing is locked up only a short way away from me".
"But what choice do we have?" Eckhart told them. "ADAM, do you have any way of dealing with the thing spawning more of these goddam creatures?"
"At this time, I am afraid not, however, I am certain that due to the recent discoveries made during this maintenance cycle, I can find a solution before the next cycle".
"That's twenty-two years away" Eckhart informed them. "You saw what happened between the last cycle and this one. God knows what else could happen between them. You have no idea what this thing really is or what it is capable of!"

Gilbey decided that this was fruitless. "Enough" he called out as he felt a slight sting in his chest, causing him to wince in pain; a wince which Eckhart took notice of. After he had composed himself, he continued. "It's stupid for us to keep arguing about this. We can deal with those things later. Right now we need to deal with Dietrich. If she gets into ADAM's mainframe, then we can kiss all eight hundred men, women and children goodbye". His saw that his words had taken root in the Doctor's mind. "If we get Dietrich back into stasis, then we can get ADAM to log this and take it up with the Admiral once we reach the Delta". He walked over to the door. It was difficult, but he managed not to show the growing pain inside of him to Eckhart. "ADAM, check the movement scanners and advise if there is any unauthorised movement on board".
After a few moments ADAM told them that there was none, which gave him a great deal of comfort as the central mass in the Sigma Bay had not produced any more of those creatures to hunt them down, at least which were moving around Section C, or D, given the short amount of time the tram shutter was open, allowing something else to creep to this part of the ship, but thankfully this had not happened, meaning that their journey to the Service Dock should be uneventful.
"I will assist in any way that I can, and I thank you for your support in this matter" ADAM's voice told them as both Eckhart and Gilbey headed out the door.

The two men had remained quiet as they headed towards the Epsilon Stasis Bay. It was clear that both of them were in deep thought as to what was at stake if they failed to stop Dietrich from disconnecting Sections C and D, as well as most likely what they were going to do about the Ouroboros outbreak if they do stop her. Not only that, but the strange and unnatural infection residing within Gilbey's chest had started to take its toll on him. He felt fatigued and weak, and there were times when he thought his legs were going to buckle beneath him, but he kept going. Every time he felt a sharp stab of pain, he hid it from Eckhart so as to not make it obvious that his situation was worsening and he was now in quite a bit of pain, despite the amount of adrenaline and pain medication he had in his system, some of which may have been starting to wear off. They still had no idea what they were going to do about the infection growing within him, and Gilbey didn't want to be out of action during their current difficult situation.

The Epsilon Bay door was already open as they approached it revealing the dimly lit room beyond. As they entered the lights grew gradually brighter and they could see the rows and rows of colonists still held in stasis inside their pods. All of which were blissfully unaware of what had been taking place over the last few hours, and for the last couple of decades as they 'slept'.

The bright white and enormous room, complete with a steel catwalk above it all echoed that of the Sigma Bay when Gilbey had entered it during the third maintenance cycle. Most of the colonist stasis bays were constructed identical to one another, housing exactly the same amount in each; two hundred people all looking to escape their dying world. It was a shining reminder of what the Sigma Bay would have looked like if they had somehow managed to remove the speck of debris that had lodged itself into Jessica Kerrigan's oxygen tube, which Dr. Reids had then sealed up, convincing him that it would be broken down in the air recycling processor, but instead, the chemicals had only transformed the organism into the horror that they faced now. It was impossible not to think of this as they stared out across the silent bay floor.

"It's so quiet" Eckhart commented, which indicated that the same thoughts must have been running through his mind as well. "All these colonists, they have no idea what we have been through, or how lucky they have been that those things didn't nest in here". He stopped for a moment to observe one of the pods displaying a green 'all-clear' status on the nearby screen. "It could have just as easily been them".

"It doesn't bear thinking about it" Gilbey told him as he continued on past rows and rows of stasis pods. "We've got to keep moving".

His mind was now on the identical bays located in Section D. They were completely unaffected by the Ouroboros and were merely suspended in hibernation until they reached the Delta, except now they were at risk of being left to drift around in space with no means to move their floating tomb. They would be trapped, unable to use the Section's thrusters as the fuel lines would have been cut and they can only be controlled from the Flight Deck, which meant that they were just going to die of cerebral hypoxias when they ran out of oxygen. It was a fate that Gilbey would never wish upon a person, except perhaps Dietrich.

The next words Eckhart spoke proved that the two men were on the same thought pattern. "How could she do this to those other colonists? They are going suffer if we don't stop her".
"I know" Gilbey told him. "We've got to get to that Service Dock and cross over as soon as we

can".

"I am just glad that Lane isn't here to see this" Eckhart admitted. "This would have broken her heart".

Gilbey could hear the sorrow in his voice, but all he could think about was seeing the poor girl being absorbed by the creature to be broken down and digested into slop. In times like this, a person would have said something along the lines of "she is in a better place" or similar, but they both knew that she wasn't, so he just stayed quiet.

As they approached the far doorway on the other side of the Epsilon Bay, a glimmer of light caught Eckhart's attention, causing him to stop still and just stare over in the direction it was coming from. When Gilbey looked over to see what it was the young Doctor could see, he saw that on one of the last stasis pods in the final row, the display screen beside it showed a red light, indicating that the colonist was deceased.

He watched as Eckhart walked over to it and tapped on the display. "Heart failure" he muttered as he went through the various pieces of data. "He died fourteen years ago".

Even though they had dealt with quite a few deaths as a result of heart failure during their first three maintenance cycles over the course of the journey, it seemed harder right then and there to see it knowing that there was a far greater threat on board. It was awful to lose so many people to becoming sustenance for that organism, but to have colonists die from the normalities of being in stasis during an interstellar voyage, just felt like a punch in the gut. It was like surviving some terrible disease, only to die slipping over and cracking your head open. It makes a mockery of everything that you are fighting for.

Staring at the body of this man; Andy Kadwill, as the display told them, with his eyes open just staring back out at them, it was difficult not to imagine how many other colonists or crew were going to die before they reached their destination, whether it was because of the creatures on board or not.

One thing they can take solace in is the fact that 'Andy' did not suffer the fate of those in Section C, or what might happen to those in Section D if they did not stop Dietrich from her plan of purging half the Eden. In either outcome, unless the creatures spread to other parts of the ship or something worse happened, Andy's body might actually make it to the Delta, at which point it could be buried in the soil of the new world.

As they were leaving, Gilbey noticed that the Maintenance Tool Kit had been removed from the wall. It looked rather forcefully, like it had been pried off with something. Scratch marks ran across the wall beside it.

"Reids must have taken it" he thought remembering how something as small as this missing plastic case and the slight damage to the wall would have been an annoyance of a task for one of the Maintenance crew to repair back on the previous cycles. Now, everyone was just content with being amongst the living. So long as the Eden holds itself together long enough to get them where they are going, who cares about a few bumps and scrapes the ship might receive along the way?

ADAM had kept his word. Every door that they needed to go through in order to get to the Service Dock was already opened for them. From the Security Office, the stasis bay, and all throughout the Kappa Wing, they never had to ask ADAM to open a single door, or wait around for the few brief moments that it took for one to automatically open. It was clear that the ship's A.I. was just as keen for Eckhart and Gilbey to reach his Mainframe as they were. They had just entered the last quarter of Section B before they would reach the Service Dock, and now the two men had started to pick up the pace a bit.

"It's not much further now" Gilbey was saying to himself as he struggled to keep up with the young Doctor, whose urgency was now becoming more and more apparent the closer they got.

Whatever had been going on in his mind after witnessing the departed colonist was now driving him to press forward. There were even a few times when Gilbey thought that he was going to leave him in the dust, which actually would not have been a bad thing as the stabbing sensations in his chest had started to become more common, causing him to stop and catch his breath.

He wanted to take a few moments to see how bad the infection had become, as he knew that since they had first noticed it after the tram incident, it had gotten a lot worse, at least the sensation he was feeling had gotten stronger and more intense over time, but he knew that the translucent skin that had developed as the infection spread, was sure to be worse.

He didn't want the Doctor to take a look at it for fear that he might say that there was no hope. Gilbey had already had the notion that he might be done for, but he was not allowing himself to be consumed by it, for fear that he would just break down and not be any help at stopping Dietrich.

They passed through an open bulkhead doorway from one corridor to another, and as they did, Gilbey read aloud the nearby sign on the wall; "Scientific Research and Development Wing", not really thinking much about what he had just read, other than the fact that he had never been down to this part of Section B before. It was only when he noticed that Eckhart had stopped dead that his brain started to process what he had just read.

"Dr. Reids' lab is down here" Eckhart pointed out but by that time Gilbey had already become fully aware of this fact.

"Holy... shit" was all he could muster.

Dr. Reids had woken up a few years after the maintenance crew had returned to stasis at the end of the third cycle to conduct research on the organism that had unintentionally smuggled itself aboard using the meteorite. It had been through his initial findings that ADAM had a vague understanding of the creatures that were amongst them, as well as it had been Dr. Reids himself that had given them the name; Ouroboros.

That had been two decades ago and he had not returned to stasis since. Everyone had been so preoccupied with the large amount of dead colonists in the Sigma Bay that they had not paid too much mind to the fact that Reids, unless he had found another spare stasis pod, would have been twenty years older, not to mention the fact that he hadn't been seen throughout this entire ordeal, which originally lead Gilbey to believe that he may have been consumed by the creature's core, similar to what had happened to Carter. When those things had emerged from the stasis bay and attempted to hunt the rest of the crew down, only Carter's voice had been mimicked by them, not Reids, which made Gilbey think that maybe the Doctor was just locked up inside his own lab instead.

Suddenly Gilbey remembered being in the Sigma wing during the third cycle. He and Graves had gone out there in their spacesuits to check the damage the meteorite had made to the ship's hull and to see about removing the debris from the area. It had been here that Reids had requested a piece of the meteor to study, which Dietrich had allowed him so long as he kept it locked up inside his lab, which is what he must have done.

"He has got a bit of the meteorite in there" he cautioned Eckhart, whose eyes grew wide in terror at the very thought of it.

"Fuck" was all he could utter.

"If he has got it in there with him, it might explain where the hell he has been this whole time". Gilbey turned and looked up towards the passageway's ceiling. "ADAM" he called out. "Is Reids located in his lab?"

A few moments passed before ADAM replied "Yes. I can confirm that Dr. Reids is currently residing within his lab".

"How long has he been in there?" Eckhart asked.

"Approximately; fifteen years, three months, one week, five days, and seven hours" the machine responded.

Both men looked at one another in disbelief at the amount of time that they were hearing.

"Surely not..." Gilbey remarked, almost stunned by the fact that not only had the Doctor been awake for twenty years, but he had spent fifteen of them locked inside his own lab. "Is he... alive?"

ADAM replied almost instantly. "Yes. Dr. Reids' vital signs are reading at weakened capacity, but not weak enough to be of any real concern".

"How weak..." Gilbey went to ask before ADAM cut in.

"I am afraid that we do not have time for this. The Senior Officer has almost opened the Flight Deck passageway door and will soon be working on the one to my Mainframe".

"Open it up!" Eckhart told the machine.

Gilbey went to grab him on the shoulder and tell him that ADAM was right and that they did not have the time to waste on this, but from Eckhart's tone, he knew that he was not going to change his mind.

"Reids might know something, some way of destroying that thing in the Sigma Bay" he went on. "Or at least help come up with a plan after we have stopped Dietrich".

Gilbey pondered the thought for a moment before giving him a nod.

"Doctor Eckhart" ADAM started to say in a manner that already told them that the A.I. did not agree with his choice.

Before he could say another word, Eckhart ordered the door to be opened once more.

Reluctantly ADAM complied and the light above the entrance to the Scientific Research and Development Wing changed to green and the door slid open. As soon as it did, an abnormal feeling crept over Gilbey, making him think that this was not as good an idea as they had originally thought. He looked over towards Eckhart and he saw a similar expression on his face as he stared out down the long dark corridor. Something was off, they could both sense it.
"ADAM" Gilbey called out. "Why are the lights out? Are the presence detectors malfunctioning?"
The entire area's lighting system should have been on. All of the lights in a wing of each Section of the Eden were connected to one another, so if ADAM was correct and Dr. Reids had remained in his lab, then one of the presence detectors there would have picked him up, so the fact that it was dark here lead Gilbey to believe that they must have been faulty.
"No" the A.I. replied. "The lighting control system is working at optimal capacity".
His response didn't seem to make sense to the maintenance engineer. "Are the ones in Reids' lab working fine?"
"Yes"
"So when was the last time they detected movement?"
The computer took a short while to respond. "The detectors last picked up movement on July sixth, twenty-four eighty-five".
"Wait a minute... there's been no movement in there for thirteen years?!" Eckhart exclaimed.
"Correct".
"But Dr. Reids has been in there this whole time... alive?"

"Correct" the A.I. repeated.

The two men exchanged a look of doubt. It was a look that said that if one of them did not want to go in, then they would not do it. They could have just gotten ADAM to reseal the door and carry on towards the Service Dock, but there was some strange curiosity that was drawing them within.

Gilbey took a deep and painful breath and stepped through the doorway into the unknown.

4ᵀᴴ Cycle — ETA: 47.7 Yrs

Part Five: Pain and Suffering

The Scientific Research and Development area was meant to be used by colonists with scientific backgrounds who were assigned there once Eden reached Delta Tauri. It was through research from this department that people could study their new world and try to discover ways to prevent the same mistakes from happening that occurred back on Earth. The new world was going to be different this time around. The colonists of this ship were planning to make it habitable for hundreds of generations to come. But as Gilbey and Eckhart cautiously moved through the foreboding hallways, past silent laboratories and offices, it felt as if the colonists would never get the chance.

Something was wrong here, they could both feel it. The lights had only just come on when the presence detectors picked them up, illuminating the whole area, but that did nothing to brush away the feelings of dread that was growing with each step that they took.

Evidence of Reids' research could be seen. In some of the labs, they could see equipment opened out of its casings, to keep it protected during the flight, and now lying motionless on the workbenches. Books were scattered around and left open on pages. One, Gilbey glanced at as he passed by the door of the office where most of them were kept, described various parasitic lifeforms that had existed in Earth's past long ago.

Most of the ship's information was stored on ADAM's system, but the Eden did keep a few old world encyclopedias on a magnitude of subjects that might help with understanding the Delta once they got there. It seems that Reids was trying to figure out exactly what this 'Ouroboros', that he himself had named, was all about. Given the amount of time he had to compile his information, and the fact that ADAM did not have much data at all, it was obvious that the entity from the darkest depths of space was unlike anything man-kind had ever dealt with before.

One of the rooms he passed by contained a few unique looking stasis pods. They appeared empty and looked like they were used for medical purposes. These were some of the only unoccupied stasis tanks located on the Eden, as the Maintenance crew knew that these were available if anything were to happen to their own personal pod, then they had these to fall back on. It was just a shame that there was not enough of them to even hold one tenth of one of the ship's stasis bays.

This whole place was foreign to Gilbey. Nothing vital to keep the ship moving was located nearby, so he had no reason to come down here unless one of the water pipes sprung a leak or something was wrong with the electrics. There were certain areas in the middle of some of the Sections of the Eden that was above their paygrade, and this was one of them. Thankfully the young Doctor appeared to know where he was going.

Something he did recognise, however, was a small Maintenance Tool Kit laying on the table in one of the labs. A couple of the items; A Bean-Saw casing, a wrench, and a dismantled Weld-Pen lay beside it. It was obvious that this was the missing Kit from the Epsilon Bay. Reids must have taken this to help with his research whilst he was out of stasis.

Just as Gilbey went to move into the lab and grab hold of the Beam-Saw casework on the side, remembering how useful the item had been previously, a voice took his attention elsewhere.

"It's through there" Eckhart announced, pointing towards a large closed steel door before him. "I have only been here once, when Dr. Reids wanted some help moving a few crates during one of his bullshit 'busy-work' projects on one of the earlier cycles".

Gilbey went over and was reluctant to open the door. His hand hesitantly hovered over the control panel beside it.

"Don't worry" Eckhart told him. "This is just the entrance area. His lab should be sealed away behind a blast door. There is a large viewing window along the wall. His whole lab is designed to be a secure place to study diseases and pathogens we might have encountered on the Delta".

His words made Gilbey feel a little better. He flicked the switch and a moment later the door slid open.

As good as his word, Eckhart had been right. As soon as they entered the entrance area of the lab, right in front of them was a large bulkhead door that appeared to be sealed. Warning hazard signs were stencilled upon it, and a terminal displaying numerous information was fixed on the wall beside it. Over to the right was a step up to a viewing platform. Here an enormous dark frosted window could be seen. Eckhart stepped over towards the terminal.

"This is one of the few doors that ADAM is unable to open, so as to avoid any miscommunication causing any outbreaks".

"I do, however, have a number of sensors and scanners set up inside Dr. Reids' quarantine laboratory" ADAM's voice informed them. "Just to monitor any situations that might develop and supply that information back to Eden personnel. I am just unable to open the door".

"The mighty ADAM foiled by a doorknob" Gilbey mocked as he stepped up onto the viewing platform.

"It is hardly a knob Gilbey" ADAM replied. "The bulkhead door is sealed by a…"

"Alright, alright" he told the machine. "It was just a joke".

"Seems like the door hasn't been opened for about thirteen years either" Eckhart said, but Gilbey was not paying him much mind, instead his attention was drawn to the large dark window, that should have shown the inside of the lab, but instead appeared to be frosted glass.

He looked back to the other side of the viewing platform and saw built in chairs, bolted to the floor, facing towards the window.

"Why is this glass frosted?" he went to ask when he suddenly noticed the dark grey colouring move. It was mist.

The entire room was shrouded in a vapour similar to that which had covered the Sigma Bay when they first entered it at the beginning of this cycle. It had left a layer of silk encrusted over the inner frame of the window. Gilbey pressed his face closer to it to look inside.

"What can you see?" Eckhart asked, not seeing what Gilbey could see as he was fixated on the data the terminal was providing him.

"Nothing. The whole room is covered in the same mist as the Sigma Bay".

His words acted like lightening that shot through Eckhart's body. He froze for a moment before turning away from the terminal and heading over to the platform to see. "Oh my god" he muttered. "That... that" he tried to say, but the words never seemed to materialise.

"That core thing produced it" Gilbey said for him, not knowing truly if that was what Eckhart was going to say.

"Could it have been vented up this way?" Eckhart asked. It was a stupid question that had just been asked in a desperate attempt to explain why the room was full of mist. There was no way that mist from the secured lab, in a completely different Section of the ship, could have found its way up here.

"No... there's another one in there".

They both stood motionless, just staring at the mist for quite some time after Gilbey's words had faded away, but they still lingered in their minds, filling their heads with terrifying imagery of what might lay beyond it.

Eventually Eckhart spoke. "How?"

"It must have grown out of the chunk Graves got for him" Gilbey replied.

"But I thought it used the colonists in stasis to thrive and grow. What's going on?"

Gilbey did not have any answers.

"Then we torch it" Eckhart proclaimed as he turned back to the direction of the terminal. "We can incinerate the entire lab from that terminal".

"You can do that?" Gilbey asked, knowing that it was most likely that the smart guy that he was could have.

"It would just need to run the same sort of bypass that I did for the tram station to get the tunnel shutter opened. We would just need a tablet to run it on".

Another horrifying thought popped into Gilbey's mind. "Reids would have his on him... in his lab. He took it everywhere with him".

It was true. The Doctor had never been more than a few inches away from it for the entire time that Gilbey had known him. Images flashed in his head of the doctor emerging from his private stasis bay with Awakening Sickness, carrying his tablet, or when he was attempting to repair Jessica Kerrigan's pod, and his tablet was on the side next to him.

"If it was anywhere" Gilbey said. "It would be in there".

"Well we'll just leave it then" Eckhart replied. "If it's been locked in there all these years, then there's no reason to go in there now to grab the tablet just for this. We can pick one up elsewhere once all this shit with Dietrich has been dealt with".

Gilbey turned to face the misty room. Through the glass he searched for signs of life but found nothing. "ADAM. Can you vent the room? Clear up the mist in there?"

If they could see what was in there, maybe they might come up with a way to deal with it then and there, rather than leaving it for later. Gilbey didn't want these things on the ship any longer and the idea of leaving one, no matter how trapped it might be for now, so close to Section A where the most important aspects of the Eden were located; the EVE Earth-Forming System, the Flight Crew, as well as the Landing Engine, made him nervous more than the core in the Sigma Bay.

"I can extract the Laboratory's air through its own self-contained cooling duct, if this is how you would like me to proceed" responded ADAM.

"Do it".

As soon as the command was given the mist began getting sucked out of the room from elsewhere. The viewing window displayed the fast flowing vapour like it was a bedsheet in the breeze. After a couple of moments the lab began to come into view. It was as if it was fading back to life from the dark grey cloud that covered it.

Machinery and workbenches started to emerge from within the haze, which was now dispersing at a swift rate, all of which were covered in a layer of translucent proteinaceous silk. Being a much smaller room than the stasis bay, the thing that had grown from the asteroid piece, which Reids had in his possession, had spread all over the area. Similar black roots that had come out of the other creature's core, were woven and intertwined all across the walls and the ceiling of the room. Unlike the ones in the Sigma Bay, these root-like stems looked more ash coloured, appearing almost decaying or suffering from malnutrition. As the last of the fog cleared, they could see why.

There, sprouting out of middle of the large desk at the far end of the room, a place where all of the roots and growths fed back to, was a shrivelled husk that had once been the central core of another Ouroboros. He remembered that the other one he had seen had a layer of black and gore red secretion over its entirety, but it seemed as if this had dried up long ago. It was nowhere near as large as the one in the Sigma Bay. Clearly this was due to the fact that it had no colonists standing motionless in stasis, not putting up any kind of a fight, for it to feed off and grow in size as that one had done. Instead it was about the size of the desk it was now fused upon.

With the mist clear, Gilbey could see all the things he was not able to before. He saw that the vines, stretching up over the ceiling, across the walls, and spread all over the floor, had small node-like buds every foot or so the closer that they got to the core itself. Heading outwards, the buds grew smaller and smaller until they were almost non-existent. These appeared to be attached to the ground, holding the creature in place, to the point where it was difficult to tell where the floor ended and the roots began, which would stop it from being blasted off into space, the same as he had done with the creature's offspring in the Cargo Hold a few hours earlier.

More mist was slowly leaking out of its form from an unseen orifice. It dispersed slowly out in thin grey wisps. Looking at it, it would have taken months before the mist could have gotten to the levels it was at when the two maintenance crew members had first come in this area.

"Is it dead?" Gilbey asked knowing Eckhart. He was the man with the extensive medical knowledge after all, except the problem was that with regards to an extra-terrestrial lifeform, both men knew equally nothing.

"I have no fucking idea" was all he responded with, which was more than Gilbey had expected from him. "It's not had enough food to sustain it" he continued, studying the entity with a terrifying fascination. "The other one had the colonists to feed off".

"But this one only had the Doctor".

"Speaking of which, where's..." he was just about to ask where Dr. Reids was, when his eyes caught sight of him.

Gilbey glanced over to what Eckhart had seen, cutting off his sentence, and at first he did not really acknowledge what it was he was looking at. It seemed as if it was just another inhuman mass amongst the others inside the laboratory, but as he paid more attention to it, shapes began to form and he began to register what he was seeing.

There had been a large grey mound that looked like part of the creature at first, but when they looked closer, they could see that it was now, in fact, what appeared to be the fossilised remains of the doctor. He was infused within, what could only be described as a tumour, which fed out of the right side of the core and had spewed out, covering Reids completely. More vines and roots had grown from this and stretched off all over the place, as the others had done.

Reids, himself, looked gaunt and withered, as if everything had been drained out of him, and most likely it probably had been. His body, arms and legs, were now thin, skeletal almost, and contorted as they blended seamlessly into the growth. His head, which was the only part not attached to the rest of the creature, was slumped forward, facing down towards the ground. Despite the fact that he had been awake for twenty years more than the rest of them, it was difficult to tell if he did look much older than he had done when they had last seen him, or if his grey shrunken skin, now looking like it could easily be stripped from his bones, had been caused when the Ouroboros had fed off him.

There were fragments of the back and seat of the chair he must have been sitting at when the abomination had sprung its attack and entrapped him. He must have been completely unaware until the very last moment as he was now facing towards the blast door, indicating that he had turned and attempted to flee when this occurred, but he had not gotten very far.

"Is HE dead?" Gilbey asked, before he realised that he was, most likely, going to get the same response as he did last time, but Eckhart remained stunned and confused as he tried desperately to think of something informative to respond with. Gilbey decided to say something as he could feel a shroud of dread taking over him the longer he stared at Reids' remains. "At least we know what happened to him".

"Why has he not been liquidated?" Eckhart questioned suddenly. "The other colonists in the pods had been melted down, yet he is still whole, more or less".

Gilbey stared at the top of the doctor's head, watching his matted hair moving back into position following the suction of air out of the cooling ducts. "He is still alive" he said. "ADAM told us that Reids' vitals were reading lower than normal, but he was alive". The words left Eckhart wide mouthed and speechless as Gilbey continued. "It's keeping him alive, feeding off of him to sustain itself as it has nothing else to eat inside there". It had free reign of any colonists in any of the stasis bays it could reach, but here, locked inside that self-contained lab, it had nothing but the withered body of an old man as its only source of sustenance.

"Let's get the hell out of here" Gilbey suggested, turning away from the window.

As he took the first step off of the viewing platform, a voice called out to them. It was a familiar sound, yet hoarse and distorted, muffled from being on the other side of the glass. "Help... me" it said.

Gilbey went back to the window and peered in. Eckhart stood wide eyed and gasping at the sight. The frail feeble remains of Dr. Reids was now facing towards them. The expression on his face spoke of the decades of pain and suffering the man had faced being slowly fed off by some parasitic entity. He was weak. They could see that Reids was trying to move his arm to reach out for them by the slight muscle movements in shoulder, but all he could manage was the slightest of twitches in their general direction. Gilbey noticed that his forearm was buried beneath a large grey vine-like tentacle that grew out of the side of the creature and was wrapped around the doctor tightly, so much so that it was now moulded to his body, making the two of them one single organism.

Reids' mouth trembled as words began to form. "Eck...hart... Eck... help" could be heard but all the while his mouth did not actually move.

Gilbey glanced over to the putrid mass behind him and knew that the words were not coming from Reids.

"Shit" the young doctor slurred never taking his face more than a few inches from the glass.

"Reids?" Eckhart was effectively Dr. Reids' protégée and, other than a few times the two men disagreed and bumped heads, Eckhart did what he was told. It must have been painful to see his former teacher in this way.

"That's not him" Gilbey told him. It was half true, it had not been him speaking, as they knew that the Ouroboros were able to mimic the voices of their victims, but the shrivelled husk that was infused with the creature was still the remains of Dr. Reids. "Remember what happened with..." he stopped for a moment and thought what good it would do to bring up what had happened to Lane at the Tram station when Carter's voice had lured her away from them and to her own demise. Gilbey was not sure how Eckhart might have reacted hearing her name now that he was face to face with one of the creatures that had killed her, but he got the impression that Eckhart was thinking the same thing. He said nothing. He just looked as if he was going to be sick. As Gilbey went to say something, the young doctor turned away and walked off the viewing platform.

"Gil...by" the voice called out once more. It was impossible for him not to look into the eyes of the frail body of the doctor. "Help me..."

"What do you want?" Gilbey asked it. He had no illusion as to who he was speaking to.

"Help... me..." he called out again.

This began to fill Gilbey with a burning rage deep inside of him. He could feel his chest tighten around the growing infection within him. "ANSWER ME!" he shouted out in an explosion of noise that took over the entire area. "What do you want?! What do you want with us?!"

Reids' head slumped back into the position they had found it in. At first it looked as if the doctor had finally passed but the throbbing veins of the vines that had entangled him, kept his body slightly moving from time to time, giving him the appearance of breathing.

Suddenly Reids' voice could be heard once again, only this time it sounded more forceful and shrilled. It stuttered a lot less. "Help, me, consume you".

As it spoke another vine coiled out from somewhere in the back and sprung itself towards the glass. It hit it with a thud, causing Gilbey to jump back, before dropping back to the ground, leaving only a smear of secretion behind.

"This man's essence is mine" it said, tightening its hold on the doctor.

Gilbey stepped forward. "Is this how you are able to communicate with us?"

"With all species" it replied.

Reids lifted his head and tried to form words once again, but none managed to materialise. It was clear that he was still alive.

"What are you doing to him?"

"We thrive off all life... their essence gives us strength" it replied.

"So you are some sort of fucking leech?" Gilbey couldn't help but ask.

Just then a weak noise could be heard. "Gilbey" it muttered, this time it had come from the doctor himself. His lips moved in time with the words, indicating that he was still conscious throughout all of this. "I can't escape".

"Reids?!" Gilbey was stunned. He could not believe that both the doctor and the Ouroboros were alive in there after all this time. "Let him go!" he demanded.

"We want more" the creature told him, but as it did it started to lose more of Reids' voice with each word, changing to something more horrifically distorted and unnatural. "Give us essence".

"Let him go" Gilbey called out again, knowing that it was not going to give up its only source of sustenance.

"No... don't" Reids called out. "My legs... I am part of it now. It won't let me..." all of a sudden he cried out in pain, turning his head upwards towards the ceiling of decaying grey tentacles that hung overhead. It was clear that the poor man had endured twenty years of pain and suffering.

"What... are you?" Gilbey asked. He had to know. Everything surrounding these creatures had been drenched in complete mystery. Everything they knew about the Ouroboros, a name which Reids himself had given them, had been learned from ADAM, based on the little knowledge he had following the doctor's early research decades ago, and what they had experienced on this cycle since they had first come out of stasis and undergone the dreadful nightmares that had greeted them.

"We consume" it responded. Its answer had been almost completely expected. Gilbey was not sure what he actually wanted to hear, but then it continued. "We were small. Shelled within the safety of the rock, feeding off of the other smalls. We are changed. Larger. A new place. A new place to consume. You... you changed us. Grew us. The air morphed us and we became what we are. But you... you provide what we need".

It was cryptic, but its words seemed to make a strange bit of sense, confirming what ADAM had already hypothesised in the fact that the atmosphere within the ship had somehow accelerated their growth from some microscopic organism that lived within the meteorite that they had crashed into. Now that they were larger and mutated, mankind appeared to be the only beings that were the right size to sustain them, and judging by what it was doing to Reids, it was able to keep its prey alive for as long as possible. There was no food of any kind in this entire part of the ship, so it must have been doing something to the doctor in order to keep him from dying of starvation.

It explained why the one in the Sigma Bay had become so enormous at least. Having a fresh supply of stationary human beings on standby, ready to be broken down and digested, allowed for it to grow as large as it had done.

Gilbey knew that this was the only chance he was going to get to have a face-to-face with one of these things, long enough at least to have an almost civilised conversation with it, and seeing how ADAM was always listening and learning, the knowledge might serve to help the rest of the crew and colonists if they did not manage to stop them from spreading. He continued to ask it more and more questions.

"Where do you come from?"

"We come from the rock, burrowed deep inside" was all it said.

Gilbey unzipped his security jacket and cautiously revealed his infection to the creature. When he looked down to see it, he saw that an area the circumference of a plate was now as translucent as the silk and slime that the monstrosity produced. Thick black veins could be seen underneath the skin, which was now agony to touch, each of which appeared to be covering all of his internal organs. He could see a slight pulsing motion, which must have been his own heartbeat, pounding away beneath it all. The red ring of sore tissue, which surrounded the entire mess, had expanded beyond his chest, circling round to either side and down over his stomach. It was taking over his entire body.

"What the fuck is this?!" Gilbey demanded to know. "What's happening to me?"

"You are nursing"

"What?!" the words sent fright all over him, worse than the pain of whatever was occurring inside of him.

It responded; "Consume and spread. Spawn and grow".

It was a virus, he knew. They were some kind of germ that spread, feeding off organic life and spawning more into whatever it could not catch.

It was then, staring into the face, or whatever the frontal part of the central core of the beast was, that Gilbey knew that he was going to die. He was now an incubator for something terrible, and he had no idea how long it would be before it butchered him from the inside and emerged. He knew that he could never go back to stasis. If he did, then he would only be prolonging the Eden's inevitable downfall. If they were going to be safe, then he would need to get off the ship with whatever was inside of him. The thought had hit him like a wall and shocked every fragment of his being. He was going to die. It was not every day that you learn such a thing. He had always been under some illusion that once they reached the Delta, once they touched own on the new world, then the other doctors and surgeons, still in stasis currently, would be able to find out what was wrong with him and give him a chance, but alas, it was not going to happen.

During this time the Ouroboros had continued speaking of how it would infect other lifeforms that threatened it, but Gilbey had not been listening. Its words were distant and confusing to him. He was still taken a back by the reality of his situation.

His eyes went blurry as he looked around the immediate area for Eckhart, but he was nowhere to be found. When he turned back to the creature he managed to make out the last few words it was saying; "We spread, but always return... return to our essence".

"What essence?" he asked, feeling as if he was going to faint. He noticed that his head was dripping with sweat as he wiped his eyes to try and clear them. "What is your essence?" he knew what essence Reids was to him, that was his very life, but what was the essence of these things?

"I am". Its voice sounded different from before. It was sharper and more direct. It had also lost its oddity of using the term 'we' whenever it was talking about itself, almost like it was talking about a collective of entities, which was most likely the case. Now it had referred to itself as 'I', and it was clear that it was the core grown from within the small piece of meteorite that Dr. Reids had requested be put in his lab for study.

Just then a split appeared in the side of the core and thick black pus started to discharge out of it, seeping downward and across what remained of the table. Another appeared on the growth right next to where Reids was now merged with the core. Both of them did nothing for a short while, other than slowly weeping black mucus, before something started to happen. At first the holes looked as if they were blinking like eyes, but soon Gilbey realised that they were pulsating as something was being forced out of them. Strange shrieks of anguish and misery erupted out of the openings, but there was something familiar to them in the dark recess of Gilbey's mind.

An obscured and shadowy grey appendage emerged from the one furthest away from Reids. It was fingerless and had no real shape to it. As it clawed its way further, he could see more black veins, similar to the ones in Gilbey's chest that ran all throughout beneath the grey skin of this arm-like attachment that was currently reaching out of the opening.

The other hole now had an entire organ hanging out of it. In one quick motion, it slid out like a baby being born and slammed onto the nest of interwoven vines below. Shortly afterwards the other one did the same and now both lay wriggling around on the floor as more muck seeped off of them.

When Gilbey pressed his face against the glass and looked down to them, he could see that they were shrivelled and malnourished versions of the spores the core in the Sigma Bay had spawned to catch him and the other members of the Maintenance Crew when Carter had first been killed.

They cried out as if they themselves were suffering from the lack of nourishment, showing their sharp and slender silver teeth, dislocating their lower jaws and exposing the opening in the middle of their face. More liquid poured out of them that frothed and foamed over their bodies before dripping on the ground. It appeared as if they were dying.

"We need you" the core spoke out once more, but Gilbey was not paying attention. Instead he was fixated upon the small variants of the abominations that had chased him throughout Section C and slaughtered his co-workers and friends, as they appeared to melt into slime in a similar fashion to how the tentacles had done when he had cut them off of one of the Ouroboros through the gate of the Cargo lift of the Storage Hold. They melted down into sludge that spread itself out over the floor, seeping into any cracks and crevasses it could find, before becoming nothing more than a repulsive puddle of liquid waste.

It seemed that starving these creatures was the only way to kill them without blasting them into space and cutting them up in the I.M.F, but that was not a solution for these unmovable cores. When they were small microscopic organisms living within the heart of the meteorite, they must have had many other bacterial lifeforms to feed upon, but now that they were the size they were, only a large enough food source would satisfy them.

"How do I kill you?" Gilbey asked abruptly as he zipped his jacked back up, determine to find a way to eliminate the threat on board the ship before whatever was happening inside of him was birthed.

It was a stupid question to be honest. Nothing in the universe was going to tell someone how to defeat them, but Gilbey hoped that it was not from our universe and did not understand that he would be able to use that knowledge against them.

"Come to us" it responded. "We'll show you". A vine slid its way up the glass of the viewing window like some sort of serpent. Everywhere it touched, it left more of the translucent silk that oozed from some unknown pore and spread itself all over the glass.

Reids lifted his head once again and struggled to speak. "The ar...teries. The middle" he managed to say before the grey vine-like appendage squeezed itself more tightly around him and he weakly cried out, struggling for breath.

"The middle?" Gilbey wondered, scanning over the mass upon the table.

It took him a few seconds before he caught sight of what the doctor was trying to tell him. Right in the centre of it, beneath a fold of overhanging tissue, not unlike that of a withering flower petal, were two arteries that fed out from beneath this flap and curled under it. It was clear that this was what he meant. Were these some major veins that were keeping the things alive? Did severing these kill the things?

Gilbey wondered how Dr. Reids might have known this, and as he did, his mind started to race with thoughts of the two entities; Reids and the Ouroboros core, sharing knowledge between one another. He knew that when the creature absorbs its target, it gains information from it, such as how to communicate with the prey's species, as well as the ability to copy its voice, but what if the sharing process worked both ways and Reids, was able to learn about these things from within. It was doubtful that these beasts kept their victims alive long enough for this process to happen, but being locked inside a completely sealed room meant that Reids had needed to be kept alive for as long as he could, allowing information to be passed over.

"That's it, isn't it?" Gilbey said softly, pointing towards the arteries. "That's how we kill you".

It was at that same moment that the most terrifying noise of all was heard. At first the sound of computer terminals and touch screen notifications were a common occurrence around the Eden, but hearing it then hit Gilbey in the face with pure fear. Not for himself, but for the other occupants of the ship and what it would mean if this creature got out. Surely it was in too weak a state to actually make it beyond the Scientific R and D area, but despite all that they had learned about these things, there was still so much that they did not know.

Light illuminated the lab, all except the silhouette of a man, as the large bulkhead door opened up.

"Eckhart! NO!" Gilbey screamed, spinning around to the door and pulling out his Weld-Pen. He ran as fast as his infected body could take him, clutching at his chest to somehow help with holding back the pain.

He could hear the Ouroboros speak. "Come to… me" it beckoned.

Gilbey could do nothing in these short moments than call Eckhart's name in hope that he could bring him back out here and seal the door.

When he finally made it to the bulkhead doorway, Gilbey stood there watching as the young doctor moved into the lab towards the creature's core.

"Eckhart... what are you doing?!" he asked but Eckhart did not respond.

At that moment the young doctor pulled out a Beam-Saw and fired it up. Gilbey wondered where he had gotten it from, but realised that whilst he was having a one-to-one with an interplanetary mutated lifeform, Eckhart must have headed back to the other lab and grabbed the tool from the Maintenance Kit there.

Reids' skeletal face glanced up towards the young doctor, who was slowly moving closer to them. "Eckh... art" he feebly called out. "Stay back", but Eckhart was not listening. Instead he kept repeating the names.

"Carter, and Graves, and Lane!" Each time he said her name, he emphasized the anger and the uncontrollable desire he had for vengeance.

Gilbey went to call out to him but instead he reached forward and took a step inside Reids' lab.

Suddenly ADAM's voice spoke out to him. "Gilbey. You cannot go in there. I have calculated that you have a forty-three point two percent chance of survival"

"What?" was all he could utter as he tried to process what the machine was saying to him.

"If you follow Dr. Eckhart into that lab, then I cannot help you, and if you were to perish in there, then there would be no one left to stop Senior Office Dietrich from executing Fail-Safe Executive Order Twenty-Eight".

Eckhart stepped closer to the Ouroboros. "... and all those colonists in Section C!" he was still listing off all those who had died during this trip as a result of these monstrous stowaways.

"Gilbey, do not go in there" ADAM pleaded.

He watched as the ceiling above Eckhart started to move. Slowly more grey vines began to descend all around him like rain in slow motion. They began closing in just as Eckhart made a dash for the core, bringing the saw out to swing at it. Gilbey ran in behind him, flicking the Weld-Pen on as he did.

"No!" ADAM shouted out, almost with a hint of sincerity of worry in his voice, but by then Gilbey had already crossed the room.

He felt that with every step, onto the malnourished tentacles and growths spreading out across the majority of the lab, the frail tissue mushed into sludge beneath his feet. He aimed the laser of the pen at some of the overhanging vines that were making their way towards Eckhart, ready to coil around him. As soon as the high intensity heat ray made contact, the Ouroboros shrieked with pain and the vines convulsed as more mucus spat out of the burns.

The creature cried out. "No!" echoing the same as the machine had done seconds earlier. Eckhart, despite one of the creature's thinner tentacles wrapping itself around his arm, still managed to swing the Beam-Saw at the beast, slicing just beside the arteries under the flap. It was a miss from what he was aiming for, but it still hurt the creature none the less. It roared worse than anything either of them had heard before, and then, as if in retaliation for the pain, they could see that it was now contorting the polyp-like tumours it had attached to Dr. Reids. His face turned to agony as it was clearly squeezing him with each spasm. The doctor looked as if he was clenching his teeth together in such agony that they were going to shatter right out of his mouth.

As Gilbey continued fending off more of the vines, which were now shaking and moving rapidly towards Eckhart. More of them were grabbing hold of him in an attempt to stop him, but Eckhart swung again at the creature, severing the muscle flap covering the arteries. The dark grey and putrid flesh chunk flew across the room and landed on the floor beside a puddle of black slime that had been the beast's spawn only a short while ago.

Now with the flap completely removed, the arteries bulged as they carried vital fluid to the rest of the core.

With these exposed, it roared once more, sending more, tentacles, thicker and armed with spikes and deformed claws, shooing out of its body and towards Eckhart in a similar way that it had grabbed Carter in the Sigma Bay. One of them drove a claw into Eckhart's shoulder, but he gritted his teeth and pressed on.

The creature must have sensed that it was now vulnerable and one slash across the arteries would kill it, so it was doing whatever it could to fight back. It must have been completely taken over by rage at this point as it showed total disregard for the victim it had held prisoner, and who had shared knowledge with it over the last twenty years, because in one quick constricting motion, it squeezed Dr. Reids enough for whatever was left inside the poor man's body rushing upwards into his head, causing it to explode in a flash of deep red blood and brain matter that was sent firing out all across the room in every direction, splattering both Eckhart, who had taken the full force of it, and even hitting Gilbey, who was quite a distance away.

Reids' body slumped forward, hanging over the grey flesh that it had been infused to. His years of suffering, as a parasite drained the life out of him, was now over.

Eckhart, now witnessing his mentor's death right before his eyes, even being covered in a majority of his head's contents, was now swinging the Beam-Saw with insane fury, slashing at whatever part of the Ouroboros core it could.

Just as Gilbey managed to stop one of the tentacles from wrapping itself around the young doctor's neck, Eckhart severed the creature's major arteries. It shrieked, but this was something different to what they had heard before. This was the sound it made when it knew it had lost.

Eckhart did not stop. He was in a frenzy and unleashing his wraith against the beast for all of the misery and heartache it had caused him and the rest of the crew of the Eden. More and more chunks of the core was flying about all over the place as the Beam-Saw sliced into it over and over again, sending sprays of black fluid all over.

The vines swung around frantically. Whether they were aiming for anything, such as trying to get Eckhart to stop, or if they were just jerking from the fact that it was dying, was anyone's guess, but in the young doctor's rage, he failed to see one of the recently exposed tentacles, with the spikes and hooked claws on, desperately swinging across the lab and in one fell swoop, sliced the top half of the young doctor's head clean off.

There was a moment of complete stillness where his body stood in the same position, held up by the vines wrapped over his appendages, where everything seemed normal. His body was still processing the fact that his head was no longer attached to the rest of his body.

It had severed him right through the mouth, keeping his lower jaw still in place. His whole row of bottom teeth could be seen perfectly and his tongue still waggled for a moment before blood began to squirt out of the sliced muscles nearby.

Once they did, the world slid back into place and time carried on as normal. Eckhart's body dropped as if he was a puppet whose strings had just been cut. Even with the vines wrapped around his arms, he still fell to the ground in a heap.

It was only a few moments later that the creature gave up his fight and finally succumbed to its wounds. The hanging vine-like tentacles became motionless ceiling decorations, as the ones sticking out of the core, which was now just a mangled mess of grey flesh coated in black gunk, dropped to the floor and the shelves and tables nearby. They crashed down with a thud, sending more slime all over.

Gilbey stood there, completely still and completely silent, just staring out into the aftermath of the carnage that had just unfolded before his very eyes.
He could see the Ouroboros core was motionless and no longer resembled anything other than a collection of mush and gore.
He saw Eckhart lying in a mound, headless, on a bed of decaying grey tentacles, slowly dissolving into black goo, his blood mixing with it and creating swirls in the forming pools.
And he could see Dr. Reids hollowed out remains, now also without his head, drooping over his moulded flesh, joined with that of the large growth which too was now slowly sinking into itself with each passing second.

They were all dead. Gilbey sealed the door behind him as he exited the lab, encasing the entire massacre within the confines of the lab. When they finally did reach the Delta and the time came for the other colonists and crew to be awoken, he hoped that no one would have to witness the outcome of the slaughter that had transpired here.

4ᵀᴴ Cycle – ETA: 47.7 Yrs

Part Six: End of the Line

The gentle reassuring, and almost hypnotic, humming of the Eden's engines roaring beyond the confines of the ship had fallen silent. The painful quiet of being alone had caused them to fade off into nothingness. It was non-existent now, and no matter how hard Gilbey tried, he could not hear another thing, no lifeforms of any kind, nor any of the hundreds of different machines operating at once to keep them alive and moving.

Now that Eckhart was gone, Gilbey had never felt more alone. ADAM had been silent for the entire trip from the Scientific Research and Development wing, to the Service Dock leading to Section A. It had felt as if the machine had been giving him time to come to terms with what had just happened, and the truth of it was; Gilbey still had not. His mind was racing with what he had learned from the creature, such as his eventual demise. He looked as the deep black veins had now started to stretch into the palm of his hands. His fingers felt numb.
He had not yet recovered from witnessing both Dr. Reids' and Eckhart's deaths right before his very eyes. The moments that their heads were either detached or burst were still playing out

over and over again within his mind. Reids' last agonising moment of suffering, after living decades at the mercy of the beast, reflected in his eyes that had made contact with Gilbey's right at the moment his head erupted in an explosion of gore, as well as the second before Eckhart's head was taken clean off from the mouth up, when he thought that the Ouroboros core had died. Both were playing on his mind, torturing him alongside the images of Graves being dragged out of the ship in the Cargo Hold, Carter being pulling into the core in the Sigma Bay, or Lane when she was absorbed by the creature's spawn and was broken down to be digested.

All of the people who had died at the hands of these things were now running rampant inside Gilbey's head. He could see the half-digested colonists inside their stasis tanks, and the puddles of slime that others had been broken down to, never having a chance to fight back against the unquestionable horror that was liquidating them over two decades.
He had tried not to think about them, but after what he had just witnessed, less than half an hour ago, the memories of seeing his friends and co-workers, as well as the people he was supposed to be keeping alive to get them to the new world, dying one by one, all of it was replaying over and over again like some torturous film inside his head that he could never switch off. He felt as if they were trying to burst out of his brain, or maybe that was just the infection taking over.

His body felt weak, and was growing weaker with each passing moment. He was dizzy, aching, short of breath at times, and just generally sore all over. He also had the feeling as if he was starting to develop a fever. All he wanted to do was lay down and rest, but his thoughts were keeping him awake.
If he stopped now, then everything would have been for nothing. Dietrich would gain access to ADAM's Mainframe and eject Sections C and D off of the Eden, killing the hundreds of colonists in stasis in the process. Not only that, but if the Ouroboros core had been truthful and he really was incubating some form of them inside of him, then he needed to make sure he was taken care off before that had happened.

Suicide had always been somehow intertwined with Gilbey's life, even from a young age. Everyone living back on Earth thought about it from time to time. He had known a few people who had done it during his life. It was actually quite common. Living in a dark tunnel beneath the ground while the very air above grows more and more dangerous, he, and the other denizens of the bunker cities would fantasise about ending it all and getting away from that godforsaken rock once and for all. But when the Eden project was announced, it gave mankind hope. A lot of people saw it as a literal way of getting away from the fate that was left for the people of Earth.

But now, with some unknown entity festering inside of him, with no idea whether it would force its way out of his body, take over his mind, digest him from the inside out, or merely pass like a kidney stone, Gilbey had to take his mind away from the tortured last moments of the other Maintenance Crew members, and start thinking about the best way to stop whatever was inside him from spreading to another part of the ship, even if that meant suicide. Because, at the end of the day, this was what was going to happen; if he did not destroy the creature or the injection within him, then it would do exactly what they had done in the Sigma Bay all over again, only this time it might spread to some part of Section A, which was the single most important part of the ship. Without Section A, the Flight Crew, the EVE Earth-Forming System, ADAM's Mainframe, and everything else that had been specifically designed to be stationed there so that even if the rest of the Eden was destroyed, the last remnants could carry on. If all of that went, then they were all going to die, and mankind would be finished, extinct, with nothing to show for it other than the inhospitable poisoned planet that they had brought upon their home.

But before all of that, before he could end his own life, he first needed to stop Dietrich from doing what she was planning. After seeing Eckhart sever the Ouroboros' main arteries, it had given Gilbey the notion that he could help fight back against them and destroy the core in the Sigma Bay, saving any of the few remaining colonists there, as well as every colonist in Section D. It would serve as his final act before he departed. He was at the end of the line, so he wanted to make sure that he did all that he could do to help as many of them as possible before his time was up.

Many of the colonists in Section C had already died at the hands of these things, but hundreds more need not. All he had to do was get there and explain it to her. She would have to listen. Severing its arteries would not be an easy task, but nothing has been easy on this mission to keep the human race going, since they first left Earth nearly ninety years ago.

When he had finally gotten to the Service Dock, he had been worried that Dietrich had sealed it down before leaving Operations. ADAM had taken care of every door between the Section B Tram Station and here, but ADAM's control could be overridden at every Service Dock from Operations, sealing them in a similar fashion to how the Tram tunnel had been. It would have hindered Gilbey too much to have to find a data tablet and try to replicate the same sort of bypass that Eckhart had created before. He was not as tech savvy as the young doctor had been, and by the time he had figured it out, Dietrich would have gotten into the Mainframe and disconnected half the ship, murdering hundreds in the process, but thankfully, she had not and the Dock was open, allowing him access back into Section A.

It had felt like a millennium had passed since he was previously in this Section of the Eden. The last time he had been here was when they had just awoken and found out that nearly every colonist in Section C had died as a result of heart failure whilst in stasis. If they had known what had been waiting for them, then there was no way in hell they would have left. If Dr. Reids had somehow learned of the creature's weak spots and provided that information to ADAM, along with any other information he had managed to acquire while infused with it, then the Maintenance Crew could have formulated a plan to get rid of them without resulting in nearly all of them being wiped out.

Of course that was a lot of 'ifs', and if everything had gone as well as that, then none of this would have actually happened and they would just reach the Delta without a hitch. Instead, over the last few hours, Gilbey had witnessed horrifying atrocities that no person should ever see.

He brushed the thoughts aside as he approached the Operations Room. Even though Dietrich was no longer residing in there, he needed to get to his own personal stasis bay for something. He was not in a good enough state to be able to stop his Senior Officer, not with the Weld-Pen running low on battery after its extensive use and not having the time to charge it, so he needed something to get the edge on her and his stasis bay provided the means.

"ADAM" Gilbey spoke. It sounded raspy from however long it had been since he last spoke. He had to cough and swallow the phlegm in his throat, which caused a sting in his chest, before he could continue. "Open it up".

"Of course" ADAM responded. His words felt strange in his ears.

The painful silence, which had been Gilbey's life now that he was on his own, was broken. It was almost like his ears popped and the sounds came rushing back. He could hear the humming of the ship's thrusters once more, as well as the noise of multiple computers running just the other side of the Operations door, growing louder as it slid open.

The Operations Room was a sight of disarray. All of the terminals were on displaying various parts of the Eden. Hard copies of the service and maintenance manuals were lying around all over the place, open at pages displaying the inner workings of the interplanetary magnetic shield generator, the cooling ducts, air recycling processors of the Sigma Bay, and the nearest airlocks and Storage Holds circled or highlighted. It is clear that Dietrich had spent her time here trying to formulate a plan to get rid of the Ouroboros on board before coming to her conclusion of disconnecting Section C.

It was probably a very logical, well thought out plan, one that was conducted without any interaction with the creatures on the ship, but armed with the knowledge of what he knew now, it was not the only way.

Stepping through the mess, he imagined his fellow companions all gathered around, as they had done on previous cycles, running ship diagnostics and checking the various on board systems. For a split second he saw Carter checking ADAM's network status, chatting away in his usual nonsensical computer talk, switching between various forms of Earth languages and binary.

After imagining Carter, Gilbey started seeing all of the other members of his team. Graves was sat in his seat right beside Gilbey's. He was a good kid and eager to learn as much as he could. He had extensive knowledge of how to make repairs outside the ship, but inside can be a bit more complex than just bolting a large sheet of steel to the hull.

Dr. Reids would have been looking on his terminal, trying to find some form of 'research' to conduct so that he didn't need to get his hands dirty, judging someone if they had come out of stasis with Awakening Sickness. Gilbey smiled slightly remembering him during the third cycle with A.S. and how ironic it was that karma had come back to bite him badly. He was a dick, but he did not deserve what had happened to him.

He could see that Lane and Eckhart were talking to one another on the far side of the room, most likely about their lives back on Earth and what they hoped to do once they reached the new world. They were the only ones who really talked much about stuff that was unrelated to the Eden and their tasks. Previously, at their free time during cycles, most of the Maintenance Crew would discuss what they were going to do next, or how they were going to finish what they were currently tasked with, or even just how they were feeling currently, that was about the extent of their social conversations. Eckhart and Lane, on the other hand, they actually talked about life after this trip; planning their future and how they were going to pioneer the new world and help lead the colonists.

And now they were all dead. They had all suffered horrific deaths at the hands of some interstellar abomination. They would never get to see the Delta and everything that they had given up their lives back on Earth for.

When he looked for Dietrich, she was not there. His mind could not seem to imagine her there with them for some reason. As he tried, the memory faded, as did the manifestations of his former co-workers, and the mess of the Operations Room came back into view.

Maybe it had something to do with the fact that she was still alive throughout all of this. She had managed to remain unharmed while she locked down most of the ship, trapping the rest of the Maintenance Crew, leaving them to suffer their grisly fates.

It was then that Gilbey suddenly realised that he could hear someone talking. It was quiet at first, hidden amongst the hums, clicks and beeping of computer terminals, but as he got closer to the centre of the room, he could hear it clear as day.

"Most likely, by the time you receive this message, me and the last survivors of Dulce will be long dead" the voice said.

He looked over in the direction of the Senior Officer's seat and could see that a holographic display was showing that of Daniel Hale; the man from the message that they had received from Earth during the third cycle. It showed his gaunt face and dark circled eyes, as he did his speech.

"I only hope that this tells you not to come back. Don't send anything back to Earth" he continued.

Gilbey caught sight of himself in the display screen beside the holograph. He and the others had been shocked by the state of Daniel Hale's appearance when they had first received the message, but now, with Gilbey's sunken eyes and increasingly haggard appearance, he actually looked worse than Daniel did. Even after a lifetime of living in the bunkered cities back on Earth, with even less access to the surface and natural light than when Gilbey lived there, it only took less than a day on board the Eden with the Ouroboros to appear even more ruined.

"I only hope that this tells you not to come back. Don't send anything back to Earth. This world is dead and you will die if you come back here" the holograph of Daniel cautioned. His words had sounded haunting when they had first heard them, but now Gilbey wished that the crew and all the colonists in Section C had stayed behind. Most of them would have lived longer than they had done on this ill-fated mission.

Daniel was, without a doubt, long dead, as well as every other person back on that rock. It was not a fate that any one of them would have wanted, but even so, it had to have been better than this.

Gilbey began to feel regret in the fact that he had gone along with the Eden project. His life as a mechanic and engineer would have continued on as it had done until one day when the Smog found its way into their city, or he died of some other natural or unnatural death, whatever came sooner. He held his hand up to his face, looking at the black infection beneath his skin spreading itself throughout his body. The life he left behind had to have been better than this.

"Hear my warning Eden. Begin your new lives and remember the horrors that you have escaped from" the holograph said.

"Escaped horrors?" Gilbey repeated almost laughing at the thought.

The Ouroboros had been far worse than anything the people back on Earth have have to deal with. He would have taken a poisonous mist over being absorbed, digested and mimicked any day of the week.

Gilbey watched as Daniel finished his message. He found himself staring at it, listening intensely to each word. "The millions of people who had died because of what our ancestors had done to this planet. Don't make the same mistake at Delta Tauri. Live... please".

He begged them to live on and forget. For all he knew, and died knowing, the thousands of people on the Eden reached the Delta and settled on the new world. The EVE Earth-Forming system rejuvenated the soil and over the years it took for the air to become breathable, the colonists awoke from stasis and lived as a community inside the docked ship, before venturing out to build houses, explore the land, and live happy and long lives, repopulating the human race and learning from the mistakes their ancestors had made on Earth.

That was fantasy. It was starting to look like it might never happen, not unless Gilbey acted.

By the time he had reached his own stasis bay, Gilbey felt exhausted. As soon as the door slid open and the lights came on, illuminating his pod, he felt as if all he wanted to do was crawl inside it and rest for a thousand years. It must have had something to do with the seeing machine, because once he had entered the room, his legs buckled beneath him and appeared to give up. He almost fell, grabbing hold of the sink counter to support himself.

He must have knocked against the sensor, because as he pushed himself back onto his feet, the water from the tap began to pour out. Gilbey took this opportunity to grab a handful and splash it over his face. It was warm. He left his hand there lingering beneath the running water for a moment before he did anything, watching it go down the drain, remembering that he had asked Carter to get ADAM to heat up the water a few hours before their cycle had begun.

When he finally did bring the water up to his face, he felt born again by the sensation of it. It slapped him awake and instantly his skin felt better for it. He did it a few more times, drenching the top of his torso and shoulders as he did.

Looking up he saw himself in the mirror. Unlike the terminal earlier, this was now a clear representation of what he currently looked like at that moment in time. Now, with water dripping off his face, he could see the full extent of the growing infection as it spread out of his jacket colour and up his neck to his beard.

He went to unzip his jacket, but, at the last minute, decided that he did not want to see what was happening to him. So long as he could stand and walk, he did no longer care what happened to his body.

"Gilbey" ADAM spoke. "How are you feeling?" Gilbey did not actually know how he was feeling. It was a strange sensation to have your body being slowly corrupted and destroyed by something feeding off of you from within. He was not sure how to answer him, but thankfully the A.I. went on. "You have not eaten anything for hours. Here, let me get you something".

Just then a satchel of coolant dropped from the dispenser beside the stasis tank. Gilbey didn't feel hungry or anything other than just pain, but he grabbed it anyway. It may have helped. He tore the top off and poured it into his mouth. It felt heavenly. He took a few peaceful and quiet moments enjoying it.

"Thanks" he said, wiping away any excess liquid that had found its way to the side of his mouth.

"You are welcome" ADAM replied.

Once that was done, it was time to get back to stopping Dietrich from murdering hundreds of colonists.

"Where is Dietrich?" he asked.

"The Senior Officer has made it into my central mainframe. She is currently trying to bypass the security infrastructure to execute Fail-Safe Executive Order Twenty-Eight".

Gilbey didn't have long. He had to get to the mainframe and stop her. He threw the packet of coolant across the room and moved over to the locker, opening it and grabbing hold of his Industrial Rivet Gun within. If only he had this when he was trapped in the Storage Hold with Graves and the Ouroboros spawn, then Graves might have still been alive. Or using it to shoot the core in Reids' lab from a far, which would have stopped Eckhart from being killed. If he had just grabbed it when they had first awoken on this cycle, then this day could have gone completely different.

There were quite a few Rivet Guns knocking around on board, but none of them had been anywhere near Gilbey's locations throughout the Eden during this whole affair. Taking the time to grab one would have cost him hours, and, at the time, there never seemed the right time to need one until it was far too late.

Well he knew that the Operations Rooms, leading to his stasis bay, was on the way from the Service Dock to ADAM's mainframe, so he was not going to let this opportunity go to waste and be caught out again.

They were designed to repair large structural damage, but they came with an intense warning about just how dangerous they truly were. Unlike normal guns, which used gunpowder to propel the bullet forward, the Industrial Rivet Gun used compressed air. It launched them out at nearly three thousand miles per hour, and had been known to kill instantly. It was practically a firearm, so most of them on board were kept behind security key coded lockers and larger maintenance kits in the lower decks of each Section, but Gilbey had the authorisation to keep one sealed inside his stasis bay in the event that access beyond the

Operations Room had been lost.

Gilbey clutched the Rivet Gun, cocking the lever on the side of it back, loading in another rivet, ready to be fired. It was too little too late, but at least he felt more prepared to face whatever next was waiting for him.

Before leaving, he look one last look at his stasis pod, knowing that he was never going to return to it. The door slid shut behind him and he pressed on knowing that the end was now insight.

As he struggled his way through the corridors of Section A, he found himself walking in Dietrich's footsteps. It was clear that this was the same route to ADAM's mainframe. It was the shortest path, which ran right beside the Flight Deck.

The enormous bulkhead door was the same type that Dr. Reids' lab had. The Flight Crew's stasis bays, along with the bridge, were all locked behind this sealed door. They were the only ones capable of landing the Eden once they broke the atmosphere of the planet, ADAM's navigation computer could only get them so far, eventually a human would need to do the final part of the job and land this ship, which therefore made them the most important people on this ship. If there was an issue on the Flight Deck, then the Senior Office of the Maintenance Crew would need to wake up the Admiral via the Operations Rooms. No personnel were allowed inside the deck during the voyage who were not part of the Flight Crew, and so, whilst building the Eden, a large door had been built to stop anyone from entering.

Admiral Walker would be the first person to be woken up. He was the highest point of authority on board the Eden, and if he somehow fell ill, or died in stasis, then one of the other high ranking Flight Crew members would be in command, all locked away safely cut off from the rest of the ship.

Dietrich had been too concerned about keeping control of the situation herself, most likely in an attempt to not make herself look like she could not handle it, so she had not even considered bringing Walker out of stasis. Gilbey wondered what the Admiral would have thought of their current situation and if he would have agreed with Dietrich's plan to disconnect half the ship, sending eight-hundred suspended colonists to their deaths, or if he would have listened to Gilbey's plan about severing the creatures arteries. It would be a suicide mission, but with Gilbey's life slowly slipping away with each passing moment, he was prepared to volunteer for the job.

If he managed to stop Dietrich from hacking ADAM's mainframe and jettisoning Sections C and D, either convincing her that there is another way, or by some other means, then they would need to wake Walker up. There was no way they could do this themselves.

As Gilbey passed by the door to the Flight Deck, proof that Dietrich had been here were evident in the tools and other equipment she had used to get into the control panel beside the passageway's bulkhead door in order to connect her tablet to it to be able to run a bypass. ADAM had sealed the doors that he could on the way to his mainframe, which had bought Gilbey enough time to hopefully stop her.

He had to get a move on. Dietrich had now entered the mainframe and it was now only a matter of time before she managed to override ADAM's control and complete her plan. Time was on Gilbey's side, which was why he had opted to grab his Rivet Gun, as ADAM's algorithms and internal network systems was a chaotic mess of code that only Carter knew extensively. Eckhart had learned a few bits and pieces from him during their downtime, which was how he had managed to write the bypass for the tunnel opening, but hacking the security protocols for the Exterior Section Connectors was far more complex, and would take time. It already took her long enough just to open the bulkhead doors ADAM had locked down in her path. It was not infinite however, and enough time had already passed. There was no telling how soon she would be done. He needed to hurry.

The passageways of the Eden felt somewhat lonelier than they had ever seemed before. Even when Gilbey had been on his own in Section C, aimlessly wandering the hallways for a way back to the Tram Station, he knew that Eckhart, Lane and Graves were all trapped down there with him, not to mention wherever Dr. Reids had gotten to, and at that point in time, he was not aware of the true extent of the Ouroboros infection and how far it had spread across the ship.

Now, other than his Senior Officer, who he was going to try and stop from murdering hundreds of people, Gilbey was truly alone.

"ADAM" he called out to nowhere in particular, just to hear his voice to try and shake this feeling away.

"Yes Gilbey?"

He was not sure how to respond. He had not planned for anything so he found himself thinking of his time in ADAM's protection. The AI was controlling the entire ship. It had only seemed like Gilbey had known him for a few months, but in reality the computer had been keeping him, and the majority of the crew and the colonists, alive for decades during their flight. Despite the fact that the creatures had managed to inadvertently find a loophole in his programming and thrived on board the Eden, ADAM had still done everything in his power to protect them. Just like now, unable to physically stop Dietrich from killing hundreds of colonists himself, he had still tried to do whatever he could to keep everyone under his care alive. He didn't need to help Gilbey and the others as they tried to escape, even with the security lock down on the system, he still tried to help the Maintenance Crew.

He does not need the humans on this ship to keep himself functional. ADAM is completely self sufficient and capable of surviving unless he suffers some major catastrophic damage, or until the nearest sun goes super nova and stops fuelling his solar panels, whatever comes first. ADAM instead has chosen to help them. Maybe it was something to do with his programming, in the sense that his sole purpose in this life was to protect the colonists and crew of this ship, but Gilbey thought that there was more to this than that. The machine had acted more concerned, and in a way more human, than Dietrich had done at least, who herself was human. Gilbey had listened to ADAM telling him and Eckhart to hurry up, and genuinely sounded concerned for the well-being of all of the remaining colonists on board.

It could have been related to the fact that Gilbey was slowly dying, but he felt gratitude towards the ship's AI and how ADAM had tried his best to look after them. He found himself thinking about how he had taken the machine for granted. They had similar AIs in operation back on Earth in the bunker cities, but nothing as technologically advanced as ADAM, so he was used to them running the show back home. ADAM was different though, he could see that now.

"Thank you" Gilbey uttered as he rested for a moment against the wall displaying a painted mural of the Eden landing on the new world as families played on the grass beneath it. The words felt strange coming out of his mouth. He had never shown any kind of affection towards the ship's AI, but he had some kind of overwhelming need, at that moment in time, to finally tell him.

"For…" he wasn't sure how to express this exactly.

"For what?" ADAM questioned. "I am merely doing my job".

Gilbey snickered, anything more would have sent excruciating pains through his chest.

"I…" he paused for a moment, thinking about everything ADAM had done for them, and was still doing for them. "It doesn't matter".

After an agonising twenty-seven minute journey across half of Section A, Gilbey had finally reached his destination. The adrenaline must have been starting to wear off, as he was now feeling more sluggish and weak than he had ever done since first being infected. He really needed to push himself in order to just keep himself from collapsing in a heap on the floor. A few times along the way, he had tried to formulate the feelings of gratitude but they never came out. Instead he found himself calling out to ADAM and telling him that he couldn't keep going, or that he could not make it.

The ship's AI had tried his best at encouraging him, saying things such as "It is only a hundred and thirteen metres to the mainframe", or "From your latest health diagnostic, and cross referencing this with your current deteriorating state, your body should be sufficiently capable of continuing".

He was trying his best to keep Gilbey motivated as best he could, but It was not the most inspirational pep-talk. Although, despite this, it somehow seemed to do the job and painfully Gilbey managed to find his way there.

He eventually found himself standing before the door marked 'USC Eden's Artificial Intelligence Core Mainframe; ADAM'. There were similar discarded maintenance and repair tools littering the entrance proving that Dietrich had been here recently. The wall panel had been ripped off of the wall and now the inner workings of the door controls could be seen. Connecting wires, that must have linked to her data tablet when she hacked into it, were still hanging there. She had reached where she wanted to be and now no longer had a need for it. Gilbey grabbed hold of his Rivet Gun in both hands. "ADAM… open it up".

As the bulkhead door shifted open, a rush of cold air forced its way out, followed by a deep blue glow that eerily bled out. In the distance, Gilbey could see flickering red and yellow lights, but the blue luminosity of the other display terminals covered the room in a mist of brightness.

There were no lights in the mainframe, other than emergency ones, purely for the fact that they were not needed, and the cold air was created by the cooling ducts here, designed to keep the hardware, that controlled the entire ship, from overheating.

Stepping inside, he found himself on a large metal catwalk inside a domed computerised vault. Wires, flashing lights and monitors littered the walls, displaying every function of the ship in a blue binary code that just seemed to run endlessly. The walkway had no handrail and just lead to a drop to the lower parts of the dome where the supercomputer's drives and processors were located. They littered the floor within a labyrinth of six foot high servers. Thick cables ran from these and crept up the walls like the veins of the Ouroboros cores. The entire room was like a cave, buried deep down underground. It was situated in the centre of Section A, acting like a heart to the entire ship.

Gilbey couldn't help but think of how much this place looked like somewhere back on Earth. It followed the same similar architecture techniques that their ancestors had used to build the bunker cities to escape the pollution that would eventually become the Gloom. Four enormous venting ducts were placed equal distance away from one another on the surrounding ceiling, amongst the hanging strips of emergency lighting and sprinklers that criss-crossed their way above it all.

The door behind him slid shut and the light from the passageway disappeared, bringing the entire dome back into an unnatural twilight. Shortly after, a series of small red lights lit up on either side of the catwalk forward to the centre of the room.
A steel staircase, about thirty foot away from Gilbey's current position, could be seen leading down to the server maze beneath them. Further along, he saw the large hexagonal platform that housed the main controls of the entire mainframe. It was the very core of the Eden, and ADAM's own existence.
Currently a holograph, similar to the one in Operations, was displaying the ship. It hovered in the air within a circular orb of light, darkening the control panels that surrounded it.

Gilbey saw slight movement through the holographic image. It was out of place here and seemed more organic than that of the cold machines that encased them. It was Dietrich. ADAM's voice called out from all around them; "Please don't do this Sir" he pleaded.

Somehow his voice was louder here than it had ever been before.

Gilbey had never been in here before. Carter had always handled anything ADAM related in the previous cycles, so to hear ADAM's voice at the very source of it was different.

"Who ordered you to speak again?!" he heard Dietrich call out. "Mute all AI audio functionalities", and with that, ADAM fell silent.

It was clear that she had deactivated ADAM's audio in the Mainframe previously, but with the addition of another crew member, they had since been reactivated. It seemed that Dietrich must have thought that this was some kind of glitch or had turned it back on whilst she interfaced with his systems in an attempt to run the bypass.

Gilbey began making his way across the catwalk towards the centre platform. He tried to be as quiet as he could at first, but due to the extent of his injuries, and the growing horrors within him causing him pain with each breath and step that he took, it wasn't long before the Senior Officer was alerted to his presence.

"Who's there?!" she called out. The words boomed outwards but the echo was lost within moments, buried within the sounds of computers and machinery.

Gilbey said nothing. He carried on towards his goal. He pulled his weapon up and began aiming it clumsily towards the holograph and the figure beyond. Gilbey was not even trying to catch her off guard.

Dietrich stepped out from behind the holograph with a handgun pointing out in front of her.

"Gilbey?" she remarked, sounding almost surprised. "Where's Eckhart?"

An image of the young doctor's head being severed from his body flashed before his eyes.

"He's dead" he coldly told her. He watched as her eyes grew wider and her mouth dropped a little. She went to speak but Gilbey didn't give her the chance. "They're all dead".

As Gilbey got a little bit closer, Dietrich appeared to have been brought back to the moment. She stepped out and pointed the gun straight at Gilbey's face. "Not another step" she demanded.

Gilbey could see her tablet in her other hand, a red cable hung out of it and lead off to some terminal somewhere in the back, shrouded behind the glow of the holograph.

"Are you going to shoot me?" he asked but before she could answer, Gilbey realised that that it was not the right question. If he was going to stand in her way, then she was going to shoot him. She had already proven what she would do to try and contain the Ouroboros threat on board. The real question he asked seconds later.

"Where did you get that from?" he said, gesturing towards her handgun.

Dietrich's eyes flicked to the weapon in her hand before turning back to Gilbey. "All Senior Officers have one sealed in their stasis bays".

Gilbey didn't know whether to laugh or become fuelled with rage. Either one would cause him pain. While Dietrich was safely locked away in Section A with her own private handgun, the rest of them have had to run, hide, and fight with whatever they could get their hands on; Weld-Pens, Beam-Saws, screwdrivers and anything else.

He took another step forward. He could feel the glow from the light of the holograph reflect upon his face. When this happened, it was clear that he had emerged from the shadows of the Mainframe and was now in clear view. Dietrich's face changed to that of someone who had witnessed something the rest of them had seen in Section C hours earlier. It was a look of uncomprehending horror.

"What the... what happened to you?"

"Was she joking?!" Gilbey thought as his mind raced with thoughts of anger and bewilderment. He pictured every pain staking moment he had endured since awakening at the beginning of this cycle.

"Gilbey?!" Dietrich snapped, bringing him back to this point in time. "What's wrong with your skin?"

He glanced down at his hand as it gripped the Rivet Gun. It were almost completely translucent, showing the blood vessels beneath it as the thick black infection had now nearly completely spread through his entire body. Only his fingertips still retained the colouring of his natural skin tone, but it would not stay like that for long.

His hands were in agony, he had not noticed before, although now that he thought about it, his entire body was throbbing in excruciating pain. He was just trying to push through it and finish what he came here to do.

"I'm dying Dietrich" he told her. "Those things in Section C... they infected me".

"Oh my god" she replied, still not taking her gun sights off of Gilbey.

"This is your fault!" he bellowed out so loud that it dwarfed the noise coming from the computers all around them. "You did this. You locked us down there!"

Dietrich's eyes turned away from him. It was clear she was ashamed. "I did what I had to do to preserve life".

"What about our lives?!" Gilbey yelled out once more, causing his chest to tighten. He felt like his internal organs were about to burst. It didn't stop him. He felt even more determined to tell Dietrich what she had done and what it had cost them. "Graves?! Carter!". She turned away from him in some futile attempt to make this easier for her. It wasn't. "Lane… Eckhart?!" he continued on. "What about their lives?! They are dead because of you". He could feel a single tear forming in the corner of his eye before slowly running down his cheek.

Dietrich turned back and looked at him. He saw her eyes flicker to the tear on his face, and then back to his own eyes. "I couldn't risk whatever it is down there from spreading!" Gilbey could see in her eyes determination and stubbornness as she attempted to justify her actions. "All of the colonists on board were at risk. I had to lock it down".

"With us trapped down there?!" A fire was now burning inside of Gilbey that was taking his mind off his pain. "You left us to die down there. Graves and Eckhart and everyone else are dead because of that".

A moment of silence passed as Gilbey let the words hang in the air as Dietrich processed the consequences of her actions.

He could feel another tear run down his cheek, he brought up one of his hands to wipe it away. His own skin was stinging to the touch. As he wiped away the tear, he glanced down at his hand and was horrified to see that it was not tears that were leaking out of his eye, but it was blood. A deep red with a fine slither of black within it. He glanced up to see Dietrich looking at him in bemused disgust.

"We could have got out" he eventually said. "We could have figured out how to stop this together".

"I couldn't risk it" she replied, stepping back and bringing her tablet up. "I have figured out a way to stop this".

"You mean detaching Sections C and D?" He could see that she was surprised he knew what she was doing here. "Jettison eight-hundred colonists in stasis to their fucking deaths?!"

"Its the only way!" she called out. "We can save twice as many colonists if we do this.

Everyone in Sections A and B will get a chance to live when we get to the Delta... They can reach the new world. It's the only way".

"No... no it's not" Gilbey told her. "The creatures... they have a weakness. They can be killed".

"You... you're ill... you don't know" she replied. "We don't know enough about them. You don't want me to do this because you are part of them now... look at you!"

"No... I'm infected... I'm dying" Gilbey confessed. "Let me help you fight them. They are linked to the big core in the Sigma Bay. That is what is causing all of this. Let me try and stop it. I know how" He could see her eyes widening with thoughts of hope. "After this..." he paused for a moment. "After I will do what needs to be done with me". His mind raced with ways that he would end his own life if the Ouroboros core did not do it first. "I won't be a problem. I can do this before the infection takes me over... but we have to act now. Just please..."

He glanced towards Dietrich's tablet and saw some words. At this distance it was a little hard to see them perfectly, but he could make them out; 'Execute: Fail-Safe Executive Order Twenty-Eight' above two boxes, one red and one green, marked 'Decline' and 'Confirmed'. Gilbey brought his Rivet-gun up and pointed it towards her head. He felt himself swaying slightly and was not sure he could even make the shot if he tried.

Dietrich saw this adjustment and squeezed the handle of her gun tight. "What are you doing?" she asked. "You're going to shoot me? I am your superior officer! Put down your gun!" she bellowed in her most authoritative voice, killing all he had done to try and convince her to see reason.

On the last cycle, if Gilbey had heard that voice, then he knew that he would have been in trouble, but right now, standing with his Rivet-gun ready to do what must be done, he could see that she was just scared, and trying to do whatever she could to grasp control of the situation, no matter how unachievable it was. It had always been like this. It had just taken him this long to notice.

"You press that button and hundreds of people are going to die" Gilbey told her. "People who just wanted to leave that godforsaken place and start again".

"I... no... I..." Dietrich was desperate to think of something to convince Gilbey otherwise, but she was stumblingly her words.

"Don't do this..." he locked eyes with her one last time. "Please". But it was not enough.

For a split-second, he thought he saw her mouth an apology; 'I'm sorry', for what she was about to do. Her hand twitched and she moved. Her finger drew near to the 'confirm' button and in that moment, time slowed down and every passing second took took three times as long.

Gilbey watched for a time as Dietrich's fingers moved closer and closer to the tablet. He knew what he had to do, and he had all the time in the universe to do it.

He rested the stock of the Rivet-gun into his shoulder and pulled the trigger. As if by some kind of divine intervention, he did not feel any pain from the infection inside of him. It was right up until the sound of the rivet discharging from the end of the barrel that Gilbey felt normal. It was the first time since this whole situation began.

Once the explosive sound erupted, time quickly caught up with itself. It seemed as if, at this moment, time moved faster than normal to compensate. The rivet flew across the Mainframe in a blur and cut into Dietrich in the same breath. Sections of her shoulder and neck separated themselves from her in a deep red mist as the rivet tore through her flesh.

Dietrich's eyes grew wide. It was clear that she had not expected him to actually pull the trigger, but this was foolish of her. She had not known, not truly understood, the struggle that Gilbey had faced in order to get to this very moment, most of which had been caused by her decision to lock herself away from the chaos, and in turn, leave the rest of her team to die.

His excruciating pain returned in a burst of agony, feeling as if every muscle in his body had ripped apart and was now torn to shreds at the energy he had used to aim and fire the Rivet-gun.

Gilbey staggered slightly but managed to keep himself on his feet.

At the same time, the tablet from Dietrich's hand fell to the ground as she brought it up to grasp at her gaping wound. The vapour cloud of gore had dispersed and now the extent of her injuries could be seen. Blood continued to pump through a damaged artery as more and more of it flowed out down across her chest, staining her overalls. The insignia of the Eden's Maintenance Crew soaked it in, turning the white, within the middle of it, a profound maroon that darkened with each passing moment.

She dropped to her knees. Her eyes filled up with tears moments before she fell back onto the steel grated floor.

"I am... sorry Dietrich" he told her as he began to walk over to her.

It was a genuine apology. After all of the deaths she had indirectly caused, and her lack of support, She had just been scared and only focused on projecting herself. If Gilbey had been the one stuck in Operations, viewing the carnage unfold from behind a computer terminal, would he have done anything different to protect as many lives as he could? It was hard to say.

It did not have to be this way. If she had given him a chance to try and destroy the core in the Sigma Bay, now armed with the knowledge of how to do it, things could have turned out differently.

"If you had only given me a chance" Gilbey said, now standing over her.

Dietrich was desperately trying to speak, but the blood in her throat was creating nothing but a gurgle as she struggled to breathe in her final moments.

Gilbey knelt beside her and lifted her torso to an embrace. "It's okay" he said softly. "I'll stop it from spreading".

Her hand reached up and clutched at his jacket. Her fingers felt like knives driving deep into his tender skin. He winced in pain, resisting the urge to release Dietrich, as her last few moments of life faded away.

He wasn't sure if she had been trying to tell him something, an attempt to hurt him for bringing this on her, or if she wanted to simply pull him in closer and hold him tight as she passed on. Either way, within a few moments he felt her grip release and the pain subsided.

He gently placed her body back onto the floor and the brightly coloured tablet beside her caught his eye. The words; 'Execute: Fail-Safe Executive Order Twenty-Eight', could be seen clearly now above the two boxes.

He stared at it for a moment, knowing that with a simple press of a button, he could send hundreds of colonists to their deaths. It must have been the same thought playing in Dietrich's mind as she came to this point, however, after ADAM locking her out of nearly every door she had come across and having to bypass ADAM's protocols in his Mainframe, the end result must have seemed more like a victory, rather than a sacrifice.

Right now, Gilbey had that same choice to make. It would have been so much easier to press the 'confirm' button and watch on the Holograph as the two sections of the ship detach and drift off into deep-space, making everything he had done up to this point unnecessary. All he would have had to do was get into Sections A or B and he would not have needed to force himself all this way and shoot his Senior Officer. But he did, and now it was time to undo everything Dietrich had attempted. He pressed the 'decline' button and the tablet went back to the menu screen.

And just like that, the colonists were saved. They had no idea what horrific fate had awaited them. Gilbey only hoped that he could stop the Ouroboros from spreading into Section D before it was too late.

He breath a sigh of relief, or at least he tried to through the searing pains in his lungs and chest.
"ADAM" Gilbey called out. "It's..." a sudden cough cut his sentence short, which eventually broke out into a small coughing fit. Each one felt as if his internal organs were being squeezed and twisted as more and more poison continued to ooze inside. He wiped away the blood from his mouth once it had finally finished. "ADAM!" he called out once more. "Fuck sake". He remembered Dietrich disabling the A.I.'s audio. "ADAM, restore all audio functionalities".
And almost instantly "Thank you Gilbey" could be heard coming from all around the Mainframe. "I am sorry that you had to eliminate Senior Officer Dietrich. I wish that it had not come to this, but she would not listen to me".
"I know..." Gilbey replied, glancing down at Dietrich's corpse as she lay staring up at the ceiling. Her blood was still leaking from her injury and was dripping through the grated floor to the computer equipment below.
"I was powerless to help" ADAM confessed. "My primary programming is to preserve life on-board the Eden. With the people in charge trying to jeopardise this, I was unable to act in order to protect them".

Gilbey reached down and picked up Dietrich's weapon and put it into the back of his belt. "Are the tram lines still operational?" he asked.
"The tram itself was critically damaged from the time you rode it, but I will have another sent to the station in Section A for you".

"Thank you" Gilbey replied.

"Are you heading there now?" the machine asked. "Are you going to Section C? To the Sigma Stasis Bay?"

Gilbey remained quiet for the longest time. His body was a wreck, but he needed to get this done before it quit on him and whatever was inside of him broke free.

He headed across the steel bridge towards the exit of the Mainframe, his Rivet-gun in one hand and the tablet in the other.

"I have no choice" he told ADAM. "I have to..."

4TH CYCLE — ETA: 47.7 YRS

Epilogue

It had felt like years since this whole incident began. From when the Maintenance crew came out of stasis at the beginning of the forth cycle, all the way forward to this moment in time, seemed as if it was time to re-enter their pods. A normal Maintenance cycle lasted for weeks, during which the team would make repairs and patch up the Eden as best as they could, spending their off-shift hours unwinding and preparing for their next shift. It felt long, but it was easy work. The team had time to discuss any issues amongst themselves, run diagnostics and liaise with ADAM in order to best approach the situation. Of course the Senior Officer in charge had the final say, but the engineers were able to put their opinions forward to come up with the most logical solution. At least that was the idea. It was why a small crew were to wake every twenty-two years to carry out routine checks and repairs. It had sounded good on paper, when the highest members of the remnant government back on Earth designed the USC Eden's mission to the new world in Delta Tauri. But they had never prepared for anything like this.

The forth Maintenance cycle had been the complete opposite to everything they had planned. How could they have known of the true horrors that awaited humanity if they were to ever leave their dying planet? Perhaps this was a sign that the human race was meant to die out and suffer the fate that had befallen their home-world.

Within a day of waking up, the Maintenance crew had learned that nearly eight hundred colonists had died of heart failure as a result of being suspended in stasis. They had discovered an alien life-form that had stowed away on a meteor shard, which had digested colonists and spread throughout the entire Section of the ship. They had witnessed one another be absorbed and broken down, only for their voices to be mimicked and used to lure their fellow colleagues to their deaths. They discovered the true nature of this organism, becoming infected, and murdered their superior officer to avoid another eight-hundred colonists dying.

Now it had come full circle and Gilbey found himself back to where it had all began; the Sigma wing of Section C. The last time Gilbey had stood in the passageway leading to the stasis bay, all of them had been together. As Dr Reids had spent twenty years being fed off elsewhere on the ship, Carter, Lane, Eckhart, and Graves had all raced here to see what had caused so many deaths, with the intention of saving the lives of any who remained. They could not have been prepared for what awaited them inside.

It had been a long and painful struggle to get back here. Gilbey had spent the entirety of this cycle hiding, running, and fighting his way back to Section A. But with the impending threat of Dietrich's plan over, it was now necessary to return to this part of the ship and finish this once and for all.
ADAM had reopened the tram tunnels Eckhart had previously locked up, and Gilbey rode it all the way here. The journey had only lasted about fifteen minutes, where as the previous journey had taken him the better part of a day to complete. Along the way he could see the aftermath of their endeavours against the Ouroboros. He saw debris at the Section B tram station, gore left over from the creature that had chased them through the tunnel, as well as destroyed pillars and floor tiles at the Section C station.
He followed the path past where Lane had been baited away from the rest of them, the darkened passageway that lead to the Cargo lift, and saw the memories as they replayed themselves over in his mind.

And now as he walked down the hall towards the Sigma Bay, he could almost hear the voices of his colleagues calling out to him. They spoke over one another, making each one of them inaudible. The noise made his brain feel like it was shrouded in a haze of dissonance. It made him go dizzy. Within moments he was on his knees, clutching at his chest above his heart. His skin had been agony to touch before, but now, he felt nothing. His pain was all beneath the skin. In fact, he could not even feel anything he touched. His hand was now completely numb. When he released his chest, Gilbey brought his hand up to his face. No longer were his fingertips the only sore skin he had. Now his entire flesh was translucent, revealing the black infected muscle within.
He still had complete functionality to it, and he could feel himself making the movements of

pressing it against the floor and lifting himself back up, but the contact between skin and the steel floor was non-existent. His entire body felt almost completely phantom to him. The feeling had slowly grown more apparent ever since he had first become contaminated back in the Section C Storage Hold, when Graves had died. Since then, as the black toxin spread from his chest wound outward to the rest of his body, the sensation in his limbs had dwindled down and become fainter and fainter with each passing hour.

This gradual state had caused Gilbey to not really notice that he was losing touch with his own limbs. It was only now, as his entire body had become semi-transparent encasing the inhuman black muscular tissue below, that he actually noticed he could no longer feel anything he touched.

He ran his thumb across the metal casework of his Rivet-gun; nothing. With his other hand, he tried to touch each of his fingers with his thumb one after another; but again he felt nothing.

This was not the case for his inside. He could feel each and every one of his internal organs tighten and stab at one another with each passing breath. Recently, however, as the infection seemed to near its completion of taking over his entire body, this pain had become less apparent. It still lingered, but it had become part of the normality of life recently, which allowed Gilbey to grow almost used to it. It was this internal agony which kept him from truly being consumed with the fact that his skin was now clear and had no sensation.

Gilbey had no idea what he had become. The Ouroboros core in Dr. Reids' lab had said that something was growing inside of him. He had no idea how long this parasite would develop inside before it needed to come out, or if it was the black infection that had spread all over his body, and he was now no longer himself, but had become one of them. It was impossible to say.

The entire growth of these organisms had come from chance to begin with; mixing with the chemicals inside the air recycling system for the stasis pods and having the ability to feed off of completely suspended colonists; who unknowingly stood by and became nourishment for it, allowing it to evolve.

Even before that, travelling hundreds of millions of miles through the cosmos, microscopically laying dormant buried beneath a piece of floating rock, the human race had never experienced life other than that on Earth. It was foolish for us to think that we were the only life in the universe.

"Are you okay Gilbey?" ADAM's voice rang throughout the passageway, bringing Gilbey back to this moment.

He was not 'okay', not by a long-shot. He knew that he was not making it out of this. Even if he was to destroy the Ouroboros core in the Sigma bay, eliminating the threat on-board the ship and ensuring the lives of the other colonists in stasis, he could not be allowed to live. For all he knew, a new core could spawn out of him and start this whole mess all over again. He couldn't let that happen. He couldn't let something as insignificant in the grand scheme of things; his own survival, go before the lives of the thousands of people on the Eden.

Gilbey ignored the computer's question. "ADAM, seal off Section C". He was too determined on his mission to pay any more attention to his failing body.

From here, he could see the end of the passageway in the distance. The black and gore coloured vines had oozed their way out of the ventilation grills above the bay's door and were now spreading themselves outward across the ceiling and the walls. It looked a hundred times worse than it did only a day ago when the team had come here the first time shortly after coming out of stasis.

It was almost like the creature knew that its end was on the horizon. It had spent the last twenty-two years metastasising throughout this section of the ship, but now, with Gilbey slowly approaching with his Rivet-gun and a knowledge of how to kill this thing, it appeared as if it was making one last desperate attempt to spread itself as far as it could. God only knew what awaited Gilbey inside.

"Are you sure?" ADAM asked. "If I seal off the tram tunnel and the Service Docks, you will be trapped here again".

"I know" Gilbey replied. "This is a one way trip ADAM". He took another look at his malformed hand. "There ain't no coming back from this. I have to try and kill this thing. If I don't, then all of them died for nothing".

ADAM was silent for a few moments. Gilbey was sure that he must have been trying to process and comprehend how he was going to respond. Even with ADAM's authentic human voice, he was still just a computer program; a binary algorithm comprised of number codes.

How could it possibly understand the idea of sacrificing yourself for the greater good, especially when his primary programming was to preserve life on-board the ship.

"Thank you ADAM" Gilbey said, bringing an end to the A.I.'s data processing. "Thank you for your help in getting me out of here, and thanks for doing everything you could to stop Dietrich from doing what she was going to do".
"There is no need to thank me" ADAM replied. "I am designed to..."
"I know it is your job!" Gilbey interrupted. "But... for a machine, you showed more empathy and concern for human life than a lot of humans I have met".
"You are most kind Gilbey" responded ADAM, almost with a hint of joyful emotion in his voice before it dropped back to its usual neutral sounding tone and he said "I am sorry you must do this".
"It's okay" Gilbey answered, catching sight of his face in the reflection of the steel handrail that turned a corner leading to another part of this section of the ship. "I don't have much time left anyway".
It looked a hundred times worse than he could have imagined. Daniel Hale; the man from Earth who had sent them the final transmission from their fallen home-world, looked almost normal in comparison to how the distorted reflection from the curved handrail showed. For a moment, Gilbey could hardly believe what had become of his face. His translucent flesh showed the true horror of what was buried deep beneath it.

Gilbey turned towards the Sigma Bay doors. It was the darkness at the end of the tunnel. Beyond that door lay his ultimate fate. Even if he did manage to survive long enough to defeat the core, he still needed to deal with himself. Yet he still had no idea how best to do it.

"ADAM" Gilbey called out. "Create a report log for the Admiral once he awakens from stasis".
"Yes of course. Maintenance log: August nineteenth, twenty-five twenty. Forth Cycle – ETA: forty-seven point seven years" ADAM announced, creating the beginning of the log that would be listened to whenever the next people came out of stasis.
He was not sure what the procedure was, given that the entire Maintenance crew would be dead by the time the Eden reached its fifth cycle. There may have been something in place that in the event of the Maintenance crew dying during stasis, then the Flight crew would be awoken. Alternatively ADAM may have just waited until something catastrophic occurred;

something would bring the end of the Eden if it was not dealt with immediately and pull the Flight crew out of stasis, otherwise the computer might just let them sleep until they reached the Delta.

Regardless, Gilbey thought it was best to leave a warning message of what had happened. ADAM would be able to fill them in on the details that he knew of. Hopefully he will be a bit more helpful than he had initially been at the beginning of this cycle at least.

He slumped against the wall, using the Rivet-gun to support himself, right on the edge of the dark. Here, the broken and covered lights, obscured by the blackened vines, had caused the final section of the passageway to fall into twilight, lit only by the stasis bay's sign above the door and the lights further along the corridor. From here, it felt like it was the point of no return. Crossing over that threshold onto the dark side meant that this was it; the end.

"Admiral Walker" Gilbey began. "Or whomever receives this message...". He paused for a moment thinking on what was best to say about what had happened. He could hear the distortion in his voice, which he knew would cause whoever heard this to be instantly concerned. "As you may now be aware...". He took a deep breath and swallowed hard. It felt like a knife was slicing downward through his throat. "We are all dead".

It was a strange feeling; recording a message that you knew the next time it would be heard, you would be long dead. In fact it could be decades before this was listened to.

"Not only that" he continued. "But every single colonist in stasis in Section C has also been killed. It happened between the third and forth cycles. You can see from the records that the Eden's Interplanetary magnetic shield Generator had issues, which caused the I.M.F to drop for a few moments. In that time something came in... a meteor. We didn't know it at the time, but it harboured something... a life-form. Microscopic at first, but it grew. It fed off of the Section C colonists and took over this entire part of the ship. Colonists died of heart-failure, which meant that ADAM did not wake us up".

Gilbey glanced over towards the stasis bay doors, remembering what had happened the first time they had gone in there.

"When we woke up we came to investigate and it attacked us. Most of the Maintenance team were killed. Senior Officer Dietrich wanted to jettison this entire part of the ship to save the lives of those in Sections A and B, but it would mean that all of those still in Section D would be lost as well. I could not let that happen". He stopped again, only for a moment, as he prepared his confession in his head. "I killed her. You see Dr. Reids had awoken earlier and become…. moulded with one?..." He did not know how best to describe it. "… in his lab, and it spoke through him. From that we learned how we could fight them. I am going to try and kill it, currently hiding in the Sigma bay. ADAM has sealed this section and will only open it following your orders… or whoever is in charge when you hear this. I can only hope that this is all over by the time you wake up, but I cannot promise that it will be. I can only hope that mine and ADAM's efforts have helped get you to Delta Tauri… and to the new world. I just wish that I could have lived to see it".

He pushed himself to his feet, gripping the Rivet-gun with both hands and crossed over the threshold into the shadowy covered area of the passageway.
"I was infected by one of those things. It has spread throughout my entire body… and we have no idea what the effects of it is. For all we know, even if I go back into stasis, another outbreak could occur and it could put more lives in danger".
Gilbey was now standing before the Sigma bay bulkhead door. He could feel the warm air emitting through the broken vent covers above. From here, he could see the gore and black coloured tentacles in all their glory. They twisted and coiled all around him. It felt as if they were drawing him inside.

"By now you must have learned that Earth is gone. The human race brought its own downfall unto itself. This mission is all that is left for us. We are… you are all that is left. Don't make the same mistakes our ancestors did. Build a better world for humanity and live". He took a deep breath. "ADAM, open it up".

As the door slid open, it took a few moments before anything came into view. In the darkness, shrouded in unnatural fog, it was almost impossible to see. The light from the passageway behind him shone through illuminating small parts of the enormous bay. He could see the pods standing uniform in rows that looked like silhouettes of monoliths standing solemnly beside one another between abnormal shapes concealed within the dark. Slight movement caught his eye, but in this light, his mind could have easily been playing tricks on him. The fear that was flowing through his brain was making Gilbey cautiously scan the abyss for any signs of the Ouroboros and the core. The fog obscured the view further, causing most of the bay to be hidden away within.

It was then that he could hear the voices. At first it sounded like air being released softly from some valve, but as the noise continued, Gilbey started to pay attention to it. It was soft and faint, but recognisable. As it carried on, the sound somehow morphed into voices that called out from the shadows.
"Save us..." it called out, overlapped with another voice calling out the words "Help... me" that ran parallel to one another. "Please...." the voices begged, beckoning Gilbey further into the stasis bay.

He knew exactly what they were. It sounded as if Lane and Carter were trapped inside the room and calling out for help from somewhere unknown, but as Gilbey noticed that there were one too many stasis pods in one row than in the others, and that a section of the room that should have been visible, even in this light, was now hidden behind a giant mass that quivered slightly as the light from the passageway touched it, that he knew that there were more of the things in here waiting for him.

He took another step inside and the voices became louder. "Help... me..." they called out. He knew it was trying to lure him into an ambush, but it also felt as if they were actually asking for help. He wasn't sure if it was the creatures calling for help, or if it was the sorrowful pleas of his colleagues begging for some kind of release from their terrible and gruesome fates.

As another voice called out from somewhere off in the distance, Gilbey realised that ADAM's log was still recording. It was clear that some of the voices had been picked up in the log, so the listeners would most likely hear the distorted cries for help.

"Admiral Walker..." Gilbey said, causing movement in the mist on the far side of the room. He brought up his Rivet-gun, ready to fire on anything that might come at him through the fog. "And the rest of you listening. Forget the past... and live a new day. This is a fresh start. It's a chance for you to start over. It has risen from the ashes of the old world we left behind. Make this worth it. Make it count. This is Engineer Gilbey of the Maintenance team on board the

USC Eden... ADAM?"

"Yes?"

"Seal the door... and end transmission".

The End

From the Author

Danny Hughes

Thank you for reading my Science-Fiction horror; Ouroboros, about humanities last desperate struggle to survive and the small group of people responsible for looking after the remnants of the human race as they face off against something that they could not have prepared themselves for.

As you might have guessed, I am a huge fan of films like Alien and John Carpenter's: The Thing, and have always been a huge fan of Science-Fiction horror in general, which has become a great influence for this book, such as the computer game series; Dead Space, and the works of Harlan Ellison.
This novel is really a love letter to this amazing genre and everything that has inspired me to try my hand at writing Science-Fiction.
I am ultimately a huge fan-boy and, throughout my life, have always thought that I would love to write a book about <*this*> or <*that*>, and to me, Ouroboros is my own personal attempt at writing something similar to all those great films, computer games, books and graphic novels that have flooded my mind with ideas all through my life.

I have always loved the idea of the 'last of humanity' on the brink of extinction doing whatever they can to claw themselves back, whether that is rebuilding in a post-apocalyptic future, colonising a new planet, or merely surviving against unspeakable odds. Stories like this have always made me wonder what exactly people would do if push really did come to shove and what they would do to survive.
I feel that this novel is a good counterpart to my previous book; Before Dusk.

Thank you again for reading this, and I would like to say a big thank you to Geraldine Hughes; for proof-reading my work, Carleyann-Claridge; for listening to my ramblings and always trying support me, Bramwell Clark and Debbie Morley, for always being my biggest fans of my amateur writing.
Jonathan Redwin,Ben Hayland-Hawkins and Greg Hughes for their ideas that have been a bit contributor to this story.

And of course Freya Hughes; who I draw inspiration from everyday. Thank you for being you.

OTHER WORKS BY DANNY HUGHES

BEFORE DUSK

ISBN: 978-1517311322

FROM THE CREATOR OF THE FREYA FABLES, DANNY HUGHES BRINGS YOU A TALE OF PSYCHOLOGICAL HORROR AND SURVIVAL, THAT IS NOT FOR CHILDREN.

STRANGE CREATURES EMERGE FROM THE SHADOWS IN THE WAKE OF A POWER OUTAGE. THEY HUNT THE LIVING AND SLAUGHTER ALL THEY MEET.
USING WHATEVER LIGHT SOURCE THEY CAN, A GROUP OF SURVIVORS, LEAD BY A GUN FANATIC TYRANT, ESCAPE INTO THE FOREST AND FIND AN ABANDONED FARM. THE SURVIVORS BEGIN FORTIFY THE FARM AND TRY TO PROTECT THEMSELVES FROM THE MONSTERS THAT STALK THEM WHEN THE LIGHTS GO OUT.

WHISPERS CALL ON THE WIND, AND DARK EYES WATCH FROM THE SHADOWS. FOR ROBERT AND THE OTHER SURVIVORS AT THE FARM, THE DARK TRUTH IS WAITING FOR THEM JUST BEYOND THE NEXT SUNSET.
AS LONG AS THEY REMAIN IN THE LIGHT, THEY WILL BE SAFE. BEFORE DUSK THEY CAN LIVE THEIR LIVES, BUT TO UNCOVER THE SECRET TO IT ALL, THEY WILL NEED TO GO INTO THE NIGHT AND FACE THE DARKNESS THAT AWAITS THEM.

THE FREYA FABLES SERIES

THE SHADOW PRINCE'S POWER GROWS ON THE DARK PLAINS OF GLOOM VALLEY. THE KINGDOM OF STORM'S-BREAK HAS BEEN PLAGUED WITH THE DARKNESS FOR MANY YEARS. FREYA; A YOUNG GIRL FROM THE SLUMS OF A KINGDOM, IS THE ONLY ONE WHO CAN STOP IT. IN A FANTASY LAND OF GNOMES, GOBLINS AND FAIRIES, FREYA IS THROWN INTO AN ADVENTURE OF UNPREDICTABILITY TO DEFEAT A DAEMONIC PRINCE FROM ANOTHER REALM THAT THREATENS EVERYTHING. WITH THE HELP OF HER MISMATCHED COMPANIONS, SHE MUST FIND THE LIGHT THAT WILL WIPE OUT THE DARKNESS FROM THE LAND.
THE FREYA FABLES ARE A CHILDRENS FANTASY BOOKS SERIES OF ADVENTURES. EACH BOOK IS CLOSELY LINKED TO ONE ANOTHER, WHIST AT THE SAME TIME BEING THEIR OWN ADVENTURE IN THEMSELVES. THE SERIES CAN EITHER BE READ TO A CHILD, OR BY A CHILD, WITH STILL PLENTY OF ACTION, COMEDY, AND DRAMA FOR ADULTS TO ENJOY AS WELL. ANY PERSON WHO ENJOYS IMMERSING THEMSELVES INTO A FANTASY REALM WILL ENJOY THE FREYA FABLES.

BOOK 1
THE PRINCE IN THE SHADOWS
ISBN: 978-1499302844

BOOK 2
THE GOLDEN LEGION
ISBN: 978-1499399202

BOOK 2.5
THE VALOUR OF SIR HENRY
ISBN: 978-1499609721

BOOK 3
THE AGE OF DARKNESS
ISBN: 978-1502879561

ALL AVAILABLE IN PAPER BACK AND ON KINDLE

DANNY HUGHES

From Harlow in the UK, Danny has always had a fondness of writing and designing even from a young age. He is a qualified computer game designer and self-published author.

He is a free-lance writer who enjoys writing all types for all ages.
He mainly enjoys writing Science fiction, fantasy, war, Zombies, and crime Noir stories, drawing inspiration from absolutely anything. He mainly enjoying designing and creating the entire world that the story is set within to help bulk out the story line of the novel itself, sometimes spending hours writing pieces of work about the lore and history of the world, some of which never makes it in the final piece.

Danny begun writing more seriously and trying to get his first book published after the birth of his daughter; Freya Iris Hughes, who served as his inspiration for his very first book series; The Freya Fables.

Printed in Great Britain
by Amazon